TROUBLEMAKERS

GILLIAN GODDEN

Boldwood

First published in Great Britain in 2024 by Boldwood Books Ltd.

Copyright © Gillian Godden, 2024

Cover Design by Colin Thomas

Cover Images: Colin Thomas

A CIP catalogue record for this book is available from the British Library.

Paperback ISBN 978-1-83561-470-9

Large Print ISBN 978-1-83561-469-3

Hardback ISBN 978-1-83561-468-6

Ebook ISBN 978-1-83561-471-6

Kindle ISBN 978-1-83561-472-3

Audio CD ISBN 978-1-83561-463-1

MP3 CD ISBN 978-1-83561-464-8

Digital audio download ISBN 978-1-83561-467-9

This book is printed on certified sustainable paper. Boldwood Books is dedicated to putting sustainability at the heart of our business. For more information please visit https://www.boldwoodbooks.com/about-us/sustainability/

Boldwood Books Ltd, 23 Bowerdean Street, London, SW6 3TN

www.boldwoodbooks.com

1

THE BEGINNING OF THE END

'No! That's not how it was!' Maggie Silva screamed across the courtroom, tears running down her face as she sat and listened to her husband Alex's whole sordid life being read out to those in court. His days of climbing up the ladder in the Portuguese mafia, from running errands and picking up money from drugs and passing on messages; to racketeering, protection and money laundering; and finally to his position as a famous assassin known as the Silva Bullet.

Alex, personally, had lost count of the people he had killed in his ambition for success. At the time he hadn't really thought about it; life had been great and he and his family were happy and well-off. But in the cold light of day, as the barristers read it out in black and white, it seemed distasteful.

Looking up at the jury, Alex could see the disgust as they looked back at him. He had led an immoral life, until his luxury lifestyle and status had come crashing down on them and the bosses had turned against him. An attempted sexual assault of his wife had led to him murdering the attacker, who was blood family of the mafia bosses, unlike him. He had done the unthinkable and thought they would see it from his point of view, but no. They had put out the contract on his life.

For the first time in his life, Alex had been the one with a bounty on his head. His only option had been witness protection. He had gone to the police and given them the one thing that only he could give them – names. Names of the five families who ran the underworld. The police had been only too glad to have Alex in their midst. They knew who he was and most importantly what he was. This had given Alex the advantage. But Alex couldn't help feeling that deep down he was just as guilty as the people he was accusing. As he looked around at his old friends, who glared at him full of hate, he realised today was judgement day. He felt ashamed of the life he had led and the very fact that he had involved his family in his circle of deceit and lies.

'Quiet! Quiet in the courtroom,' the judge shouted as he banged his hammer down. 'Mrs Silva, you will get your chance to speak, but for now be quiet or I will hold you in contempt of court.' Maggie's neighbours, Mark and Olivia, held on to her hand tightly.

'Leave it, Maggie. It's their job to make Alex look bad,' Mark whispered in her ear. 'Come on, let's go outside for a bit, get a coffee or something. You don't want to hear this.' Mark nodded towards Alex before standing up and leading Maggie out of the courtroom. Maggie felt she could see the relief in her husband's face as they left.

Once stood outside the claustrophobic courtroom, Maggie wiped away her tears. 'He's not a bad man Mark, but it's the world we lived in... although that's no excuse I know.' Tears rolled down her face once more.

Taking Maggie in his arms, Mark looked at Olivia, his wife. Neither of them knew what to say. They had only just found out about Alex and Maggie's past themselves recently; how they had both had connections to the mafia and how Alex Silva had once been a hitman. It all sounded like something out of a movie and things like this didn't happen in Sevenoaks. Mafia hitmen didn't just turn up and run the local pub, but that was exactly what Alex Silva had done.

'What did you expect Maggie? Surely you didn't think they were going to speak well of you in there. Those men are on trial for terrible crimes and they're going to be sent away for, well, forever,' Mark stammered, not knowing what else to say. Alex was his friend, and he wanted to stand by him and his family, but even Mark had to admit it didn't sound good. He could hardly believe that quiet, friendly Alex had been mixed up with the big guns and had once been a loyal member of their gang. It seemed impossible, although, once he thought about Alex's mannerisms and quiet ways, he saw the possibilities. Alex was a closed book; the James Bond of the neighbourhood who never gave much about himself away. Now, Mark realised why. They had seen the news and photographs of a very different Alex wearing sharp suits and drinking champagne with the very men he now stood next to in the courtroom. Maggie was in photographs, too, draped in furs and standing beside celebrities and famous actors, a far cry from the woman they knew in her jeans and T-shirt working behind the bar of the local pub.

Olivia proffered another handkerchief. 'I don't know about these things Maggie, and I don't pretend to. I've only ever seen the *Godfather* movies, but even I realise people don't like to hear of people killing each other and running drug rackets.' Mark winced at Olivia's words. She was trying to help, but was missing the mark.

Maggie blew her red nose, wiped away her tears and smiled weakly at them both. 'I know, and I thank you both. But it's a hard pill to swallow when everyone is curious about our lives. They've even questioned Alex's old school friends and neighbours in Portugal. His mother has been dead for years, but now they are tarnishing her memory by saying Alex worked for them to keep his mother comfortable. It must be tearing him apart.'

'Come on, there's a coffee shop around the corner, let's go there and get away from these nosey journalists.' Mark and Olivia both linked an arm through Maggie's and walked out of the court to the nearby coffee shop. To their surprise, no one paid them any attention and they were able to get their coffees in peace.

Maggie hadn't eaten properly for days. She couldn't stomach anything and every morning, she felt sick. Sick at the thought of the day to come. Seeing her children, Dante and Deana, suffer. Watching them rely on her for support when truth be known, she couldn't even support herself. But they were the only thing that made her get up in the morning. She was their mum and if it wasn't for the children, she would have hidden under the duvet with a bottle of vodka and stayed there. Deana was losing weight, but put on a brave face and Dante never said a word. That was worse. They were having to live with all of this and yet none of it was their fault.

'It's going to be over soon Maggie. Any ideas of what your future holds when it is? What happens next?' Mark asked as he drank his coffee.

Maggie welcomed the hot steaming liquid and shrugged

as she put her mug down. 'I don't know. Part of it is up to the brewery and what they decide, but until they do, I don't know if we have a business or a home. Nothing is for certain. We're right back at the beginning, not knowing what the future holds for us.'

'It's always darkest before dawn, Maggie love,' Olivia butted in. Mark felt like kicking her under the table.

'You're going to find out soon enough Maggie. But be warned, this is the peak of it. After the court case, you are going to have to try to get your lives as regular citizens back on track. But after everything you've already been through that should be a piece of cake. Think ahead Maggie, don't look backwards. Alex is more worried about you than he is for himself and I've promised him I will keep an eye on you and the kids.'

'Thanks again, Mark, but did you hear what they said about me? I sound like some scarlet woman.' Sipping her coffee in silence for a moment, Maggie thought about what they had said inside the court room. How the mafia bosses had accused her of flirting and making enemies amongst the men that worked for them. That all of this bad feeling was Maggie's fault. That Alex was her puppet who'd believed her lies and acted upon them in his own private vendetta, threatening the mafia bosses for his own gain. That this was somehow all her fault. Maggie began to cry again.

* * *

The jury had looked at Alex with disdain. The expensive barristers had made him sound like a very ugly, unlikeable man. No one would show any empathy for him; as far as people were concerned, he was evil, and deep down he admitted that he probably was. But there were worse crimes committed in the world. He had never hurt a civilian going about their business or mugged old ladies in the street. But he was a professional who worked for an organised crime family. That meant only one thing – he was damned!

Alex had been cross examined so many times in the witness box, his head spun. The webs of lies the gangland bosses and their barristers had weaved to try and trip him up had been astonishing. They had even claimed that he had been the mastermind organiser and executioner and that it had been himself who had set up the entire drug circuit. How, once the heat had been turned up and the police were on their tails, Alex had gone into a witness protection programme to cast the blame onto others who were all innocent, following his orders.

Paul Pereira, Alex's old boss, had been the *real* mastermind and had been a powerful man, but Alex now saw him through different eyes. Dare he say it, he thought to himself, 'grown-up' eyes. Back in the day, he had been blinded by loyalty, money and status and Paul had provided all three. Alex had enjoyed being part of the family, always having someone to rely on. Something he had never had at home until Maggie came along.

These days, he thought to himself, people would call it grooming. He had been no more than a kid when he had been pulled into Pereira's world and had quickly become the envy of the other kids on the block. Dropping off packages for the families and selling their stolen goods and drugs on the streets, had earnt him cash to improve his appearance and ease his mother's burden. He had been welcomed with open arms and had willingly joined them, doing their bidding without question. He had been known as the Silva Bullet – a man with no conscience.

Alex felt nauseous. The more he listened to the stories about his past, the more he made his mind up to do the right thing. He didn't like this Alex Silva any more. He wanted to be the family man. Even though he knew his former life would always be buried deep down inside of him, he felt he was being given a second chance and he wanted absolution and forgiveness from his family. He needed to take account-ability for his actions. He was no innocent in all of this and if he was going to point the finger, then he needed to point it at himself first.

When it had been Paul Pereira's turn in the witness box, he had been asked why things had turned out like this and why he thought Alex had turned on them. Paul had openly told them that it had been because of a quarrel with his brother who had been accused of trying to rape Alex's wife Maggie. Paul had laughed and tried to brush the whole thing off as an absurdity, questioning why Maggie had made such a big deal of it. 'She would have got over it.' He had laughed, full of bravado. 'After all, that is what women are for.'

But it seemed Paul's remarks had turned the tides. The women on the jury felt sorry for Maggie. She was living as a victim because her husband had protected her in the only way he knew how. Pereira's barrister had stood rooted to the spot, trying to think of something to say to retract his client's stupid outburst. But the die was cast.

At last, after much deliberation, the judge read out the sentences. Paul Pereira received a 125-year prison sentence. As his sentence was passed, Paul had raised his head slightly and looked directly at Alex from underneath his dark lashes, mouthing the words, 'Fuck you.'

Alex looked towards the back of the court and saw a familiar face sat in his usual seat. Each day John – the new godfather and mafia boss – had turned up dressed immaculately in an Armani suit. Once sentencing had been passed on Pereira and the other gangland bosses on trial, John stood up, catching Alex's eye and giving him a slight nod. Their deal was done. None of the prison sentences were below a hundred years, which was exactly what John had wanted. With all of the other gangland bosses out of the way, the crime syndicate needed a new leader and John had been duly selected. He was the big boss now.

Breaking into his thoughts, the judge asked Alex to stand. He had been warned that he could be facing a long prison sentence, despite his intel on the others, and he waited with bated breath. Looking up, he spied Maggie above him in the gallery, where she had been for every day of the trial. His mouth felt dry and he moistened his lips. His heart was pounding in his chest. He had seen his old associates just get hundred-year sentences. Pensively, he waited, expecting the worst.

'Mr Silva, taking into consideration all of your co-operation with the police and the fact that you gave yourself up and have lived in hiding for almost two years, the court feels that you have already served a prison sentence. However, the court feels you should carry some sentence and so I am sentencing you to...'

Alex closed his eyes tightly and grimaced. Considering all of the hundred-year sentences that had been given out, he waited for his.

'Mr Silva, are you listening?' the judge asked when she saw him with his eyes shut. Opening them, Alex nodded. 'As

I was saying, I am sentencing you to two years, suspended sentence. You are free to go.'

Alex stood wide eyed and rooted to the spot. Turning to his own lawyer, Alex saw his shrug still not quite taking in what had been said. This wasn't what he had expected. He thought his legs would give way, but he was determined to face it out.

A thought flashed through his mind. 'May I speak your honour?'

Confused, the judge made everyone be silent and gave Alex the opportunity to speak.

'I want to leave this courtroom a free man. I want a clean sheet. I want to go home and rebuild whatever life I can with my family and leave the past behind. We've had this witness protection programme and court case hanging over us for two years and now I have a suspended sentence hanging over me. I would prefer to serve those two years and then I can leave the past behind.'

Gasps of surprise sounded around the courtroom as Alex spoke. Then the courtroom fell silent, waiting to hear what other surprises Alex had in store. Frowning, the judged leaned forward, talking to Alex on a one-to-one basis. 'Are you sure Mr Silva that you would rather serve your prison sentence now? Normally, people who stand before me want their freedom, not incarceration.'

Alex's heart pounded in his chest. 'Yes, your honour. It's the only way I can start afresh and leave the past completely behind me. By serving my sentence, it's over. At last, it's over,' Alex croaked. He knew Maggie would hate him for this and wouldn't understand. But to him it made all the sense in the world. Also, hopefully, his time away would give time for the dust to settle.

How could he go home and just stand behind the bar and pull someone a pint of beer as though nothing had happened? He had laid in bed, night after night and thought about it. This was his way of giving Maggie and the kids a fresh start in life. If they still wanted him once he got out of prison then so be it. He felt sick at the idea of Maggie turning her back on him after everything they had been through, but this was her chance to rebuild her life. Two years was a long time and times change. Who knew what the future would bring. Only time would tell.

'Very well then Mr Silva. May I say, I admire the fact that you are prepared to pay your debt to society.' The judge looked directly at Alex for a moment and leaned forward, resting his elbows on the desk and smiling. 'Good luck Mr Silva.' He nodded towards the awaiting police. 'Take him down.'

Alex saw Maggie stand up in the court, shouting and screaming his name. 'Alex, don't do this!' Tears rolled down her face. Looking up, he felt a sense of betrayal overwhelming him. Blowing her a kiss, he did his hardest to hold onto his composure as he was quickly led away to the cells below the court, leaving her voice ringing in his ears as he left her there. He was heartbroken, but knew it was for the best. He loved her and wanted to give her this chance without dragging her down with him. The thought of leaving her sobbing in her seat made him want to cry himself, but he fought the tears back with a heavy heart.

* * *

As everyone filed out of the courtroom, only Maggie and Mark sat there. With her head buried in her hands, Maggie sobbed so much her body shook.

'Maggie?' Mark whispered beside her, putting his arm around her shoulders. 'Let me take you home.'

Bleary eyed, she brushed away her tears and wiped her face with her sleeve. Mark was sat beside her, his face solemn. Wiping away the snot from her nose, Maggie sniffed. 'Where is home, Mark?' she croaked. 'Everyone knows we're criminals, and I'm a criminal's wife. The good guys hate us and so do the bad guys. They will kill Alex in prison... don't you understand?' She fell into his arms, sobbing.

'If I know anything about Alex, it's that he will survive. You're all survivors Maggie. Christ, I can't imagine what hell you've all been through.' He sighed, patting her back as he comforted her. 'But, you're not alone Maggie. You have me and Olivia and you have your kids. Stay focused, you have a lot to live for. Alex knows what he's doing. And when we can, we will visit him and lift his spirits, but you know Maggie' – Mark squeezed her hand tightly – 'the only way to really lift his spirits, is by knowing you're okay. He'll worry about you night and day, but he needs to stay focused too. The only thing you have in prison is time. Time to think and time to worry. Come on, let's get you home.'

As his words sunk in, Maggie stood up. Although her legs were still shaky, she took his hand and followed him out of the courtroom in a daze. She knew he was right, but inwardly, she cursed Alex for not telling her his plan. He had known all along that he would serve whatever sentence they threw at him and had never discussed it with her. She hadn't had the chance to prepare herself for the outcome or say a proper goodbye. It was all a mess. Tears rolled down her face again as Mark drove her home. 'What am I going to tell the kids?' she asked sadly.

'The truth, Maggie. It will be all over the internet by now anyway so they'll probably already know. Here, take this.'

Mark had lit two cigarettes and handed her one.

'We'll have to move, Mark. We can't stay here. I presume the police might help us find somewhere. I really don't know now.' Maggie shrugged. 'I don't know anything any more.'

'What's the point in moving?' Mark snorted. 'Christ, Maggie, your faces have been splashed all over the news. Where are you going to hide – on a bloody desert island? Stay put for Christ's sake. One place is as good as another. Fuck them all. You've paid the price for whatever you've done. Everybody has skeletons. You might as well go home and open the pub as usual. It's your name above the door. Just don't make any rash decisions without speaking to the kids first.'

Inhaling on her cigarette, Maggie looked out of the van window as they approached the pub. It seemed desolate. Day in and day out, there had been crowds outside just waiting for photos of the mafia wife and her kids, but it was all over now and already they were losing interest.

'I'm not sure if the brewery will even let us stay. But thank you, Mark. Thank you for being a friend.' Maggie smiled and opened the van door to get out.

'Do you want me to come in with you?'

'No, I have to get used to doing things on my own now. Thank you.'

'You're not alone. None of you, and Alex would have my guts for garters if he thought I wasn't being a mate and seeing you were okay. Don't blame him, Maggie. Don't let it eat you up. Us blokes are dumb fuckers and do the wrong thing sometimes. Have a strong drink and get some rest.'

Maggie nodded and gave Mark a weak smile as she walked away as though the weight of the world was on her shoulders.

2

LIFE GOES ON

Walking into the pub, Maggie felt weak. She prepared herself to face the usual barrage of journalists with their flashes on their cameras, shoving microphones in her face, but all the strength had left her body and she had no fight left in her to give. Opening the door, she looked around, but saw that there was only a handful of regulars in. Confused, she glanced at Phyllis who was working behind the bar. 'Where is everyone?'

'This is everyone Maggie. Come in, put your feet up.' Phyllis smiled. 'You look like you need a large brandy. Let me pour you one.'

Averting her eyes from the customers, Maggie sat down on a bar stool in front of Phyllis. She didn't feel her legs would carry her any further. 'Has it been like this all day?'

'No, it's only recently gone quiet. I guess the ghoul mongers have had their fill for now. It will perk up again, don't worry, love. And you don't need to tell me anything, I've already heard all about it. Take this.' Handing Maggie a glass of brandy, she gave a wagging finger. 'Down in one my girl and then go and have a lie down. We can finish up here.' Phyllis smiled and patted Maggie's hand. Doing as she was told, Maggie held the glass and let the warmth of the brandy bite and soothe her throat. She almost felt like crying again. Phyllis's kind, comforting words touched her in her vulnerable state.

'Where are the kids?'

'No idea where they are. Maybe Deana has taken Dante out for a breath of fresh air to get him away from everything. Maybe they felt that you needed time on your own. Who knows what goes through the minds of kids today? They'll turn up when they're hungry.' Phyllis shrugged and laughed. 'Go and have a lie down, love, or even run yourself a warm bath. Let all the troubles go down the plug hole. That's what my mum used to say anyway.'

A weak smile crossed Maggie's face. 'I think I will. Thank you, Phyllis. Why don't you close up early? With these few people it's not worth the electricity.'

'I'll do no such thing. Now you scoot! I won't hear any more of this defeatist nonsense.'

Doing as she was told, Maggie wearily climbed the staircase. Her mind was in turmoil wondering what was happening to Alex now. What was he thinking? Her head ached and her eyes felt swollen and tired. 'Alex,' she muttered to herself. 'Oh God, Alex, why did you do this?' Running her hand through her hair, she couldn't make her mind up whether to be worried about Alex or be angry at his selfishness. It was her that had to hold the family, their home and livelihood together and face the scandal he had created. Alex was locked away in his cell hiding from the world, leaving her to face all of this alone. Suddenly, she felt bitterness wash through her. 'Fuck you Alex Silva, you selfish bastard!' she shouted at the bedroom door as she kicked it wide open. With a start, she stood there open mouthed.

'Well, I've heard better entrances Maggie.' Wide eyed, Maggie stared at the well-dressed man sat on her bed smoking a cigar.

Maggie held a hand to her chest, to try to stop her heart from pounding, 'John,' she breathed. 'What are you doing here?'

'Waiting for you. Shut the bedroom door.'

Nervously, Maggie looked at John sat on the bed. Suddenly, that awful day when Matteo Pereira had cornered her and had tried to rape her flashed through her mind. Quickly, she scanned the room for any kind of weapon to defend herself.

'Maggie, take it easy. I am not here to harm you, but to help you. I came up here because there are too many ears down there. All I want to do is talk to you.'

'What about? I saw you in court, John. Did you hear what Alex did?'

'Of course, but then he was never a man for half measures. Being Alex, he thinks the only way to end this is to serve his own sentence and not have a suspended one hanging over him. He's honourable Maggie and you will see that once you're feeling yourself again. But, for now, I've come to assure you that Alex will be okay. I have made provisions for him in prison. I know he can protect himself, he's a survivor. He knows the rules and will keep his head down. In the meantime, there is you and the kids. I've assured you of his safety, now I need to assure him of yours.'

Relaxing slightly, Maggie walked over to the dressing table and sat down on the stool in front of it. 'How do you propose to do that, John? There is nothing you can do for me now. I'm a lost cause. I don't even know if I'll be able to stay here.' Resting her elbows on her knees, Maggie let out a deep sigh and rubbed her face. Turning slightly, she caught sight of herself in the mirror. 'God, I look like a hundred-year-old shit. I'm not even forty yet, but I look like an old woman.'

'I doubt the brewery will make you homeless Maggie. You're still a mafia wife and the landlady of one of their pubs, which brings its own celebrity status. People are always going to be talking and whispering about you. And they are businessmen, and businessmen don't sack their star turn. And if they were going to, they would have already served you notice by now. Here, take this.' Putting his hand inside his jacket pocket, he pulled out a bundle of money and threw it on the bed. 'There is ten grand. Pay your bills. Take the kids for a holiday or something. It's time to come back into the sunlight. Your life sentence is over.'

Puzzled, Maggie looked at the bundle of money held together by an elastic band on the bed, then back at John and met his eyes. 'Why are you doing this John?'

'Because Alex would do it for me. He always had my back and he's taken a big fall for me, Maggie. And, like an elephant, I don't forget.'

Shaking her head, Maggie pursed her lips together. 'I don't need your money, John. I don't want mafia money! That's what got us into all this in the beginning.'

John stood up and inhaled on his cigar. Walking over to the dressing table, he flicked his ash into an ashtray there. 'Keep the money for now in case you need it. If you don't use it then you can give it back to me when Alex comes out of prison. But it's there if you need it, and so am I. I don't want our meetings to be common knowledge, but you know how to find me if you need me.' Comfortingly, he put his hand on her shoulder and squeezed it. 'You'll be okay, Maggie. You're a survivor too.' Turning, John tentatively opened the bedroom door slightly and looked around, checking there was no one about. He turned towards Maggie and gave a slight wave, and stealthily left the way he had come, without anyone seeing him.

Maggie looked at the money on the bed. Standing up, she picked it up and opened a drawer, throwing it in. Looking up at the clock, she realised how late it was getting and realised that there was still no sign of the kids. Panic rose inside her and all kinds of thoughts flashed through her mind. What if they had been kidnapped or killed? Adrenalin started to race through her veins, making her more alert. Standing up, she ran to the bathroom and splashed her face with cold water. Looking up into the bathroom mirror, she stopped dead.

'Mum, are you okay?' Her daughter Deana was stood behind her.

Quickly turning, Maggie gripped Deana's shoulders and pulled her towards her. 'Where the hell have you been? Where's Dante?' Maggie half shouted.

'He's on his way up. Phyllis said you might be asleep or something and we didn't want to disturb you.'

'I've been out of my mind with worry. Anything could have happened to you!'

Prizing herself away from Maggie's tight hug, Deana stood looking at her mum. 'We know what happened with Dad. Is he okay, are you okay?' Tears brimmed on her lashes, and she sniffed hard to fight them back. 'It's not going to be the same around here without him. I'm gutted Mum.' Suddenly Deana burst into tears and deep sobs wracked her body as she fell back into her mother's arms. 'I miss him already.'

Trying her best to comfort Deana and find the right words, although she was uncertain herself about Alex's safety, Maggie remembered what John had said. 'It's okay Deana. You know your dad, he's going to be okay. Well, I hope he is,' Maggie sighed.

'He might be fine, but what about us?' Deana and Maggie parted and looked at Dante who was stood on the landing outside the bathroom with his arms folded.

Wiping her tears with the back of her hand, Deana glared at him. 'Don't you give a shit about Dad?' she snapped.

'Of course I do, but he's no fool. He wouldn't put himself in a position he couldn't cope with, would he? He's not stupid! And he's not some naïve young kid starting a prison sentence. He knows what to expect. He's starting the first day of a different life from today and so are we. So, we might as well get used to it.' Dante shrugged, although inside Maggie guessed that he felt just as helpless as they did.

Holding out her arm towards him, Maggie beckoned him over. 'Group hug Dante. You're right, we have to go forward.' Ruffling his dark hair that resembled Alex's, she smiled. 'Since when did you become so grown up, eh?'

'Since I realised that I'm the man of the family now and we can get through this. Let's make Dad proud and realise his sacrifice hasn't been for nothing. We are Silvas and together we are invincible.'

Entering their little triangle, they all put their arms around each other and hugged for a moment in silence. The air was tense and none of them knew what the future held, but this was the deck of cards they had been dealt and they had to play them.

'Mum, you go and have a good long soak and get rid of those panda eyes. Me and Dante are okay, even if he is keeping a stiff upper lip.' Casting a furtive glance at Dante, Deana winked. 'Aren't you, Mr Head of the Household?' She smiled.

'I think I will Deana. I'm bushed. What are you two going to do?'

'We'll watch Netflix and avoid the news. After all, we're all over it!' Deana scoffed. 'You know, you could even give Gran a call. I'm sure she would want to hear from you. Better still, why not ask her over here to visit. It makes no difference now we're no longer in hiding, does it?'

'I hadn't thought of that,' Maggie mused. 'That might be a nice idea.' Maggie walked towards the bathroom, and shut the door behind her, turning on the taps.

Deana pulled Dante's shirt sleeve. 'Come on,' she whispered. Walking into the lounge, she turned the television on, with the volume up even louder than normal.

'Dante, we need to talk about Luke. What do you think of him?'

Standing up, Dante shut the lounge door. 'My, what a cool liar you are, Deana. You're as devious as a snake. As for Luke, I don't think he was that pleased to see us, especially after what he's just learned about Dad. Maybe he thinks our mafia connections are going to "jump him" or something. Although, I could see his point when he said we were known faces and he and his brother like to keep a low profile. It makes sense.'

Luke had been an acquaintance of their dad before the court case, but hadn't known the extent of Alex's past crimes. Deana and Dante were hoping Luke could help them in this new life they were now having to navigate and that they could pick up exactly where Alex had left off. But with their dad pulling his stunt today, that now felt in jeopardy.

'He'll get over that. Luke knew Dad wasn't squeaky clean. I suppose it's just come as a bit of a shock that Dad was involved with the gangland bosses to such an extent. But my proposals were good, weren't they?' Deana asked hopefully. Weirdly, excitement ran through her veins at the prospect of putting her plan into action.

Unlike his sister, Dante was a thinker and not impulsive. Some would describe him as the strong and silent type but Alex had just called him moody. Adjusting his horn-rimmed glasses, he nodded. 'There were some holes, Deana, but generally the plan is sound. But at the end of the day, it's up to Luke. They are his contacts and although we might have plants Deana, who are we going to sell them to? Do you have names of people who want to buy, because I don't.' Dante shrugged. One of the last jobs Alex and Luke had been involved in had been acquiring a large quantity of cannabis plants. Deana wanted to make sure that when the gear got sold, she and Dante would get their cut.

'First things first Dante. Tomorrow, I'll convince Mum to use some of Dad's stashed cash to buy all three of us new mobile phones. That way, she won't panic when we're not around like she did today.' Deana winked. 'We haven't got Dad around any more and we're no longer in hiding. Then, with or without Luke, we step out into the twenty-first century with our own mobile phones like grown-ups and find new contacts.'

'Is that all you care about Deana – things? Mum's heart is breaking in the bathroom, and all you want is a mobile phone!'

'We have freedom, Dante, and I intend to make the most of it. I'm sick of being treated like a caged animal!'

'Until you end up joining Dad in prison for selling drugs.'

Dante's voice, much older than his years, stopped Deana's excitement. 'Look, he seems like a good bloke, your Luke. But I don't think he's happy that I'm a school kid, and he looks at you like he fancies you. So I think it's up to you to convince him we're a dynamic duo, or trio. But... I'm in Deana.' Holding his hand up, they gave each other a high five.

A big grin crossed Deana's face and her eyes lit up. 'Thanks, Dante.' Raising her arm, she held up her fist. Dante did likewise, and they pushed them together as part of their pact. 'But Luke doesn't fancy me.' She blushed. 'Anyway, even if he does, it doesn't mean I'm interested in him, does it?' She pouted, her cheeks heating slightly.

Dante pulled his glasses down to the edge of his nose and looked at Deana. 'No, course you don't Deana, whatever was I thinking. And that blush of yours isn't too much blusher either,' Dante said sarcastically, and burst out laughing.

Playfully, Deana reached for a cushion and hit him with it. 'Shut up clever clogs. We'll go and see him again in a couple of days when he's had time to think about it. We've put the idea in his head, and he just needs to weigh things up a bit before he jumps in. He will go for it though, I'm sure of it. He's just uncertain about our ages and the baggage we bring with us. So, let's use our baggage, not trail it behind us like sackcloth and ashes. We're hardnosed mafia kids, whose dad was an assassin. That will make them think twice about not paying for their goods. Let's just chill out tonight, I'm knackered. I'm going to order a kebab or something. What about you? I wonder what Dad's having for dinner and what he's doing now.' Her voice cracked as she finished speaking.

'He's probably wondering what we're doing, Deana. We'll soon get a visiting order, and Mum will feel better when she sees him. Either that or she will murder him! Dad's probably shitting himself having to face Mum's wrath, so he'll want it over with as soon as possible. She can be one scary, angry woman when she wants to be. A bit like you Deana.' He grinned. 'Order a couple of pizzas as well and get Mum something too.'

3

DECISIONS

'Hey greaseball, super grass! You moving in?' As Alex walked through the prison to his cell, he heard the shouts from the landing above. Leaning over the landing were a couple of inmates glaring at him and banging their tin cups against the metal bannisters, encouraging others to join in. 'Super grass!' they all chimed while banging their cups so loud it was deafening.

'You wanted this, Silva. You got it.' The prison guard left Alex standing at the bottom of the staircase to walk alone up the stairs, while blowing his whistle and shouting to the inmates to be quiet. Although his heart was pounding in his chest, Alex remained calm. He had known what to expect when he walked through the prison gates – life was going to be hard. Meeting the governor for his induction had been an experience he wouldn't forget. As he walked and tried blocking out the roar of screams and abuse, Alex thought about how it had only been a couple of days ago, but already seemed like a lifetime ago.

Standing in a line-up with other prisoners about to start their sentence, the governor had invited him into his office. Puzzled, Alex had entered, not knowing what to expect. Was it a trick? Was someone in there waiting for him?

Sitting at his own side of the desk, the governor had offered Alex a chair. 'I'm not going to mince my words, Silva. I appreciate you want to pay some kind of sentence for your many crimes, but I want no trouble from you or the people you mix with,' he said with a stoney expression. 'Friends of yours, who have friends very high up, have requested that you have an easy time of it. A cell of your own. A good job, preferably away from others. And extra money for whatever needs you have. Cigarettes, chocolate... whatever.' Throwing his hands in the air, the governor stood up and walked to the window, looking out. He could see some prisoners in the yard, walking and talking and he let out a huge sigh before turning back towards Alex. 'My superiors have asked me, or rather told me, about how your time in this place should go. Personally, I don't agree with it, but that's the way it is. So I would appreciate you not squealing to your friends that your treatment here isn't good enough. If you have a problem, I would rather we keep it between ourselves to sort out.'

'Do you mind if I smoke, sir?' Knowing that he wouldn't, Alex took out his cigarette packet and lit one. He didn't bother offering the governor one. After all, cigarettes in a place like this were gold dust and he was quite sure the governor could buy his own on his way home. Blowing the smoke into the air, Alex looked him squarely in the face. 'Now, I won't mince my words either, sir. I suppose I half expected this, and I realise the predicament you've been put in... is not nice. I also appreciate that some of the Spanish or

Portuguese in here will want my blood. These places are ghettos. Every landing has its own gang and there is always a top dog.' The governor was about to butt in, but Alex stopped him. 'I've done time in prison before, sir. I know how it works. But if I am going to get any respect from these men, it won't be by hiding behind my friends or your bosses in the home office. So, I will take the beatings they hand out until they get tired of it, although I'm not saying I won't fight back of course.' Inhaling on his cigarette again, Alex felt his next sentence would shock the governor into silence. 'I will serve my time like any other prisoner. I don't want special privileges handed out by my contacts, but instead, from my behaviour in here. I will keep my head down and do my time, but I don't expect it to be easy.' Inwardly, Alex felt he was putting a noose around his own neck by refusing all the special privileges requested for him, including a cell of his own. His hands felt sweaty, and he couldn't deny he felt a little nervous – afraid even. 'I want to earn their respect and possibly even yours. Is that fair enough?'

Quite taken aback, the governor looked at him surprised. 'Are you sure about that?'

'Absolutely, sir. Although, I'm not refusing the extra cigarettes or chocolate.' He smiled. 'I have chosen to do this and I will do it properly, beatings and all.'

Alex had taken the wind out of the governor's sails, and he could see it. A nervous laugh escaped the governor's mouth and he threw his hand up in the air, letting out a huge sigh. 'Well, I really don't know what to say, Silva. I'm not sure if you're absolutely bonkers or have a death wish. Most of the men would bite my hands off for the opportunity I'm offering you.'

'I appreciate that, sir. But you wouldn't respect me, would

you? You would do your job and go along with things, but seeing me would make your skin crawl, wouldn't it? Your hands will have been tied by my contacts and yours, and you wouldn't appreciate that. Not a man of your standing. And after a lot of years being the governor of this place and many others I presume.'

'I started off as a young prison warder thirty years ago, Silva.' The governor smiled, as though reminiscing to himself. 'And I don't have a blemish on my record. I'm fair but firm and I like things running smoothly.'

'So do I, sir. I'll let it be known you did your best, but I'm a stubborn fool on a death wish.' Alex laughed. 'I can handle myself, sir.'

Spying him up and down, the governor nodded. 'I presume you can, Mr Silva. A man like you with a past like yours wouldn't have amounted to much if he couldn't. And for the record, Silva, you have already earnt my respect. I don't do this often, but...' The governor held out his hand to shake Alex's, who did likewise. 'Good luck Silva. You can leave now.' Alex stubbed out his cigarette and stood up. Taking a breath, he walked to the door and opened it. He knew he had already broken one barrier with the governor, now he had to prove himself to the rest of the inmates.

Now, hearing the noise above him as he walked up the staircase to his cell, he looked up. Whistles and hollers filled the landings, much to the annoyance of the guards who were trying to calm down the situation. Strangely enough, Alex didn't recognise any of the faces. They certainly weren't from any of the circles he had mixed in and he couldn't understand why they were taking his situation so personally. Seeing his cell door was barred by a couple of men smoking their roll-up cigarettes, Alex stared at them and waited for them to move so he could enter.

Blowing smoke into his face, one of them spoke. 'So super grass, you think you're a hard man, do you? Well not in here you're not. Jonesy has got your card marked. Not so hard without a gun in your hand, are you?' The man then spat in his face. 'This is to let you know that whoever you were, you're nothing in here.'

'Yeah, watch your back you greasy bastard,' said the other one, smirking. 'Who knows what might happen to you in here?'

Moistening his lips, Alex slowly wiped the spit off his face with the sleeve of his prison uniform. 'Well, I'll be careful how I pick up the soap in the showers then, if it's my back I need to watch.' Pushing his way through them, he walked into his cell and shut the door. Sitting on the lower bunk bed and letting out a huge sigh, he rubbed his face. He felt tired all of a sudden.

His thoughts went to Maggie and the kids. He didn't want to send a visiting order yet. Things needed to calm down first. He didn't want her walking into the visitors' room while the other prisoners sneered at them both. And he didn't want the kids coming at all. He realised that would cause a stir, but he felt it was for the best.

Seeing his cell door opening, Alex expected the worst and instantly his hackles rose, but instead it was his cell mate.

'No need to look like that Silva. I live here too.'

Alex lay back on his bed and put his arms behind his head. 'Indeed, you do.'

Shutting the door his cell mate stood beside his bed. 'Look mate, we all know who you are and why you're here, but we have to live together. It makes life easier if we get on.'

'Now why would you want to do that? Everyone in here hates me and yet you want to be my friend? I don't think so.' Alex felt like a fly in a spider's web.

'You know, Silva, I've done time most of my life. Petty thieving mainly, house burgling and stuff. You can't do the time, don't do the crime. The same goes with you. This is not an open prison, but it's better than some I've been in. You've been lucky. I gather some of your associates are in maximum security.'

'Yeah, I feel lucky,' Alex muttered, not wanting to get drawn into conversation.

'The point is, we got caught and ended up here. But you've rocked the boat, Silva. There is always a pecking order in places like this, I'm sure you know that...' The man tailed off. 'People don't like getting hurt and so they comply for their own safety. It makes life easier.'

Alex closed his eyes. 'So, where are you in this pecking order of yours?'

'Nowhere. I don't count. I keep out of everyone's way and mind my manners when needs be. Sure, I will give the people in charge my chair at the dining table, or in the cinema room if that's what they want. I don't rock any boats. The man at the top is called Jonesy. He's a big criminal and quite the celebrity. He doesn't want anyone being friends with you and has made his threats quite clear. Your celebrity status went before you, which makes you a threat. We knew who you were and what you'd done before you came in. Some have taken a grudge because you're a grass. Then there's the foreign lot.' Suddenly, as though remembering that Alex was one of the foreign lot, he blushed. 'Erm... sorry no offence, like. Well, they don't see you as one of them. You know there is nothing worse than a grass and you're a super grass. You've got balls though; I will give you that. By the way my name's Harry Fiddler. Fiddler by name and career,' he laughed. 'Do you want half of my tangerine super grass Silva?' he joked while peeling it.

Opening his eyes, Alex looked up at the man above him. He was in his fifties with salt and pepper hair, and casually took prison in his stride as though it was an occupational hazard. Spying the tangerine, Alex looked at him. 'You eat your half first.'

'Why, don't you trust me? Do you think I've poisoned it like Snow White and the apple?'

'That's no apple and you're not Snow White.' Alex grinned.

'Fair point.' Once his tangerine was peeled. Harry split it in half, counting the segments to make sure it was even, and popped his half in his mouth and chewed. 'Well, I haven't collapsed yet,' he said, holding out the other half. Alex glanced up at him and waited a moment, then reached out his hand, took the tangerine and popped it into his mouth. It tasted good. Something so simple tasted like paradise in comparison with the shit food he'd had lately. 'So, Fiddler, what do I owe you for half a tangerine?'

'Nothing, if you don't want to. As I said, I'm just trying to make life easier for myself. I've been given a special dispensation because I have to share a cell with you. I'm supposed to ingratiate myself with you and find out more about you. The mole, if you like. I've no idea what they want to know unless you've got millions stashed away somewhere they want to know about...' Fiddler's brows crossed. 'You haven't, have you? Anyway, it might be best for my health if we don't look too matey beyond this door, eh?'

Still tasting the tang of tangerine, Alex nodded. 'That's fair. No point in making life shit for the both of us. No, I don't have millions stashed away. I'm a pauper. Everything was taken away from me, and I mean everything,' Alex stressed. 'So, you can tell them that. This is one of the best hotels I've stayed in since I went into witness protection two years ago.' He laughed.

'Christ, you are poor. Welcome to the Wandsworth Hilton!' Bending down, Fiddler held up his hand and gave Alex a high five. 'How come you're in a category B prison when you're only doing a couple of years?'

'I thought people in here didn't ask questions? I could say the same about you,' Alex retorted.

'I'm here because I can't be trusted, although I will be downgraded soon. Only got eighteen months out of five years to go. Did a runner from the open prison last time. Heard the wife was ill and the governor wouldn't let me visit, so I legged it while working on the farm area.' Fiddler laughed. 'Tell you what though, I made sure I had a few pints of bitter before they came for me. Tasted like amber nectar it did, barely touched the sides.' Smacking his lips together, he grinned.

Alex sat up; it felt like years since he'd had a conversation. 'I suppose I'm classed as high security. Maybe the authorities think Al Capone is going to come running through the doors with a machine gun pointing at my head.'

'Well make sure they know what bunk you're in, so they don't get mixed up with mine.' Fiddler laughed. Hearing the warders shout, Fiddler looked at Alex. 'Dinner and cocoa time. You ready for another encore and round of insults?'

'Absolutely. It lightens the boredom for everyone, doesn't it?'

Fiddler spied Alex. 'A bloke like you knows how to handle himself, I'm sure of that. Why don't you fight back? Give them a taste of their own medicine?'

'Because they want me to. And bullies hate being ignored. Well, that's what I'm always telling my kids. I won't rise to it, unless I have to. Come on, let's see what shit they will serve me up tonight.' Alex grinned and slapped Fiddler on the back. Suddenly things weren't looking so bad.

4

ALLIANCES

As Dante and Deana sat around the breakfast table, they could see their mother had something on her mind. She had talked and talked for hours about Alex, and they felt they knew what was coming. 'I've been thinking about what you said Deana. It makes sense... I suppose.'

Deana's brows furrowed. She had said so much to comfort her mum over the last few days she couldn't remember what she'd said.

'About the mobile phones. I'm a single parent now and don't have two pairs of eyes to keep an eye on you. We should be able to keep in touch, in case you're going to be late or something. Or if I'm held up with whatever.' Maggie shrugged. 'I just need to get my head around this single parent business, I'm not used to it.' Sniffing hard, Maggie shook her head to dismiss the tears brimming on her lashes.

'Dad's not dead Mum and he hasn't left us forever.' Deana put her hand on Maggie's and patted it comfortingly, while casting a glance at Dante. This was music to Deana's ears.

'I know, it's just that we haven't heard anything from him yet. I was sure we would have had a visiting order by now.'

'We will,' Deana assured her. 'You know Dad, he never rushes into anything.'

Nodding her head, Maggie carried on. 'Anyway, I'm going to take over running the bar again. Poor Phyllis and Pauline have taken the pressure off me for too long and it's not fair. I need to show my face as landlady. The brewery hasn't said I'm no longer the landlady and I was sure one of their representatives would have been round by now, giving us notice or taking my name from above the door, so we take it as read that we still have a roof over our heads. So that's one box ticked. Also, I have a job, which is another box ticked. The police have been in touch and apparently they will still be on call if we need them, which I hope we won't!' Maggie stressed. 'But that's a little security, should we need it.'

Listening intently, Deana pursed her lips together. 'Why are the police going to be still sniffing around?' With her own projects in mind, that was the last thing Deana wanted.

'They are there as back-up if we need help from our old enemies. Or new ones, I'm not quite sure.' Maggie shrugged. 'Some people are on witness protection for life, Deana. They've got off lightly with us since your dad came out into the public eye. It's part of the contract. We are still under their umbrella if needed. It doesn't hurt to have back-up Deana. Anyway, how are things at school and college? I haven't really asked lately; I've been too wrapped up in my own wallowing and it's time I snapped out of it.'

'Everything is just fine Mum. We've had hurdles to cross, but it will blow over,' Deana said quickly, before Dante could speak.

'So why did the school ring me Dante and ask if you were

okay? It seems you've taken a bit of stick lately and you've handed some out apparently.'

Dante lowered his eyes to the table and blushed slightly. 'We're handling it, Mum. Same as you. It's not been easy, but we never expected it to be, did we? At least we don't have all those journalists hanging around now; that was the hardest part at school. Having your life splashed all over social media. Not having phones then probably did us a favour. They couldn't troll us or send nasty messages.'

Deana glared at Dante; the last thing she wanted was for him to put their mum off the idea of getting them mobiles, but he carried on. 'But we might as well have worn targets on our back. We've been picked on, bullied and snubbed by everyone. That's what you want to hear isn't it, the truth?' Unlike Deana, Dante felt honesty was the best policy. He knew their mum could see right through them, and that she wanted their honest thoughts in this Silva family meeting.

'Thanks Dante.' Maggie smiled. 'Saying "fine" all the time doesn't quite cut it, does it? But we'll get through this together.' Maggie squeezed his hand across the table. 'Right, well I'm going to have a shower and slap some make-up on to get rid of these dark circles. I know I look like shit, I don't need telling. I'm also going to take your advice Deana and invite Grandma over for a few days. If nothing else, it's another pair of hands behind the bar!' She laughed. 'I think we should also go and buy your mobiles. Although I'm not stupid. Yours are going to be pay as you go. I am not running up countless bills because you're playing games.' Hearing the familiar groan from Deana, Maggie shrugged. 'You either want one or you don't Deana.'

'No that's fine Mum.'

'Right then, now that's settled, we'll crack on.' As Maggie

left the room, Deana turned towards Dante with a great big grin across her face. 'Sorted!' Giving him a high five, she pushed a piece of toast in her mouth and jumped out of her chair. 'I'm not bothering with a shower. Quick spray of Febreze under my armpits and pull my jeans on. We're going shopping Dante and then later we're going to see Luke.'

'Febreze? You're putting air freshener under your armpits? You dirty cow!' he shouted after her as she ran laughing down the hallway to her room.

* * *

'Afternoon, Luke, we thought we'd pop by and see how you are?'

Standing in the doorway, Luke folded his arms. 'Well, I'm not going to say I didn't expect a second visit. You're predictable Deana. Like a dog with a bone.'

'Nice to see you too. Are you going to put the kettle on? It's a long way from home, this place,' she asked, ignoring his slight.

'Sure, why not? My brother Kev is here. He's doing his weekly visit to Mum.'

Once they were inside, Luke walked into the kitchen and switched on the kettle. Dante stood behind Deana surveying the situation. Deana tried to look like she was bubbling with confidence as she made herself comfortable and sat down at the table.

Before she'd opened her mouth to speak, a man entered the kitchen. 'What's going on bro? Who are Pinky and Perky? You two Jehovah's Witnesses that have come to the wrong door?' Dante saw Deana's eyes light up as she looked this young man up and down. He looked like Mr Supercool in his mirrored sunglasses, leather jacket and designer jeans and trainers. His hair was dark brown and went past his collar, flicking out everywhere.

'This is Alex Silva's daughter Deana and son Dante. You remember I told you about them?' Luke blushed while looking down at his own stained, baggy T-shirt and jeans. He'd had a late night and was still feeling the after-effects.

'Oh, yeah. The cannabis. The dealing mafia kids,' boomed Kev as he sat down opposite Deana. 'Well, blondie, why don't we start by you telling me what you've got to bring to the table that would interest me? I mean me, not Luke. We're partners, you're outsiders wanting a cut. Alex isn't around any more and so we should class him as a sleeping partner – got it?'

Dante could see Deana was a little out of her depth. Apart from being swept away by Kev's appearance and blushing like a schoolgirl, his matter-of-fact business manner had stopped her in her tracks. Dante felt it was his time to step forward. He wasn't impressed by Kev's appearance, or his smart mouth. Pulling out a chair, he sat beside Deana, opposite Kev.

'You want to know what we have to bring to the table? I can answer that. Nothing. Absolutely nothing. Just give us our goods and we will leave. Your sleeping partner's goods, I should say.'

Kev's jaw dropped. In front of him he saw a young school kid, but with an adult's mouth. He remembered meeting Alex once and recalled his calm manner that exuded authority. Now meeting his son, he felt there were possibilities. Luke had told him it was Deana's kid brother, but this was no kid. This was someone who had a mind of his own and the balls to match it. To save face, Kev burst out laughing. 'You've got balls kid, I will give you that. So, you want your half, do you? And just what are you going to do with it?' he asked sarcastically.

'Sell it. The same as you, erm, Kev, is it? We need the money. Dad's in jail and you know why, so I won't go into details. We need money and so do you, by the looks of it.' Dante paused and looked Kev up and down, then reached over the table and took off his sunglasses. 'Yeah, just as I thought. You have an expensive habit; your eyes are already spaced out.' Kev glared at him, then turned towards Luke. 'Forget the fucking tea and sit down.'

'You didn't tell me that the Brady Bunch here had visions of their own. They don't want to be partners. They want the lot, don't they? Especially smart mouth here,' Kev spat out, glaring at Dante.

Reaching forward and quite out of the blue, Dante punched Kev in the face, almost knocking him off his chair. Kev howled and put his hands up to his now bloody nose. 'Stop the smart remarks junkie man. We're here to either work together or collect our plants and work alone. The four of us could make a wider network and more drops. Luke is still in hiding by all accounts, even though I know for a fact that my dad shot a couple of the blokes resembling the description of the ones that nearly killed your brother. I know that, because I saw it for myself. So, that's another strike for us and another debt you owe the Silvas, Luke. I presume those dead blokes have bosses who want rid of you as well, so maybe you'll need to stay in hiding for a little bit longer?' Dante shrugged and sat back in his chair.

Dumbfounded, Deana turned towards him. 'You saw all of that? Does Dad know? How come you never told me?'

'I doubt Dad knows, Deana. And I never said anything

because I was being nosey and got more than I bargained for.'

Half smiling, Luke had opened the freezer and passed Kev a bag of frozen peas for his nose. 'Keep it down will you. Mum's in the lounge.' Remembering Luke's elderly and disabled mum, Deana said, 'Shall I go and say hello? She might remember me. Are you making her a drink? Maybe I could take it through?'

'Yeah, she'd like that.' Luke handed Deana the cup of tea and smiled. 'She will remember you.'

After a few minutes talking to Luke's mum Deana walked back into a very different atmosphere. Kev, Luke and Dante were laughing and joking with each other; it seemed they had overcome their differences.

'So, have we all kissed and made up then?' she asked, hating being left out of the joke.

'The gauntlet is laid Deana. We need to prove ourselves. Kev appreciates we can't go into the nightclubs selling stuff. But we can drop off and make new contacts. There must be a whole gang of cannabis smokers at your college who might want something a bit cheaper. I've already got a contact in mind. Do you have cocaine Luke?'

Surprised at the question, Luke nodded. 'Why? I thought you were only interested in cannabis?'

'Because I'm friends with someone whose dad likes the odd sniff apparently. Maybe it's time he got himself a new dealer with a discount. We'll start cheap, undercut the others.'

'That kind of thing causes arguments Dante. We don't want trouble.'

'It's a buyers' market Luke. And we're selling.'

'Dante's into science and chemistry. He reckons he can cook meth,' Deana butted in, not wanting to be left out.

'Meth? Do you think you can?' asked Kev, leaning forward, very interested in what he was hearing.

'Possibly. There are just a couple of hitches though.'

'Oh, here we go. That usually means you can't and you're all wind and piss,' sneered Kev.

'No, that means I have nowhere to cook it, or freeze it. And it could take a week or so to get the ingredients. It's easy enough. Also, there's the initial layout for the ingredients. After all, I'm just a school kid. Where would I get that kind of money?' Dante laughed.

Kev's eyes widened. 'You can cook it here,' he blurted out. 'We can sell meth mate. Christ, we can always sell that stuff. But it has to be good.'

Luke started to laugh. 'Let's not get ahead of ourselves, Kev. Let's start with the weed. The seedlings are downstairs in the basement. I'll take you down if you want. The other plants are at the allotments waiting to be sorted out and bagged up. I have a mobile phone with contacts the Liverpudlians we used to deal with used to sell to. People message us to see if we're working and place their orders. That's when we deliver. We stay in the car and call them a minute or so before we turn into their street to let them know we're there. The people come to us. Can you deliver?' Luke asked.

'Yes, we can deliver. Do you get a lot of trouble?' answered Dante.

'Sometimes. But you two don't drive. How are you going to deliver? What are you going to do? Spend all night on the bus?' He laughed.

'That's our problem, Luke. I have said we can deliver, and we will.'

Deana cast a sideways glance at Dante. She hadn't thought about that and was unsure about the hole Dante was digging for them.

'We could only do a few nights a week though. Not every day. We have to keep our own cover. College and stuff.' She blushed. She hated thinking she sounded like a school kid in front of Kev. He was so grown up and handsome!

'Well, we're not Tesco Deana,' Luke retorted. 'They message us and if we answer we do. And it's not just nights. Some people work nights and want their stuff delivered in the day time. Could you do that?'

'Dad didn't work days, did he?' Deana spat out. 'When are you two going to do some work?'

'Ah, now were getting to it. Don't worry, me and a few mates will organise the club scene. People always want something to make the party go with a swing. Kev here has got a drug den people pay to go into. He needs a supply though. And that's where MasterChef here and our plants come in. We have contacts and all you two have is a few plants and a delivery service after school.' Satisfied, Luke sat back and waited.

'Fair point. But we also have a partnership, and we will be keeping Dad updated when we visit him in prison. After all, we're looking after his interests. Let's not argue amongst ourselves. Let's give it a probationary period, shall we?' Dante said. He could see they were going around in circles. There was no trust at this point and only time would tell if this was going to work. 'We have to get back. Here are our mobile numbers. Call us when you have something to deliver.'

Luke saw them both to the door and waved them off, saying he would be in touch.

Deana was bursting with excitement as they left, but

Dante squeezed her arm. 'Not a word yet. Let's get to the bus stop first.' Looking up, she could see Luke and Kev looking out of the window, watching them walk up the path. 'Don't look like an excited kid Deana,' he whispered. 'We have to be grown-ups now.'

* * *

As Alex walked out of the showers a feeling of foreboding came over him. Usually, at this time of the morning other prisoners were shouting for those using the showers to hurry up, so they could use it. But this morning it was deserted. Drying himself off, he looked up into the mirror and saw someone standing behind him. A cold shudder ran through him. He'd known this was coming and was prepared for it, but it didn't stop him feeling nervous.

One huge burly man walked in followed swiftly by two more. Swallowing hard, he turned towards them. 'Morning,' he said nonchalantly, although his heart was pounding in his chest.

'It's time you got your comeuppance, Silva.' The burly man punched his fist into the palm of his other hand.

'Do I bend over or kneel down, gentlemen? What come-uppance do you have in mind?' asked Alex, hoping it was a physical beating and not sex.

'We might do that later. Hearing you squeal like a Portuguese pig could be funny.' He grinned. 'But for now we've been told to teach you a lesson.' Swiftly, the burly man punched out and hit Alex in the face, knocking him backwards onto the sinks. 'Hold him,' the burly man shouted to his mates, as Alex stood there defenceless. They grabbed Alex's arms tightly while the burly man threw punch after punch, pummelling him. Alex heard a crack and knew one of his ribs had broken, making him groan in pain. Standing there wet and half naked, with only a towel around his waist, he winced as one of them, he couldn't see who, kicked him in the groin with their large leather boot, making him howl.

The burly man reached into his shirt pocket and took out a homemade wooden knife carved to a point and stabbed it hard into Alex's shoulder. He screamed in pain. Blood spurted out like a fountain. Adrenalin kicked in and freeing his arms a little, Alex elbowed one of the men holding him and kicked out at the other one. Once he heard him scream, Alex knew he had kicked him in the groin as the man held his balls and bent double. Using the moment of opportunity, Alex lunged forward and grabbed the burly man with a hand on either side of his head. Swiftly, he leaned in and chewed off the burly man's earlobe and spat it out. The wet shower floor went crimson with blood as the burly man howled in pain. His mouth full of blood, Alex felt dizzy and weak.

Suddenly, whistles were heard, and two guards ran into the showers to see what all the screams were about and seeing the bloody sight before them that resembled a massacre, they radioed for assistance. More guards ran in. Seeing the burly man with half of his earlobe missing, and the sea of red covering him and his uniform, they looked up at Alex with horror as he swayed back and forth. His mouth was dripping with blood and his face was smeared with it. Quickly, the guards shouted for them all to get down on the floor and handcuffed their hands behind their backs, before making them stand up. Seeing Alex's nakedness, one guard wrapped the blood-stained wet towel around his waist.

Alex could barely stand. 'Leave that wooden spear, or whatever it is, in his arm. Don't take it out or you will cause more damage,' he heard a warder shout. Alex's body felt on fire and his eyes were closing. The aftermath of the beating he had just taken made his body shiver and the searing pain from his ribs made it hard for him to breathe. He ached everywhere. He could barely see through the slits in his eyes and the blood on his face, but, inwardly, he felt satisfied that he had fought back and caused some damage. Then he slipped into a black veil of unconsciousness.

Blinking hard, Alex woke up, although his eyes were swollen and he could barely open them. He didn't recognise his surroundings. Everything was stark white. Gently, he touched his chest and felt the bandages covering his ribs, covered by a cotton sheet. Trying to move his aching neck to the side, he saw trollies and nurses and realised he was in the prison hospital. His head was pounding. 'Well look who's awake. Welcome back to the land of the living.'

Squinting hard, he followed the voice and saw Fiddler standing beside him. 'I work in the library and hand out books in the hospital 'ere. Well, two nurses and an over-worked doctor they bring in twice a week,' he scoffed, 'and books, well, we hardly have any.'

Swallowing hard, Alex tried licking his swollen lips. His throat was dry, and he could barely whisper. 'How long have I been here?' he muttered.

'Two days in here and two in the big hospital in civvy street. The governor had to inform your wife, just in case. Apparently, they had to give you some blood, too. Think those two were going for the jugular but hit you in the shoulder instead. Thank goodness. In my opinion, if you're going to get a hitman, get one that's been to Specsavers first.' Fiddler grinned, trying to make light of the situation. As he looked down at Alex's purple, bruised face, he winced.

'How do you know all of this?' Alex croaked. Thinking about Maggie seeing him like this made him feel sick. 'Did my wife come to the hospital?'

'Presume so, not sure. I know all of this because I make it my business Alex. Still, you have earned yourself a new name. Alex the cannibal they are calling you now.' Fiddler laughed. 'Old one ear doesn't look any prettier than you. At least the chef knows you're not a vegetarian now.'

Seeing that Alex was rousing, a nurse came forward.

'He's waking up nurse, thought he might like a book,' explained Fiddler.

'He won't wake up properly for a while considering the number of drugs we've had to give him. He lost a lot of blood, but you can leave him a book if you like.'

Putting a book down on the bedside table, Fiddler looked at Alex. 'See you later,' he mouthed as he walked on with his trolley.

As the nurse felt his head and took his blood pressure, Alex realised the men had meant to kill him. He felt groggy and tired and found it hard to keep his eyes open. Before he drifted back off to sleep, his last thought was: if that home-made knife had pierced his jugular just inches above where the knife had gone in, he would most definitely have bled to death. And he would never have seen Maggie or the kids again.

5

NEW GOALS

Maggie knew she looked worried as she put the phone down, but she tried to hide it from her mum, Barbra, or Babs as she was known to everyone, who had recently arrived for a visit. 'Has that governor been on the telephone again? How's Alex doing? For goodness's sake, if he did his job properly and kept an eye on his inmates, he wouldn't have to ring you all the time updating you!' Babs scoffed. 'It's a bloody disgrace; the man can't just do his time in peace.'

Rolling her eyes at the ceiling, Maggie wondered if it had been such a good idea inviting her mum at this time. She had missed her a lot over the past couple of years and at times she had yearned to have a talk with her, but now Maggie was too exhausted. 'Alex is a lot better, Mum. Apparently, he's woken up and is being checked over. The governor has said I can visit whenever I like. But what's the bloody point, Mum? I was nearly a widow, and for what? Because Alex stood in that courtroom and volunteered to go to prison. He knew it was going to be a rough ride. Well, I hope he's learnt his lesson!' Hurt and upset, Maggie couldn't hold it in much longer.

'Come on, Maggie love. You've had a shock and it's natural you're upset. Why don't you go and visit him? It might cheer him up.'

'I'm not upset, Mum. I'm angry, bloody angry. He brought this upon himself, on all of us. After everything we've been through, he's probably going to die behind those prison walls – and for what? All that hiding and worrying has been for nothing. His bloody stubbornness will be the death of him. Well, if they think I'm turning up with grapes and kind words they're bloody wrong!'

'Shush, the kids will hear you, Maggie. I take it you haven't told them any of this, because they haven't said anything to me.'

'No. I haven't.' Tears of anger and frustration fell down Maggie's face. 'I'm not telling them their dad nearly got himself killed.' Babs opened her arms and Maggie fell into them, sobbing on her shoulder. 'He should come home now Mum, surely?'

'He can't come home yet, Maggie, you know he can't.' Babs gently patted Maggie on the back. 'He would look like a coward who's done a runner and we both know that's not him, love. There, there now, love. Come on, dry your eyes. We don't want the kids seeing you like this. Questions will be asked. Although, you should take that governor up on his offer and go and see Alex. Put his mind at rest that you're on his side and put your mind at rest seeing him awake again. Give it another day or so, but go, Maggie love, go and see your husband.'

Nodding, Maggie dried the tears from her eyes. 'You're right, I suppose. I can't desert him now, can I? As much as I hate him at the moment, he is still my husband and we've been in this together from the beginning. But why did he have to decide to go to prison?'

'Because he had a lot to prove, Maggie: his self-respect, his pride. He's not hiding any more. Okay, it hasn't gone as planned, but he is showing that mafia lot that he isn't scared to stand on his own two feet without their backing. Hell love, that lot couldn't do anything without each other. Well, your husband has stood alone and weathered the storm, like a man. Now brush yourself off and let's get down in that bar.'

Hearing a voice behind them, both women instantly stopped talking. 'Knock, knock. Is this women's business or can I come in?' Looking up, Maggie and Babs saw Mark standing in the doorway. 'Just thought I'd pop up to see how the invalid was doing?'

'If you mean my prick of a husband, Mark, then apparently, he's awake. I don't know much else.' As an afterthought, Maggie narrowed her eyes and looked at Mark. 'Please tell me you haven't broadcast all this during one of your drinking sessions?'

Taken aback, Mark looked almost wounded at Maggie's words. 'For God's sake Maggie. There's no need for that. I haven't said a word, not even to Olivia. I wouldn't; you confided in me for Christ's sake.' Letting out a huge sigh, Mark turned to walk out, but Maggie stopped him.

'Sorry Mark, I'm just a bit stressed and I haven't told the kids about Alex yet. I don't want them to know about this, they've had enough on their plate lately. Where are they anyway? Is your George home from school yet?'

'Dunno, just got in myself and thought I'd pop by to see how Alex was. They should be home though.' Looking at his watch, Mark frowned. 'It's already after five. George will be having his dinner now. The kids might be at mine; I'll go and check.'

'No, it's okay, I'll give one of them a ring on their mobile. At least that was a good idea. It helps me keep a check on them.' Maggie bid Mark farewell and went to find out where the hell her two kids were.

* * *

Deana danced excitedly outside the gates of Dante's school as she waited for him. 'Christ,' she tutted when he finally emerged. 'What have you been doing in there? All the others left ages ago.'

'Finishing my essay. I like the peace and quiet and the teachers don't mind. They usually stay to do some marking or whatever. There's never peace and quiet at home with the barmaids and kitchen staff clanging around all the time, plus the punters and now Grandma. I thought she was only coming for a few days but she's brought three suitcases with her, which isn't a good sign,' he groaned. 'Anyway, what are you so excited about and why are you here? My big sister picking me up from school! Doesn't exactly do much for my street cred does it?'

Deana's face was flushed with excitement. 'There are loads of deliveries to be made! Here are the addresses and a list of what they want. We have to go to Kev's place and pick up the goods tonight... there is a snag though.' Deana's heart sank when she scrolled down the rest of the message, which she'd overlooked in her excitement. Shoving her mobile phone in front of Dante's face, she pointed at the message. 'Look, that's your big mouth, Dante. You said this wasn't a problem.'

Craning his neck, Dante looked at Deana's mobile and read the message. Puzzled, he looked at her, not quite understanding her reluctance. 'Yeah so, what about it?'

'We need a car, Dante. A bloody car! All these addresses are quite a distance apart.'

'So, we'll get one.' Dante smiled. 'Christ, Deana, for someone with a big mouth and an impulsive nature you've just fallen at the first hurdle. I can drive. You can drive. So, we'll hot wire one. Better still, well take one of those old bangers Mark has on his driveway. No one will notice, not even him, and at least it's not traceable to us. Find some balls Deana. This was your idea!'

Biting her bottom lip, Deana paused for a moment. 'Sorry Dante. You're right. We can do this. I was just having a wobbly.'

'Deana, we can't afford for you to be having a last-minute wobble. We have to prove ourselves or we prove we're two kids who are full of shit. I've got pride even if you haven't. Now, do you have the address of Kev's place?'

Scrolling down, Deana read the message again. 'Yeah, I've got it. Shit, it's in the real shitty part of town. Everybody talks about that warzone and warns you away from it at college.'

'Well, I didn't expect the Ritz. I fancy some chips, then we'll work out our plan. We need a good excuse for going out tonight. Both of us together.'

Thinking for a moment, Deana looked around for inspiration. 'Actually yeah. I do have a plan. There is a fair going on at the moment. We could use that as an excuse for tonight but we need something more regular. So let's go home and suggest the fair. Mum's going to be behind the bar with Grandma, anyway. We need this money, if only to pay for another cement mixer for Grandma's make-up.' She laughed.

Rolling his eyes at the ceiling, Dante let out a laugh. 'I know, she must get up at 4 a.m. to put it on, layer by layer. I can never make my mind up whether Grandma resembles Peggy Mitchell from *EastEnders* or Pat Butcher. Possibly both! Whoever said less is more, never saw Grandma's make-up routine.' The pair of them burst out laughing as they entered the chip shop and ordered. 'And if she pinches my cheeks again and calls me "Dante Boy" I will scream. Grandma visiting was not one of your best ideas Deana.'

'Yes, but at least Mum has something else to take her mind off things, and Grandma has a whole new pub to impress with her barmaid skills. Even though she's pissing everyone else off.'

As they walked home eating their chips, Deana's mobile rang. Looking at it, she saw it was their mother. 'Hi Mum. I know, I've just seen the time. I will call you back on WhatsApp video.' Ending the call, Deana smiled. 'Let her see what we're doing. It makes it look good. We're just good, honest kids walking home with a bag of chips.' Suddenly their mum's face popped up on the mobile screen. 'Say hello Dante.' Deana held up her mobile while they both stood waving at their mum. 'Hi Mum.' Dante grinned.

Obviously relieved at seeing them both safe and sound, Maggie smiled. 'Well, I won't worry about dinner then. As long as you're okay. No problem. See you both soon.' Maggie blew them both a kiss and ended the call.

'You didn't mention the fair, Deana,' Dante snapped. 'Don't you think you should have said something?'

'That comes up when we're home. One step at a time. We've answered her call, she's seen we're okay and she's happy. Our little request won't be a problem.'

'And if she calls us and there is no fair? Are you going to video call her then, in a stolen car and a bag of cannabis?'

'Christ's sake Dante, who can hear their phone at a fair with all that music? Also, the internet will probably be really bad, too.' She laughed and grabbing him by the shoulder, frog marched him, making him drop his chips. Flinging her own onto the ground, she started running. 'Come on slow coach, it's going to be a long night!' she shouted after her as she raced ahead.

*　*　*

Maggie stood behind the familiar bar serving the usual customers, who had eventually started to come back. She knew the place held a stigma now, but their thirst and social life came first and slowly the old faces from the neighbourhood started walking back through the doors as though nothing had happened. As she overheard them chatting to their friends, Maggie noticed that none of them mentioned Alex's name once. It was as though their latest venture had never happened, which felt surreal to Maggie as she was still very much living the nightmare.

Pulling Phyllis to one side, Maggie asked if she could speak to her in private. Together they walked into the staff room-cum-lounge where they all had their breaks.

Phyllis stood stoney faced with her arms folded. 'You don't have to say anything. I presumed as much when your mum turned up with all her baggage and started bossing us around the bar. You're sacking me, aren't you?'

'What? For God's sake, Phyllis. No way am I sacking you. You've been my rock and if my mum's bossing you about, I will deal with it. What I was going to say, is I know that your sister in Portsmouth has been unwell lately, but you've stayed and run this place in my absence. Why don't you go and visit her, on full wages of course and you don't have to take the leave from your holiday allowance. This is just to say thank you.'

Taken aback by Maggie's words, Phyllis stood rooted to the spot. 'Oh, well, I didn't expect that. You've taken the wind out of my sails a bit Maggie. I don't know what to say,' she stammered. 'And will I have a job to come back to?'

'Of course you will! I wish I hadn't suggested it now. It was meant as a good will gesture.'

'Then I will take it as one. I wouldn't mind seeing her for a few days to see if she's okay. Maybe I'll be able to bring her home with me.'

'That's sorted then. Go when you want and come back when you want. And I mean come back,' Maggie stressed. 'I'll be doing the same for Pauline when you get back and will tell her later. It's the least I can do for all your loyalty.' Maggie also thought about putting a little extra in their pay packets from Alex's savings. They had kept the pub going between them while she had almost fallen apart. 'Anyway, what's my mum been doing?'

Making a face and raising her eyebrows, Phyllis let out a sigh. 'Giving orders, changing things around, standing at the end of the bar gossiping like the landlady and then telling us – not asking us – to go and pick up dirty glasses. We do that anyway, Maggie. It's part of our job,' Phyllis blurted out. It seemed to Maggie that she had been bottling all of this up and it just came tumbling out. Clearly disgruntled by the fact that Maggie's mum made her feel inferior, Phyllis's face turned sour again.

'Leave it with me Phyllis. Mum has run a pub all of her

life and it's a hard habit to break, eh? Well, she will have to get used to the fact that you're my staff, I'm the landlady and she is my visiting mother. I will sort it – promise.' Maggie reached across and gave Phyllis a hug, which she returned. 'I've taken my eye off the ball. Sorry love.'

Hearing the back door slam shut and a stampede going up the stairs, Maggie smiled. 'Sounds like the kids are home.' About to leave, Maggie turned to Phyllis again. 'Your job is always safe here, Phyllis – don't ever doubt it. I'm glad we had this chat.'

Walking upstairs and into the kitchen, musing to herself, Maggie felt it was time to put her 'mother' hat, on. She'd been the wronged wife, the landlady with staff problems and now she had to step up as a mum. Would she ever get five minutes to herself, she wondered? 'Well, how are you two? Did you have a good day?' Maggie asked.

'Yeah, I was going past Dante's school and thought I'd wait for him, but Mr Swot here stayed behind and did homework, that's why we're late,' Deana scoffed.

'Good for you Dante. It's good to know that, with one thing and another you haven't let things slide.' Maggie patted him on the head and ruffled his hair. 'How are your college studies going Deana?' Seeing Deana make a face, Maggie didn't push it.

'Where's Grandma?' Dante asked suspiciously.

'She's in the bath making herself look beautiful for tonight.' Maggie laughed. 'What do you fancy to eat or have you stuffed your faces with chips? Not much of an advert for the chef of this place is it if you would rather eat out.'

'Actually, Mum.' Flashing a glance at Dante, Deana looked at Maggie, feeling now was the time to bring up their night out. 'There's a fair on not far away. Could we go there and get some hot dogs and stuff? Some of the girls from college are going.'

'What, and you want Dante to go with you? Well, that's surprised me. Won't it be just you and your friends?'

'No, there's a crowd of us, and he'll only moan about it if you don't let him. It's just we don't have any money,' Deana lied, sulkily. 'And everyone's going Mum.'

'Well, I'm okay with that if you are. No need to put the hard done by act on for my benefit, Deana. Although I'm not happy it's a school night.'

'It's Thursday, Mum. Friday and Saturday are the last nights, and it will be rammed and the prices will go up. Plus, there will be all kinds of weirdos and trouble. Usually is on the last night of those things.'

'Fair point. Do you want to ask George to go with you, too?' Maggie asked Dante and Deana almost choked on her cough. 'For Christ's sake, Mum. I don't mind taking my little brother but I'm not taking the bloody street of kids. I'm not the local babysitter.'

'Okay, keep your hair on, I was only asking.' Maggie smiled. 'Yeah, you two go and enjoy yourselves. I can always ring you if I want you. And you two can ring me when you're coming home.'

Furtively, Deana and Dante looked at each other. 'Absolutely Mum,' they both chimed.

6

A NIGHT TO REMEMBER

Once Maggie had given them some spending money, and Babs had pulled them aside and given them a little extra in case they needed it, Deana and Dante left for the fair.

'Well, how are we going to steal one of Mark's cars without him noticing?' Deana scoffed. 'Why don't we just get the bus to a supermarket and hot wire one of the cars parked there?'

'Ye of little faith. I've already sorted it while you were getting changed.' Smugly, Dante cast his eyes to a car that wasn't parked outside Mark's house, or in his driveway. Following his eye line, Deana shrugged. 'Whose is that?'

'Mark's fixing it, but he doesn't have the room for it on his drive, not with all the other cars he has. And I just happen to know that Mark's having a few of his mates round tonight. They will all be getting pissed in his garden so no one will be taking any notice of what's going on. Anyway Deana, supermarkets have cameras and someone might see us.'

'So do some of our neighbours, including the pub.'

Deana was half excited about their mission and also a little pensive.

'Come on. It's now or never.' Quickening his pace, Dante walked up to the car. Trying the door handle, he was surprised that Mark hadn't even locked it.

'What if it won't start? Has it got any petrol?' Deana butted in.

'Only one way to find out, sis. Now move your arse and get in,' he snapped.

Just as Alex had shown him, Dante pulled out the wires and put them together. As the pair of them held their breath, the car started up immediately. Looking down, Dante smiled. 'This is even better, just in case we're a bit rusty at driving. Look, it's automatic.' Laughing, he put his foot on the accelerator and drove on without a backward turn.

'You haven't checked for petrol!' Deana half shouted, as she looked around to see if anyone was watching.

'Half a tank.' Dante smiled. 'Now get Mr Google Maps out and type in the postcode to Kev's warzone.' He laughed.

Driving along, Deana laughed excitedly, too. 'We've done it Dante, we've bloody done it!'

'Christ, you weren't kidding when you said it was a warzone.' Even though the headlights were on, Dante couldn't help peering closer through the windscreen as they arrived. Looking at the surroundings as they turned into a block of flats, he spied burnt-out cars and overflowing skips. A lot of the windows in the flats were lit up. Some soiled net curtains hung at the windows, others had nothing.

'I don't like it. This place gives me the creeps. God knows who's around here.'

'Yeah,' he muttered. 'You mean like drug dealers and thieves.' He smiled in Deana's direction.

'Christ, Dante, stop being so flippant. It's pitch black out there, even the street lights aren't working. Put your full beams on so we can see where we're driving to.'

'Nope. Full beams will attract attention. This lot will probably think we're the police or something. Look on the side of the block of flats. That's the name you said, isn't it?'

'Yeah, Zeus Tower.' Deana laughed nervously. 'Omg, look at that one. Hercules Tower. They are all named after Greek mythical legends or something. Well, they look around the same age. Park behind those skips if you can.' Deana pointed. 'This place is desolate, but when we come out, this car will be on bricks. I guarantee it.'

Trying his hardest to see in the darkness, Dante was tempted to put on the full beam headlights but thought better of it. He heard a scrape on the side of the car and knew he'd brushed against one of the skips. 'Shit!' he moaned. 'I can't see a bloody thing. Sorry.'

'Not our car. Not our problem. Just make sure I can get out; back up a bit.' Feeling a little braver now, Deana was eager to get out of the car, see Kev, and get out of there. It was going to be a long night considering all of the addresses they had been given. Thankfully, Dante had methodically worked his way through the addresses and put all the postcodes in order, which would save them a lot of time.

'Is this a stereotype or what? Why are the lifts always broken in these places? I've never heard of a high-rise flat lift working yet, not even on the telly,' she moaned.

'What floor is it?' Dante's heart sank as he looked at the double doors at the side of the lift covered in graffiti. Presumably this was the staircase and those were supposedly fire doors, which he doubted.

Giving him a weak smile, Deana replied, 'Ninth floor.'

'Oh, well it could be worse. It could be the top floor. I thought we would be picking the stuff up from Luke's house. Not this dump. Why is there no one around?'

'Would you walk around here at night? Cos I bloody wouldn't. As soon as the lights dimmed, I'd be indoors with the doors bolted. Come on, let's start climbing.' Pushing the fire doors open, they both winced and almost gagged at the smell of dried urine and vomit on the stairs.

Shaking his head, Dante covered his mouth with his arm. 'Fuck this, I've had enough. Let's go. If we don't get mugged we're going to faint from the fumes!'

'Don't be such a coward. We're visiting, not living here. We've stolen a car, driven to a warzone and now the stink of piss and tobacco is imbedded in our clothes. At least let's show our faces, Dante. Come on,' Deana stressed. 'I'll message Kev and let him know we're here.'

Stopping at a door, they both noticed there wasn't a number on it. Not wanting to make a mistake, they looked down the corridor counting the numbers. 'This one has got to be it.' Suddenly the door opened, and standing there in his mirrored sunglasses and combat jacket and trousers stood Kev.

'You found me then.' He grinned. 'Come on, you need to get started. People are waiting.' Following Kev into the flat, Dante looked around. 'It's an opium den,' he whispered, standing even closer to Deana. His eyes hurt and started watering in the foggy, smoky room. The more he wiped them, the more they stung. It was claustrophobic, and instantly he started sweating, it was so hot. Through the mist, he could see people scattered around in corners on the floor, as Kev led the way. Some were conscious, some not, but each one was either smoking something through glass pipes, sniffing something or shooting up. The place was stark, with just a few deck chairs scattered around. Dante could feel the bile rising and felt sick.

Kev walked them towards the balcony and opened the sliding doors and stepped out. Dante almost jumped out, trying to breathe some fresh air into his lungs.

Chewing hard on his gum, Kev grinned. 'Not your scene schoolboy? Never mind, you will come to like it. This is my office; sit down.' Ignoring Kev's sarcasm, Dante and Deana looked around at the balcony and noticed a couple of folded up deckchairs resting against the wall. From where the balcony started to the ceiling above them was netting. Noticing Dante looking, Kev said. 'That's to stop the pigeons flying in and people jumping off, Dante. They still do it anyway.' Kev smiled.

Opening up the deck chairs, they sat down and waited for instructions.

Taking off his mirrored sunglasses, Kev kicked over a leather holdall. 'In there you've got mushrooms, cannabis, coke, speed and heroin. You also have four hundred ciga-rettes. We get them cheap and we have more if need be. These are your orders. The sandwich bags are in there, so that it looks like you're delivering a takeaway. It's corny but it works. One of you drives, and one of you has the bag. You never and I mean *never*, get out of the car. Don't give a fuck what they say or if they are having a heart attack on the pave-ment.' Giving them a glare and wagging a warning finger in their faces, he repeated himself. 'As you get to the top of the street you ring them, that gives them time to come out of their front door. Then you wind the window down, take the money first and then hand them the bag. No pleasantries. I don't give a fuck about the weather or their health. You just drive away – got it?' Kev put his sunglasses back on, and then, as an afterthought, said, 'You are driving, aren't you? For Christ's sake, please tell me you're not on skateboards or something!' Then, he burst out laughing.

'What do you drive, Kev? I didn't notice where your car was parked,' Dante couldn't help retorting to Kev's mocking words.

Faltering, Kev stammered slightly. 'I don't drive. I'm usually off my head on something, so I don't drive.' Looking Dante directly in the face, he nodded. 'Fair point snotty. Just joking. So, you've got wheels, nicked I presume. That's your business. You do it whatever way works for you – okay?'

Deana and Dante nodded in unison as they listened intently to Kev's words of wisdom and experience. He had obviously done this many times.

'On a brighter note, Dante the man. Here's a bag for you.' Kicking the bag with his foot over to Dante, Kev folded his arms and grinned, looking very pleased with himself. Feeling a little better with the cool evening breeze clearing his head and eyes, Dante looked down at a bigger holdall, puzzled. 'What is it?'

'Everything you need to do some cooking, MasterChef. You're going to use Luke's kitchen as we said, but you need to take the stuff with you tonight. I don't want it hanging around here. Lots of thieves and vagabonds here.' He laughed and slapped his knee at his own joke.

'I will go at the weekend, if that's okay?' Dante asked. Casting a glance towards Deana, Dante noticed how quiet she was. He couldn't understand that bolshy Deana didn't have anything to say. And then he saw the almost girlish grin on her face as she listened to Kev and laughed at his jokes, which in Dante's opinion weren't very funny.

Lighting a cannabis roll-up, Kev waved his hand in the air nonchalantly. 'Yeah, whenever mate. That's between you and Luke. Just one of you let me know when it's ready to try. Do your best, eh? This stuff isn't cheap.'

Nodding, Dante stood up and pulled Deana by the shoulder of her hoodie onto her legs. He wanted to leave and get started, although he dreaded walking back into the flat again to find the front door.

'Drop the money off at Luke's as well. I'm not saying I don't trust you but... well, I fucking don't!' Kev laughed and Dante cringed when he saw Deana laughing too.

'No, but you trust me with this bag of chemicals, don't you? Luke will get the money,' snapped Dante. Irritated by Deana's blatant flirting and Kev's insults, he walked through the balcony doors. Holding his breath and with his hand over his mouth so he didn't inhale the smoke, Dante marched towards the front door.

'Hey, what about me?' Deana called after him. Giving Kev a quick smile, she picked up both bags and followed her brother.

As they got back to the car, pleased to see it was still in one piece, Deana read out the first address and telephone number. 'You didn't have to be so rude to Kev in there Dante. It's just his way.' She shrugged as Dante drove off.

'I wasn't the one being rude. Now be quiet, I'm listening to Google Maps,' he snapped. Before they turned into the first street of the address given, Deana called the number and informed them they were five minutes away and to meet outside their house. Rummaging through the bags she took out a brown bag, which looked like it contained a sandwich or burger, which was the disguise for whatever drug it contained. To the outside world they looked like delivery drivers for a takeaway firm.

At the gate as they pulled up, a man greeted them. Dante pulled down his baseball cap and adjusted his glasses to make him look older and opened the window. The man reached through and held out a wad of notes and took the bag. 'Thanks,' was all he said before he turned to go back up his pathway.

'Christ! That was easy, Dante,' exclaimed Deana, grinning from ear to ear.

'Well, we're not going to sit and discuss the weather, are we?' He laughed. 'Come on, which one's next?' Deana had already typed the addresses into Google Maps and so clicked on the next one to bring the directions up.

Before long, they had done twenty of the drop-offs, all the same routine. Deana looked down at the bag full of money. She couldn't believe it. She wasn't stupid, she knew dealers made money, but seeing it with her own eyes like this amazed her. 'This is the last one, Dante, then we'll get a real burger or something. I'm starving and my stomach thinks my throat's been cut.' As Deana made the call and they drove to the address they saw two burly men come out of a house and walk to the kerbside to meet them, as the other customers before them had done.

'Here you go mate.' As one of them threw the wad of cash through the car window towards him, Dante's gut feeling told him something wasn't right. He wanted to drive off, but the money was in the car and they couldn't leave without giving them what they had paid for. Snatching the brown bag out of Deana's hand, he held it through the car window.

Suddenly, one of the men grabbed Dante's wrist and

pulled his arm through the window, while trying to pull the car door open. Dante had cleverly put the child locks on in the car, so the door wouldn't open from the outside, but as the burly man pulled his arm through the window he nearly pulled it out of the socket. Dante screamed in pain and Deana screamed at the man, but as she looked up, she saw the other man going around to her side of the car. He started pulling at the door handle and banging on the window for her to open it.

'Put your foot down on the accelerator Dante!' she screamed, but it was too late. The man at her side of the car took out a small hammer from underneath his coat and smashed the window, shattering glass all over her and the inside of the car. Deana did her best to shield herself with her arms, as remnants of the glass embedded themselves in her hair and clothing. The man reached in and opened the door from the inside, roughly, dragging her out onto the road and letting her fall to the ground in pain. Getting in from Deana's side of the car, the man half knelt on her car seat and shoved Dante's head into the car window. 'The money; where is it?' Looking around, he saw the bags on the floor in front of the front seat and swiftly picked up the money and got back out of the car, shaking off bits of glass that had got onto his clothing. 'Fucking dealers! Sending kids to do a man's job.' Both men shouted and laughed. Standing beside Deana, he gave her a swift kick in the stomach making her double up into a ball and wince in pain. The man who had hold of Dante loosened his grip and put his hand through the window. Grabbing Dante by the back of the neck, he rammed his head into the steering wheel. Then, once they had got what they wanted, the two men walked back up their path, opened the front door and slammed it shut.

Struggling to get up, Deana hobbled to Dante's side of the

car. Seeing his blood-stained face, where his nose was obviously broken, she burst into tears. 'Oh, for Christ's sake, Dante, are you conscious?'

Seeing him nod, she let out a breath of relief. 'Open the car door and move over. You can't drive. We need to get out of here.' Dante did his best to slide across to the passenger seat, but blood streamed from his nose and mouth and his arm ached. He hoped it wasn't broken, but the man had twisted it and pulled it so hard, he wasn't sure. Pain wracked his body, and his head throbbed. Deana got into the still running car and put it into drive, putting her foot down.

Almost blinded by her own tears, she didn't know where she was driving to, but just wanted to get away. Casting a glance towards Dante, she could see his blood-stained shirt and jacket as they soaked up the blood dripping from his face. 'Dante! Are you okay?' she shouted in a blind panic. Her heart was pounding, and she felt herself trembling as she tried keeping a grip on the steering wheel.

'No, I'm not fucking all right. Look at me! I think my nose is broken,' he muttered, as he spat blood out of his mouth. Seeing a small cul-de-sac, Deana pulled into it and stopped. Reaching over, she pulled Dante towards her and hugged him, covering herself in his blood. 'Oh my God, Dante, I thought they were going to kill us. They've taken all of the money. Look at us, how do we explain this to Mum?' she wailed.

'Are my front teeth broken?' asked Dante, opening his mouth towards Deana. His gums were red with blood, and she could hardly see in the darkness. 'No, I don't think so. They look okay to me, but I can't see properly with all the blood in your mouth. Here, drink this as mouth wash.' Reaching into the glove compartment, Deana took out a bottle of water and handed it to him. Taking a huge mouthful, he rinsed it around his mouth, before spitting it out onto the pavement. 'We could go to Luke's and get cleaned up before we go home.'

While Dante was still rinsing his mouth out, he shook his head. 'We can't. We've lost the money. We've been robbed Deana and there's no one we can report it to. It's what Kev and Luke suspected. We're two kids not up to the job. We've fucked up on our first outing.' Feeling more himself now, Dante got out of the car for some air and poured the rest of the water from the bottle over his head and rubbed his face with the flap of his shirt. 'There was a good few grand in that bag, Deana.' Letting out a huge sigh, he rubbed his hands through his wet hair. 'At least my glasses aren't broken.' He half grinned as he rubbed his arm and tried waving it around to get some sensation back into it. He knew it wasn't broken now and felt pleased about that.

'We could borrow some money out of Dad's stash and give them that to cover our backs?' Deana reasoned. 'At least we know what we're up against with these druggies now.' Getting back into the car, they both sat in silence for a moment contemplating their near escape with death. At last, Dante spoke. 'We blame the fair Deana. One of the rides jolted forward and I hit my face on the metal safety bar. That could explain me. What about you?'

'Just a kick in the stomach. Winded me, but a few cuts from the glass, I think. Nothing much.' Feeling a little calmer, she nodded her head. 'Okay, the fair ride. Shit like that happens all the time. Now what about the money? We have to pay that back. We've tried and failed Dante. We're not Dad. I'm sorry I dragged you into this mad-cap scheme. I really am.'

'Don't be. I came along with you. We are going to get that money back Deana. I don't know why, but I have a feeling your beloved Kev has set us up. Testing us. Surely if those blokes steal off the drivers, they wouldn't go back to them? They wouldn't be on their mailing list, would they?' he stressed. 'Think about it. And I heard their sarcastic remark about kids doing a man's job. We've been tried and tested and Kev possibly already knows about it. How come they only took the money bag and not the bag of chemicals? Look, it's still here.' Dante pointed to the bag beside his feet. 'They didn't know what was in it. It could have been full of drugs, but they never took it. Why not?'

'Are you always so calm and rational, Dante?' Deana smiled. 'But you're right. That holdall is zipped and they didn't even look inside. It could have been full of money for all they knew. So now what?' Feeling disappointed that Kev would set them up like this, she felt foolish for flirting with him now. She had made herself look like a silly schoolgirl in front of him and Dante. All the while he had known what was going to happen to them. She felt embarrassed and hurt.

'If those two fat bastards want a war, they can have one Deana. We're going back to get our money, but first we need to get something and get rid of this car. We can't drive around with a smashed window; it would attract too much attention. And if the police saw it, we're up shit creek.'

'Going back? Are you serious?' Deana exclaimed, not believing her ears. 'That bang on the head has made you stupid. For Christ's sake Dante, we can't go back there and demand our money back. They will beat the living daylights out of us. Look at us already. I do agree about the car though.' Deana looked around it. There was glass everywhere, the window was smashed and there were traces of Dante's blood in it. 'At least the seats are leather; we could clean the blood off. But it's late and we have to get home. I'm surprised Mum hasn't called already.'

Turning towards her, Dante glared at her with a determined look on his face. 'We're going home to make our excuses and alibis and then we're going back. Those druggies don't sleep till sunrise. Look at Kev, he's like Dracula, always wearing dark sunglasses. Daylight would probably kill him. I agreed to your scheming ways, now you agree to mine. We're in this together. Do you want your own back or are you going to let those fat bastards get the better of you?'

Nervously, Deana smiled at him. Starting up the car engine, she was about to drive off when Dante stopped her. 'Leave this here. We'll take one of those.' Deana looked out of the windscreen to where Dante was pointing at some parked cars. 'What about the blood? It will have your DNA all over the place.'

'Torch it. It's secluded enough around here. Come on.' Getting out of the car, Dante walked towards the few cars in the cul-de-sac before he spotted a small Renault. Deana watched as he fiddled about with the handle. The alarm flashed orange for a moment, but once Dante got in, it stopped. Suddenly the engine burst into life, and he drove past Deana and stopped at the end of the cul-de-sac. Deana searched the glove compartment. She needed a lighter and suddenly wished she smoked. Dante looked at her. 'What's the problem?'

'No lighter. How are we gonna burn something without a lighter?'

'Use the car lighter. Get some paper or something.' Doing as she was told, Deana pushed in the car lighter. After a moment it popped out and glowed orange. Seeing a discarded twenty-pound note on the floor, she held it close until it caught fire, then held it towards a throw cover blanket on the back seat. Instantly, it caught fire. Grabbing the bag of chemicals, she got out and ran to the car Dante had stolen.

'Oh my God, what happened to you?' Maggie half shouted when she saw them both.

'It's okay Mum. We're both okay. It was just an accident at the fair.'

Maggie almost pushed them both up the stairs with Babs hot on her heels. 'What happened? What accident?'

Deana went on to tell their well-rehearsed story about the fair ride jolting and Dante banging his face on the safety rail. Almost distraught, Maggie ran to the cupboards for antiseptic and asked if he needed a doctor. 'I think it might be easier if I jumped into the shower. I'm covered in blood. It looks a lot, but it's just from my nose and lips.' Dante smiled. 'I'm okay really. It was an accident and half my own fault for not paying attention and holding on tight enough.'

Seeing that he seemed okay, Maggie smiled. 'Well, if you're okay, go and have a shower and then we'll assess the damage. You're bleeding, too, Deana. Is your face cut?'

'No, the blood is from Dante's nose when I was looking after him.' Deana hoped she had got rid of all the glass in her hair. Once they had got out of the car, she had taken off her top and jumped up and down while shaking her hair. 'But I will have a shower after Dante.'

'Christ, one night at the fair and they look like they've been in a massacre. Who's in charge of that thing? Surely there are regulations about safety.'

'Let it go, Maggie. We'll patch him up once he's out the shower. I bet he was showing off in front of Deana's college friends. Trying to be macho or something.' Babs laughed and winked at Maggie. 'He's at that funny age boys go through.'

After his shower, Maggie inspected him more closely. 'Your nose is cut and swollen, and boy, are you going to have a couple of black eyes. Christ you must have taken one hell of a bang, Dante. You're not feeling faint or drowsy, are you? You could be concussed. Maybe we should go and get you checked out.'

'No, Mum, I'm okay really, I am,' he assured her. 'Just a few aches and pains. Think I'll go for a lie down.'

'Take some paracetamol, love. I'll look in on you later.'

Dante's blood almost froze. 'No, Mum, no need if I'm asleep, you'll only wake me. I'm not a baby.'

'Okay love. But shout for me if you want anything. I'm just going to check the bar, and I'll be up myself in a minute.'

'I'm bushed too, Mum. I'm going to bed. Night both.' Disappearing to her room, Deana shut the door until she heard Maggie and Babs go back downstairs. Then she walked back into Dante's room. 'We can't go back out now. Mum will definitely look in on you Dante.'

'Put some pillows under the duvet. If she sees I'm asleep she won't come in. You do the same. We haven't got long while she cleans up downstairs, come on.'

Quickly dressing, Dante and Deana crept downstairs and stood near the umbrella rack in the hallway. Reaching down, Dante took out the shotgun his dad had hidden there when he still lived here. 'Do you have one Deana? We've got to look like we mean business.' Shocked, Deana stared at Dante and nodded. Going back upstairs, she got the gun her dad had given her and walked back down to Dante. Once outside, she turned to him. 'You're not going to kill them, Dante? We can't do that. Why are we carrying guns for Christ's sake?'

'We won't have to. They will shit themselves when we turn up with these. Let's find a car.'

'What if they use them on us Dante? We don't know how many blokes are in that house,' Deana reasoned, while trying to catch up with Dante as he quickened his pace ahead of her.

'That's a chance I'm prepared to take. We have to think like Dad, Deana,' Dante snapped. 'We have to stop this before it gets worse. We need that money back and I'm going to get it. We're not pushovers; we're Silvas and we've faced worse than a couple of dealing druggies who thump kids.'

'Spose so,' said Deana half-heartedly. She wasn't sure about this, but it was too late now. She had agreed to go back with him.

After hotwiring another car, Dante turned into the road they had been attacked in. 'Make the call Deana. Tell them their delivery is here. Let's see how many come out of that house this time.'

Frowning, Deana turned to him. 'You're going to warn them we're here?'

'Yes. They'll think it's a game. Come on, let's see their reaction.' He grinned.

'You're off your head Dante. I think you did suffer concussion. This is a stupid idea.'

'Have you got a better one? Shall we just go and knock on the door? How do you propose we get in?'

'Fair point.' Deana sniffed and made the call. The raucous laughter on the other end of the phone annoyed her. She had put it on loudspeaker specially for Dante.

'Are you taking the piss! It's Mickey and Minnie Mouse

come back for more. They've probably brought all their school mates to beat us up!' the man on the other end of the phone shouted to someone and burst out laughing, Presumably the friend he was with. 'Yeah, we'll be out in a minute.'

Casting her a sideways glance, Dante looked at Deana. 'See. They think we're a joke. We're going to show them that we're not.'

Dante parked a few cars up and doing his best to conceal his shotgun, walked towards the house. He could see all the lights were on and he ran up the path and stood with his back against the wall beside the front door and pointed to Deana to stand at the other side of the door. 'Remember what Dad used to say,' Dante whispered. 'Always take your enemies by surprise, and we have an advantage. I bet they've been smoking or sniffing something to weaken their senses.' The door opened and the two men came out laughing, while drinking a can of beer. Swiftly, they walked up the path, unable to see Dante and Deana at either side of the doorway in the darkness. Turning their heads from side to side, looking for the car, the two men stood at the gate with their beer cans in hand.

Suddenly Dante crept forward and held the shotgun to one of their heads. 'You were right boys, I've brought a friend.' Swiftly turning, the men found themselves looking down the barrel of Dante's shotgun. Deana followed suit and walked out of the shadows with her handgun. 'Indoors you two,' she ordered. 'Don't fuck with me; my hands are trembling, and I might just press the trigger by accident,' she warned. Casting a furtive glance towards each other, the two men walked forward, back into the house.

'What do you want?' one of them asked sarcastically, once they had got back into the house. Seeing Dante's battered face, he grinned. 'Been in a fight, kid?' He looked at the gun pointed at him. 'You two haven't got the guts. Are those things even real?' He laughed and with one swoop of his hand slapped Dante across the face making him stagger backwards. Deana cocked the trigger of her gun and shot the man who had hit Dante in the foot. 'Yeah, they're real fatso,' she snarled above his screams of pain, as he fell to the ground holding his leg. Then she pointed the gun at the other man. 'Which foot do you dance on big boy, or do you want to do the one step?'

'Hey, hold on kid. There's no need for violence. You've shot him in the foot! Look at him bleeding all over my wife's carpet.'

'We want the money back,' said Dante, once he'd recovered from the blow he'd received. 'Hand it over and we'll leave.'

'What are you going to do: kill us both?'

'If that's what it takes mister. Who are you going to complain to, the police?' Dante laughed. 'Do you think they'll send someone like me to prison? It could be my disturbed background that made me snap and as for the guns, well, we found them in your house.'

Angrily, and knowing he was cornered, the man kicked his friend in the stomach. 'Shut up,' he shouted. 'I'm trying to think. Look, Kev said two kids were dropping off some stuff for him; he wanted to see if you were up to it, and you weren't, were you? Kev will get his money, so you two can stop playing gangsters now. Put the guns down and go home and we'll say no more about it.'

Dante glared at Deana; his gut instincts had been right. Kev! He'd laid down the gauntlet to teach them a lesson. Wide eyed, her jaw almost dropping to her chest, Deana stared at Dante. 'Kev will get his own message from us. But now the money if you don't mind. Get it! We will deliver it ourselves.'

'It's behind the sofa.' The man pointed.

Not turning their backs on him for a moment, Dante grinned. 'Nice try. Now go and pick it up and hand it to us.' Unsure of what they were capable of, the man nodded. Walking behind the sofa, he picked up the bag that he had stolen and threw it on the floor towards them. 'Open it,' Dante ordered.

'For Christ's sake,' Deana muttered and looked down at the man on the floor. 'If you don't shut up, I will shoot you in the mouth. You're getting on my nerves.' Looking around, Deana saw a child's small soft toy and picking it up, she rammed it in his mouth. 'You! Open that bag now and stop pissing around.'

Crouching down, the man looked up at Dante and Deana with their guns pointed to the back of his head. Sweat poured down the side of his face, and he brushed it away with his arm and unzipped the bag. Deana and Dante both looked down at the contents. Nodding to each other, Dante reached down and picked up the bag. 'Well, we'll be going now if that's okay with you two. But in future tell all your druggie friends not to fuck with us. Pay up and take their stuff, that's all we ask, because in future we will be carrying our friends with us. We're even now, but if you want to take this further speak up now.'

'No kid. Let's just leave it at that.' Looking down at his friend, he saw he was now breathing heavily, with saliva dripping from the sides of his mouth, while almost choking on the soft toy. 'It's him with the bullet in his foot not me. I didn't want any trouble, just a bit of fun. Rough you up a bit like.'

'What about you, fatso?' Deana shouted at the man on the floor. 'Are you coming after us?'

The man shook his head wearily, tears rolling down his cheeks. 'Come on,' said Dante, 'we're leaving. And you two, remember this night. His foot is just a taster of what could be, thanks to our mutual friend Kev. If I were you, I'd seek your revenge there!'

Cocking his head towards Deana, they both walked out to the car in silence.

Once inside the car, they looked at each other and let out a huge sigh. 'Well, that went better than expected Dante,' said Deana, relieved it was over.

'We're not finished yet. Now we go back to Kev's and strike while the iron's hot.'

'What! Why?' Wide eyed, Deana stared at Dante. 'Haven't you had enough for one night? We need to get home.'

'Not until I've settled this – *we've* settled this. We're going back. Look at my face. Look what Kev set us up for. Anything could have happened to us Deana. Those two bastards weren't just having a bit of fun roughing us up. We were sport to them, and I won't be taken for a mug by anyone, or used as a bloody punch bag!'

Doing as she was told, Deana drove to Kev's place. 'Are you sure about this Dante?'

'I am. Pick up your gun. We need to be the ones they fear, not the other way around. Let's show them we mean business.'

Walking into Kev's den of smoke, Dante squinted his eyes until he found his target. Grabbing a tentative Deana by her hoodie he dragged her in front of Kev. 'We've got your money you slimy bastard, but we're keeping this lot for all the trouble you've caused tonight.'

Kev took off his glasses and let out a low whistle. 'What happened to you? Your face looks twice the size it did three hours ago.' He grinned.

Both Dante and Deana could see that Kev was spaced out, his pupils were large, and he was slurring his words.

Dante took out his shotgun from under his jacket and pointed it towards the ceiling above Kev and fired. Plaster and dust rained down on Kev's head and body, making him jump out of his chair.

'What the fuck!' Kev shouted. Everyone else turned, startled by the noise of the gun fire and ran around the room looking for shelter once they saw Dante with the shotgun in his hands.

Kev put his hands in the air and shouted out, 'Calm down everyone, it's okay. Just an accident.' Glancing at Dante, he mouthed, 'Put the gun down.'

Looking around at the panic-stricken room, Dante lowered his gun. 'Are we partners now Kev or what?' Slowly, Kev nodded his head. 'Sorry mate. We're quits now, eh? Take the money, you've earned it. I had to know if you could go through with it. It can get rough, but I see you can handle that.' Nervously, Kev held his hand out to shake Dante's. 'Mates?' he asked.

Raising one eyebrow, Dante stared at him. 'Partners,' said Dante and shook his hand. 'Come on Deana, we're leaving.'

As an afterthought, Deana turned back and walked up to Kev. 'I might have flirted with you a little, but always remember, Dante's my brother and he will always come first. Be careful nothing happens to your brother or mother because of your careless, thoughtless ways Kev.' With that, Deana slapped him across the face and walked quickly to catch up with Dante.

Once back in the car they both looked at each other and burst out laughing. 'Christ what a night. Did you see Kev's face?' Deana laughed. 'Christ knows what the neighbours upstairs thought. How much is in that bag, Dante? I didn't know you intended to keep it.'

Although his face was still swollen and painful, Dante laughed. 'Too bloody right I'm keeping it! My face has earned it and now Kev knows we mean business. I'll give Luke his share; I don't believe he was involved in this. Anyway, I want to use his mum's kitchen and see what I can cook up. I would say there's about six thousand pounds if my reckoning is right Deana. That's two grand each.'

Deana nodded. 'That's fair Dante. I don't believe Luke knows about tonight's set up either, but I think there is probably more in that bag than you think. That last drop we did was fifteen hundred.'

Dante ran his hand through his hair. 'I'm tired Deana and my body and face hurt. I need some sleep.' Grinning up at her, he smiled. 'If this is a night out at the fair with you, I think I'll give it a miss in the future. Come on, let's dump this car and go home.' Still laughing, Deana started up the engine and drove off into the night with their bag full of money.

7

LAYING THE FOUNDATIONS

Feeling a thud in his groin, Alex looked down to see a bunch of grapes on his bed. Then he heard a familiar voice. 'Well, stranger, I thought I'd come and see the walking wounded.' Alex looked up from the prison hospital bed and saw John stood there, pulling up a chair to sit beside him.

Feeling much better, Alex smiled. 'How the hell did you get in here? More to the point, how did you know I was here?'

'I have my ways.' John grinned. 'Good to see you're still alive and kicking, but I've come to give you a wake-up call. Stop being so proud Alex, it doesn't suit you. Maggie looks shocking, and you still haven't sent her a visiting order, have you? You decided to put yourself in here and she's having to cope with it. Time to be fair on her and the kids.'

Stunned, Alex sat up in bed and let John's words sink in. Up till now, it had all been about himself, his pride, his beliefs. He hadn't really thought about the impact it would have on his family.

'Do you know if she's okay?' Alex asked, suddenly concerned.

Giving him a knowing look, John tutted and reached out for one of the grapes. 'Now and again I get one of the boys to pop in the pub for a drink and see how things are. That's the good thing about a pub, anyone can walk in unnoticed. But if you want to find out how she really is, invite her here yourself. Don't let her last memory of you be in a shroud Alex.'

Alex let out a sigh and cast his eyes down to the off-white sheets. 'I admit, it was a close shave. I knew it was coming though and I did retaliate. I've barely let anyone get the better of me.'

'You against a thousand men?' John raised his eyebrows and cocked his head to one side arrogantly. 'I hear you got a few blows in, but what about next time?'

'I don't need you to babysit me, John. I intend to visit the man who set me up once I get out of here. I'm going to the organ grinder, not his bloody monkeys!'

'I don't need to babysit you, Alex. I'm here and word will spread and that's enough. But I agree, you have to front this out. There's a bounty on your head, but it's time you reminded these so-called "hard nuts" that no one is going to pay it. Which reminds me, Paul Pereira hung himself in his cell. He couldn't cope with the idea of being behind bars for years on end with no light at the end of the tunnel. But now Paul is dead, everyone is crossing sides and changing allegiances. Thankfully, it's all mine Alex, and you and I go way back. You would have my back, I don't doubt that for a second.'

'So, Paul couldn't cope with life on the inside then. Are you sure he hung himself?' Alex asked suspiciously.

John held his hands up and laughed, 'That was either his own doing or some enemy he had made. Nothing to do with me.'

'So, what do you want from me John?'

'Sort yourself out first, then we'll talk. And then sort your family out too, you selfish bastard.' John let out a loud guffaw, ignoring the nurse's glare.

'After all this, I don't intend going back to my old ways. I owe it to my family. Those old ways are what put me in here and kept us living in hiding for all those years.'

Raising one eyebrow, John wagged his finger at Alex and smirked while reaching for another grape. 'No Alex, you put yourself in here, don't kid yourself – or me – for that matter. You volunteered to serve time when you could have walked away from court that day. I know that, and so does Maggie. Pride before a fall, eh?'

'They needed time for the dust to settle without me there. After all that hype I couldn't go back to the pub and just start serving pints of lager as though nothing had happened. I doubt even the brewery would have let Maggie stay with me there. I needed to be out of the picture for a while. It was the only way.'

'Most people go to the costa del crime Alex, skipping off into the sunshine.' John laughed. 'But you come to prison like a martyr.'

'Yeah, but they have to come back to England to face the music at some point, too.'

'Like you're going to have to go back and face the music when your sentence is finished.' For a moment they both stared at each other in silence. Alex realised John was right. He had just delayed the inevitable.

'It's your business not mine Alex, but you hadn't thought that far ahead, had you? For fuck's sake Alex, wake up! Stop being a selfish prat. You're a celebrity – use it for your own ends. Don't hide away in here rotting and smelling of disinfectant. Send out the visiting orders to friends, family and anyone else you can think of. Give your interviews to the journalists before you leave. Make your presence known and then when you are released it won't be news any more. Oh, you may get a mention and some comments on social media here and there, but you will be yesterday's news. The novelty will have worn off. On the other hand, if you hide away in here in silence and suddenly turn up again, people will be interested. They will want to know about your life in here.' John looked around at the white emulsion walls and shrugged. 'Don't make the journalists rich. Sell your story! Everyone else does and I know I bloody would. And you've got nothing to lose any more; now is your chance to make money.'

Alex listened intently to John's wise words. John was right; he hadn't thought about what would happen when he was released from prison. Would he turn Maggie's and the kids' lives upside down again? All this sacrifice would be for nothing if he did. 'You make a fair argument John, and it's taken on board, believe me. Maybe I've had my head in the sand for so long now, all I do is hide from the public eye. How're things in your world anyways? Is life at the top just as you expected?' Alex grinned.

'Better Alex. Now I give the orders. And it's updated to the twenty-first century. Not like those old men running it. It's still demanding money with menace, racketeering, prostitution, drug dealing and murder, but it pays the bills.' John laughed and his laughter was so infectious, Alex burst out laughing too.

'Pays the bills my arse John!' Genuinely, Alex smiled at

John and nodded. 'It's good to see you mate. I'm glad you came, even if you have eaten most of my grapes.' He looked down at the half-empty bag. 'You've given me a lot to think about, thank you.'

'Good. Then I've done my good deed for the day. Let's hope it brings me some absolution when my time comes amigo.' Standing up, John reached out his hand to shake Alex's and held it for a moment as they looked at each other intently. 'Many's the time you've covered for my stupid antics Alex and saved my life without any thought of pay back. We're friends and always will be. We need to look out for each other.' With that, John released his grip and turned to walk away, leaving Alex with new decisions to make about his future.

* * *

'I'm applying for my driving licence, Dante. It will make life easier. I'll need a few lessons, and then I will have to pay for the theory test. Christ, it's going to cost a fortune. But first things first, let's get my provisional licence and then we're half legal on our nights out.'

'You'll need the driving lessons to get rid of all those bad habits you've picked up. Driving with one hand on the wheel, over the speed limit. You're not exactly a nervous driver are you, Deana? But good idea – how are we going to explain the extra cash though?'

'I'm going to tell Mum I've got a part-time job shelf stacking or something. I don't know, I haven't thought it through yet, but either way it will be in the evenings after college.' Deana gave Dante a knowing wink and grinned.

'And what about me?' asked Dante as they both sat in the

beer garden of the pub, talking in hushed whispers. It seemed like the only peace and quiet they got these days. There always seemed to be someone around invading their privacy.

'I've thought about that too,' exclaimed Deana excitedly. 'You could get a paper round, delivering newspapers and such.' Drumming her fingers on her chin, Deana looked around for inspiration. 'Or, what about a job doing stacking like me?'

Rolling his eyes, Dante looked at Deana's excited flushed face. 'Firstly Deana, nobody reads newspapers any more, they have the internet. Secondly, shelf stacking? No, if I say I want a job, Mum will give me one in the kitchen, which means I'm going nowhere fast.'

'Mmm, fair point Dante. Why would we be looking for jobs when there are jobs here? I see what you mean. But, on the other hand, you could say that you live here and don't want to work here as well.'

'Let me think about it, but it does have promise as an idea. When are we delivering again?'

'Friday night. So, we've got two days to come up with an excuse for your disappearance. And this time no mistakes. I've spoken to Luke and said you would take his share when you go back to the house. How's your cooking doing?'

'Time will tell Deana. I did my research, followed the instructions and the first batch is now in the freezer at Luke's house. It's only a small tray size, I didn't want to waste the chemicals if it didn't work out. Fingers crossed. My only problem is who do we test it on?'

Deana burst out laughing and gave him a playful punch. 'Kev of course! Christ, I doubt there's anything he hasn't taken or sniffed. He'll try it, trust me.'

'It was good fun cooking it at Luke's actually,' Dante mused. 'It was nice just having my own space and a bit of peace and quiet with no one shouting for me to do something. His mum's nice too.'

'That's it! Oh God Dante, it's looking us in the face. Luke!' Deana shouted excitedly.

Puzzled, Dante took a sip of his orange juice. 'What are you going on about Deana?'

'Your new friend Luke who you are just spending time with, hanging out. Mum hasn't met Luke. She knows the name but not the man himself. And it doesn't have to be the same one Dad knew, it's just a coincidence. Anyway, Luke looks about ten years old.' Deana scoffed. 'He's your new buddy. After all, it's not exactly lying, is it?'

Grinning, Dante nodded. 'That's not bad and closer to the truth to remember too. And if Mum picks me up, she can also meet Luke's mum and won't suspect anything at all.' Giggling mischievously, they raised their fruit juices and chinked their glasses together.

'Hey you two. What are you cooking up, huddled together like two peas in a pod?'

Startled, Deana turned around and saw Mark approaching them waving a piece of paper in the air. 'I've had a letter off your dad. It's a visiting order.' He beamed. 'I'll pop in and tell your mum.'

'Dad's sent you a visiting order?' Deana's brows furrowed, and she looked over at Dante. 'He hasn't sent us one. Why you and not us?'

'Oh shit! Your mum's not going to be happy, is she? Maybe I shouldn't say anything.' Blushing slightly under his beard, Mark looked down at the ground.

'Well, you can't not say anything now, can you? We

know for starters and God knows who else you're going to tell – big mouth! What I want to know is why you and not us?'

'Well, erm, I don't know Deana,' said Mark, embarrassed by his boasting. 'Look, why don't you take it? It can be easily changed to your name.'

Hurt and disappointed, Deana glared at him. 'No, you go and see him. After all, it's you he wants to see – not us!' Angrily, she stood up from the garden bench and strode indoors.

'Don't worry about her Mark. She's just disappointed. She's been wanting to visit Dad since he went to prison. I think you should go and tell Mum though; before Deana does, I mean. It will be easier coming from you. Deana will twist it and make it sound worse than it is.'

Looking at the visiting order in his hand, Mark nodded at Dante. 'I suppose so.' With sunken shoulders Mark walked towards the pub doors.

Dante watched Mark walk away and said to himself, 'Time to go in and face the battlefield.' He could already hear the shouting in the hallway as he approached the pub and opened the door. Deana was stood there, face flushed, raising her voice at Maggie. 'Dad's sent him a bloody visiting order. Why hasn't he sent us one?' she shouted.

Flustered by Deana's outburst, Maggie stood there stoney faced. 'I know he's sent Mark a visiting order Deana. Your dad called me and told me. We will go next time, but it will do your dad good to get some gossip from Mark about the boys. It's going to be hard for your dad seeing you. Let him work up to it slowly and prepare himself. Write to him, but nothing too sentimental or private – the letters are all read and checked before they get them.'

'You knew and you're okay with it? What about you? Don't you want to see him?'

Maggie could see how upset Deana was but tried her best to calm her down and recalled her earlier conversation with Alex. He had sounded chirpier on the telephone and after skirting around each other for a minute, he had said he would send them a visiting order, but that he would also like to send one to Mark. Weighing things up in her mind, Maggie had felt it would be better if Mark went first to give time for Alex's bruises to disappear before the kids saw him. To her surprise, Alex hadn't argued about it. He hadn't wanted Dante and Deana seeing him in prison, but he had obviously thought better of it, she mused to herself while Deana kept on ranting. It would be another month before the next visit and as much as she yearned to see Alex, she wanted to see her husband alive and well, not the battered man he was in hospital. Anyway, she chuckled to herself, Mark would do him the world of good and make him laugh. It would be a happy visit and that was what she wanted for Alex. Apart from that, she wanted to prepare herself and the kids for the shock of seeing Alex in prison. He sounded a lot better though, and as angry as she had felt when he had deserted her, a warm glow filled her body. Suddenly, she had felt that they would get through this, and it would make them stronger. After his call, she felt better. There was something positive in his voice that reassured her.

'Deana, love, come into the staff lounge for a minute and stop shouting in the hallway near the bar. Everyone can hear you.' Sulking and tearful, Deana followed Maggie. 'Sit down Deana.' Seeing Dante enter the room, she offered him a seat, too. Realising Mark had made himself scarce, she felt able to speak freely. 'It was my suggestion that Mark should visit first. It's going to be your dad's first visit and I don't want to make it a sad one. Do you understand? We have each other, your dad doesn't have anyone in there.'

'Well,' Dante interrupted, 'what's another month? Deana's only upset because she has things she wants to tell Dad. Like, she's got a job stacking shelves at a supermarket. And she's applying for her driving licence.' Giving Deana a furtive glance, he stopped her ranting immediately.

Stunned, Maggie said, 'You've got a job Deana? I didn't know you were looking for one.'

'Yeah, one of the girls from college got a job and told me about it so I applied. I didn't want to say anything until I'd heard from them.' She brushed away the tears from her reddened face, partially glad that Dante had told their mum of her plans.

'There's always work here love, if you want it?' Trying not to show her disappointment, Maggie forced a smile.

'That's just the point Mum. This is a proper job, it's not just my parents' pub I'm working in. Anyway, I'll work here when I have time.'

Seeing that Deana had already made up her mind, Maggie realised Deana wanted to make her own way in the world now. 'So, what about this driving then?' she asked.

'Well, I'd like to drive and thought it might even be easier for you. I can always pop to the wholesalers or do your errands for you when you're busy. Two cars are better than one and my job will pay for the lessons.'

'As long as you don't take lessons or buy a car from Mark.' Dante laughed, trying to make light of the situation. This worked, as they all laughed together.

'So, where is it, this supermarket? I'm not prying, I know you're your own woman now. I'm just asking.'

'Other side of town. Bit of a crap area, but it's a new supermarket, that's why they want the staff.' Deana filled in as many details about her job as possible, even giving a name of a known supermarket that she had seen near Luke's house.

'Okay then, it sounds as though you have it all in hand. Congratulations. When do you start?'

Deana was trying to think on her feet when she was saved by Dante again. 'She's got the induction this Friday night and then she's starting next week. Or maybe over the weekend, you said, didn't you?'

'My goodness, you two have had your heads together, haven't you. I thought you couldn't stand the sight of each other!' Maggie raised her eyebrows. 'Okay, well if you need picking up or anything, let me know. Your dad will be very impressed with this new work ethic, Deana. Good on you love.' Standing up, Maggie gave her a hug. She couldn't believe how grown up her children had become all of a sudden and realised at some point she had to loosen the reins and let them become adults.

'I can always pick you up on the way home, Dante. Didn't you say you were going to ask Mum if you could go to your new mate's house to play on his new PlayStation?'

'Really?' Maggie queried. 'I didn't know you had a new friend Dante. You kept that quiet.'

'I bet it's a girl,' Babs butted in. She had entered the room to be nosey. 'He's at that funny age now, where he's taking an interest in women,' she scoffed, giving them all a knowing look as though she knew better.

'Well, it isn't a girl and I'm not at a funny age,' Dante snapped. 'I know what women are. God knows I live in a house full of them exchanging their beauty tips on shaving their legs and dying their hair. His name is Luke and he's one of Deana's college mates actually. We met that night of the fair. We share the same interests, so he asked if I wanted to pop round his house one night.' Dante shrugged, as though it wasn't important. 'I suppose I could go Friday; it's not far from you is it, Deana?'

'No, and then I can make sure my little brother gets home safe and sound. Can't I, Mum?' she purred, almost sarcastically, to give it some authenticity.

'Well, that's you two sorted then. And don't be too hard on Mark, Deana. Remember this is for your dad. Just like you two, he has a friend. You're going to make new friends at your supermarket and Dante has... Luke, is it?' She questioned. 'Well, come on Mum, back to the bar. The war's over.'

'I still say it's a woman,' Babs chirped up, while she followed Maggie back into the bar. 'I'll just put a bit more lippy on Maggie, out in a minute.' Taking out her lipstick, she stood in the hallway looking in the mirror and applied yet another layer of red gloss. Admiring herself, she walked behind the bar.

Dante instantly stood up and shut the door. 'God, how much lipstick does she need? She spreads it like jam!'

'The only jam around here, is you, you jammy bastard. Piping all that stuff out in one go. I was going to work up to it slowly, but no, you just blurted it out and it worked!' Standing opposite him, Deana held up her hand. 'High five Dante. Definitely high five!'

'You okay about Dad now?' Dante asked with concern. 'You didn't take it very well, but I see Mum's point. Mark will make an impact on the fellow inmates!'

'Yeah, I suppose so. It pisses me off though. Let's just hope

Mark hasn't fixed any of their cars in the past or there will be a prison riot when they see him.' Deana laughed.

Now she had other things to think about, she was prepared to let it go. Dante had worked a blinder with their mum and they had their excuses to leave the house at night. Inadvertently, Mark had done them a huge favour! So, what did she care any more? She would see her dad soon anyway, and during that time they would be making a lot of money!

8

OUT WITH THE OLD AND IN WITH THE NEW

As Alex walked into the prison dining room for the first time in what seemed like forever, an eerie silence was cast over the room. Alex could hear the sound of his own boots as he walked towards the food counter, picked up a tray and stood in line. No one spoke, only the servers continued behind the counter as they picked up a ladle and poured the food on his plate, which looked like a lot of gravy, and not much else. Then there was some kind of sponge with custard, Alex couldn't make out what it was, but that wasn't his purpose for being here and frankly, he didn't care about the food.

Most of the inmates who were sat at tables had stopped eating and raised their heads to look at Alex but averted their eyes when he looked at them. His bruises were a yellowish colour now, but he felt a lot better and much more in charge of the situation. It was this man Jonesy he wanted to see. The man who everyone supposedly feared in here. He had organised the heckling and the beating and his name had come up with most of the conversations he'd heard, especially from his cell mate.

Spotting him, Alex walked directly towards his table. Jonesy was busy eating and ignoring everyone else's curiosity. Alex glanced at his food and saw that it looked a lot more appetising than the slop he'd been served up. Obviously, he put his own food orders in, or had it brought in especially for him.

Two men who were sat at the table stood up as Alex approached. Still carrying his tray, Alex calmly looked each of the men directly in the face. His chillingly calm voice seemed to echo around the room as everyone strained to hear. 'You're not afraid of little old me are you boys? It's just a friendly chat I want with your Mr Jones.' Alex kept his voice monotone and offered respect by calling Jonesy, mister. Glancing across the room, he could see the guards watching him. They were already holding their radios and, on the alert, waiting for trouble. 'Let him sit,' said Jonesy to the two men that barred Alex's path.

As they parted, giving him an evil glare, Alex looked at the Formica table with just Jonesy sat there shovelling food into his mouth like there was no tomorrow, and almost burst out laughing. Alex sat down opposite him and spied him curiously. He was around thirty, Alex supposed. According to hearsay, he was inside for murder but, as no one really knew the details or asked questions, that was as far as Alex knew. True to form, his head was shaved, and he was tattooed all over his head and arms, possibly to make him look more intimidating. He also had a large black, waxed moustache, which he was obviously proud of and took great pains over. He looked like he worked out in the gym on a regular basis, although in a place like this there wasn't much else to do in your spare time. Alex made a mental note to check it out and make use of it himself.

'Mr Jones, I think it's time we had a proper talk. We seem to have got off on the wrong foot. Presumably, you've heard the whispers that there's a bounty on my head, but in your clouded delusions ask yourself who would pay you for my demise? Have you thought about that?' Alex waited a moment for his words to sink in and watched as, slowly, Jonesy put his spoon down on his plate.

'So, you think you're a hard man in here, do you? You're nothing. I rule the roost around here, not some super grass immigrant who hides away for an occupation.'

'Well said. But now it's my turn. Send anyone to do your dirty work again and I will bite your balls off and use them as earrings. Us immigrants are like that. We have no boundaries.' Alex's eyes flashed like dark jewels in his face. Trying to keep his anger under control, he gave an inward sigh. 'You have had your pound of flesh and made your point, and I am prepared to let it go at that, but enough is enough. If you want me dead, then do it yourself Mr Jones. Show this lot that you have some balls worth biting off. But trust me, I still have friends in very low places who would carry out their revenge, even after my death. And death doesn't bother me, but what does, is that you don't have the guts to do it yourself. So here is my deal; take it or leave it.' Alex knew word would have spread about John's recent visit. Seeing Jonesy avoid his stare and look down at his plate, proved the point he had made. 'You can keep your reputation in here, I'll not take it from you, although I could if I wanted to,' Alex warned. 'You are still top dog, and we steer clear of each other. But I want no more heckling or stupidity. I just serve my time and leave. You will be well shot of me, I'm sure of it.'

'And if I don't agree?' Jonesy asked tentatively, showing a bravado Alex knew he didn't really feel. Quickly glancing up at his two friends stood with their backs to him, he dropped his voice so they couldn't hear. 'You wouldn't be the first inmate to threaten me or the last. How do I know you'll keep your word?'

'Well, that's up to you, but whatever you throw at me I swear I will throw back, but to you and you alone,' Alex warned and glared at him, while pausing to make his point. 'I won't take my anger out on those dishing it out, but to the one that ordered it. You, Mr Jones, and if I am not around to be able to carry out my threats, my friends will. Sleep well in your prison bunk Jonesy, because you never know when I might turn up,' Alex stressed. 'For every beating you order, I will beat you to a pulp until there is nothing left to beat. As I say, I don't care, never have. I was the Silva Bullet and torturing and killing people was my occupation. What's yours?' Alex's threatening, chilling voice seemed to have struck a chord with Jonesy and Alex felt there was no more to be said. He stood up to leave, but then, as an afterthought, he sat back down again. 'In future, tell the chef to serve his slop to some other poor bastard, I don't like it.' Alex left his tray, containing his plate full of food, on the table. Pushing past the two men, he walked away, back to his cell, in silence.

* * *

Pulling Deana aside, Dante whispered in her ear. 'Tell Mum you're working tonight, Deana, I need to go to Luke's house. That meth will be frozen by now and will need smashing up and we'll get Kev to try it.'

Confused, she frowned. 'Smashing up – why?'

'Well, it's in a slab. The mixture is poured into a baking

tray then frozen. Now it needs smashing up so that we can sell it by the gram.'

Stunned, Deana let Dante's words sink in. 'How do you know if it's any good?'

'Well, I don't, do I? That's why it needs testing. I've followed all the instructions, although they are a bit vague. Only one way to find out and the time is now.'

Holding her mobile to her ear, Deana feigned a phone call just loudly enough for Maggie to hear. She knew Babs would be listening too. God knows if a fly walked up the wall in the next room she would hear it, Deana mused to herself. 'Yes, sure, I can do that. I will come after college for a few hours if that's okay.' Pretending to end the call, she waited.

'Who was that and where do you think you're going on a college night?'

Smiling to herself, Deana was glad that Babs was nosey.

'Did you hear that, Maggie? Deana's going out on a college night, and she hasn't even asked you.' Standing in the doorway like some matriarch with her arms folded and her heated rollers in, Babs waited for Maggie to enter the dining room where Dante and Deana were having breakfast. 'She's got some boyfriend stashed away, I bet. God knows what teenagers get up to these days.'

'Are you going out love? You know I don't like you going out late on a college night. You'll be tired in the morning.'

'I'm not going out!' Deana snapped. 'Well, not like Mrs Nosey there is suggesting. It was the supermarket and they wondered if I could do a few hours after college, that's all. I won't be late Mum, but I can go straight there so there's no point in me coming home first, is there?'

'Would you mind if I tagged along? I told Luke I'd swap one of my games for his,' Dante butted in.

Putting on an act for her mum and Maggie, Deana let out a big sigh. 'Christ, I can't fart without you lot wanting to know what I'm doing. Yeah, might as well, and I'll pick you up on the way back.'

'I'll pick you up if you want. It will save you catching the bus.' Maggie suggested.

'It's all right Mum, we'll manage. You do have a pub to run, and it won't be late,' Deana emphasised. 'Although you do have super barmaid there putting off your customers.' Giving Babs a glare, she bit on her toast.

'You cheeky bugger. I wouldn't have dared to speak to my grandmother like that when I was your age,' snapped Babs.

'Can you remember being my age, Grandma?' Seeing Babs' just about to retort, Deana averted her eyes and looked directly at Maggie. 'Is it okay with you, Mum? I don't want to keep turning them down or they will stop offering me the shifts.'

Maggie could see how much it meant to Deana, and with Dante to pick up and drop off, she didn't think she could come to too much harm. Nodding, she agreed.

'I see your point. Make a good impression and all that. You have your mobiles, so text me when you're leaving, and I'll know that you're both safe. If you need a lift, everyone can cope for an hour while I pick you up. Although, I realise, it's not the cool thing, having your mother pick you up. And don't be too late. If not you, Dante needs his rest. It's a school night.'

Standing up, Deana put her arms around Maggie's neck. She was almost tempted to stick her tongue out at Babs but realised she had served her purpose. 'Thanks Mum. We won't be late. Promise.' Once Maggie and Babs had left the room, they could still hear Babs tutting and complain to

Maggie, but they grinned at each other. Their plan had worked and now they could get on with the business in hand.

'Hey Alex!' Mark shouted and waved as he made his way to Alex's table. The prison visiting room was full as Mark, ignorant of the other prisoners' stares and amusement, pulled out a chair and sat down opposite Alex, throwing handfuls of chocolate bars on the table and a couple of cans of cola. A smile crossed Alex's face. Mark was just what he needed. He was loud and full of excitement as well as his usual bravado. 'Have some chocolate mate, I think I've emptied that vending machine.' He laughed loudly. 'Sorry lads,' he shouted to the others. 'You'll have to wait until they fill it up again.' Taking the wrapper off a chocolate bar, he handed one to Alex. 'The old place isn't the same without you, Alex,' Mark boomed, not realising the loudness of his voice as everyone else spoke in whispers to each other.

'Good to see you Mark, thanks for coming. I wasn't sure that you would.'

'Why not, you prat! We're mates. I've done my time in one of these places.'

Alex had to smile; he remembered Mark telling him that he had served six months in an open prison once for assault when he had been working as a bouncer. A far cry from what he was doing in this place. But this was Mark's badge of honour and he loved to boast.

He took a bite of the chocolate and let the fizziness of the cola soothe his throat. It felt like nectar after what he'd eaten lately. 'Well, thanks for coming. So, what's the news?'

'What? You mean apart from Maggie being pissed off cos

you're here, Deana being pissed off cos I'm here and your mother-in-law driving everyone bonkers with her opinions? Yeah, everyone's okay.' Mark let out a belly laugh and sat back in his seat. 'Olivia is driving me mad. She's on a new fitness regime, which means I'm on it too. No more kebabs for me. Well, at least for the time being anyway. Work is going okay, although a car I was fixing was stolen and the police found it burnt out on the other side of town somewhere. Not good for my reputation Alex.'

For the first time in what seemed like a long time, Alex laughed. Mark was just the tonic he needed. He knew he'd have to face the family sooner or later but wanted to work up to that. Glancing around the room, he could see his inmates having conversations with their families. But there didn't seem to be much laughter. Unlike Mark, who lit up the room with his personality. Alex noticed that even others in the room were paying more attention to Mark's gossip then their own.

In no time at all, the visit was over. Alex's face ached with laughter. It had been a great visit, refreshing even and a real boost. Mark ended his visit with a big bear hug, even though the warders frowned upon it. Alex was still smiling as he walked back to his cell.

'Hey Silva,' he heard someone shout as he was just about to climb the stairs to his cell. Turning around, he saw Jonesy sat at a table with a mug of tea. As Alex looked at him, he noted that he hadn't had any visitors today. He looked like he had been sat there a while with his drink, musing away the time until everyone came back.

'Yes?' Alex answered politely. Looking around him, he saw the other prisoners cast furtive glances and almost halt their footsteps as they waited to see what was going to happen.

'Do you fancy a game of checkers?' Jonesy asked, ignoring the stares from the others.

Alex realised that this was the olive branch and it must have taken a lot for Jonesy to summon up the courage to do this publicly. He'd obviously taken what he'd said on board and decided to let it go. 'Why not? That sounds good.'

As the warders shouted for everyone to move on in case of a scuffle, they seemed surprised to see Alex sat opposite Jonesy, setting up their board game. After this, Alex went about his usual routine and never once tried to hold court or tread on Jonesy's toes as promised. He was still the leader of the prison and Alex let him get on with it. He had bigger goals in mind. He had a family waiting for him. and now, thanks to Mark's visit, he also realised he had good friends to go home to.

Mark nearly burnt the rubber off his wheels as he braked outside the pub and ran in to see Maggie. 'He seems okay, Maggie. In quite high spirits and laughing with me when I joked with him. He's eaten enough sugar to have him bouncing off the walls for the next year! Yours and the kids' turn next. Trust me, it will be okay.' Mark omitted to tell Maggie about the dark rings around Alex's eyes and the remnants of bruises yellowing.

'Oh God, Mark, thank you.' Maggie almost fell into Mark's arms and burst into tears. She was relieved to hear that Alex was okay and that Mark had cheered him up.

'You know me, Maggie, anything for a mate. And Alex is my mate.'

'Indeed, he is Mark.' Maggie smiled. 'Go into the bar and have that well earnt drink I'm going to pour for you and the finest cuisine that the Silvas can offer. Give Olivia a call and invite her here, too.'

'Erm, no. I don't think I will bother her,' Mark stammered, remembering Olivia's fitness regime and diet. If he was going to get a free meal from the carvery, he intended to enjoy it without counting the calories!

Maggie grinned widely as Mark sat at his table with his plate piled high, beckoning his friends to join him for a drink while telling them the tales of his visit with Alex. His voice got louder and louder as he boasted about being the 'chosen one'.

'Just how many free meals does he think he's going to get out of one visit? God knows he will dine out on that visit for years to come,' Babs snapped. 'His story gets longer and longer with each pint of beer that he drinks.' Sarcasm dripped from Babs' mouth. She had made it clear that she didn't like Mark's brusque, burly ways and the fact that he lowered the tone with his 'grease monkey' hands and clothing.

'Leave it, Mother. If you can't say anything nice, don't say anything at all.' With that, Maggie poured Mark another drink, while Babs, cheeks pink from Maggie's scolding, picked up a glass and started polishing it in silence.

9

DEVIOUS MINDS

Deana, Dante and Luke all stood together at the freezer. 'Have you looked at it, Luke?' asked Deana inquisitively.

'No, I've waited for you. Well, Dante, the proof is in the pudding. Shall we see if it's a catastrophe?'

Pensively, Dante waited. He didn't speak, but just held his breath in expectation. His mind was in turmoil, wondering if he had done everything right. He went through the ingredients again in his brain.

Luke opened the freezer drawer and took out the long silver baking tray about an inch thick and put it on the worktop. Slowly Luke took off the cling film that covered it. 'Well, something has frozen.' Each in turn, they stared at the clear frozen liquid.

'Will it melt if we smash it up?' asked Deana, unsure of herself and not knowing what to expect.

Smacking his lips together, Dante shook his head. 'It shouldn't. It's like toffee. Once it sets, that's it. Unless heated up and then it will go soft again, but not watery.'

Luke gave out a low whistle. 'Blimey Dante. This is as

clear as glass. I've seen some before that looked cloudier, frosted even, but this, I'm really not sure. Let's see if it breaks up. Talking of toffee, I have one of those toffee hammers Mum uses. Bit old fashioned but she likes it.' Luke shrugged. 'You go first Dante; let's take it out the back so Mum doesn't hear it. Fingers crossed mate.'

Walking out to the overgrown back garden, Luke laid the tray on the path, closed his eyes and hit it with the small rock hammer. Instantly it cracked. When he hit it again it started breaking up into small pieces that looked like icicles once he'd finished.

'How much smaller should we make it?'

'If it's any good Kev will smash it into grams of powder. We need to get him to try it first. Only his nose will tell us the outcome. Hang around here for half an hour while I give Mum her tea and then we'll go and see Kev. In the meantime, we'll see if it melts and that will answer another question.'

Luke ran out and bought fish and chips for everyone, then carefully buttered some bread and put a tray together for his mum. 'I usually eat with her, but you can have yours in here if you prefer.'

'No way Luke. She knows we're here. Can't we all have fish and chips together? The company might do her good,' exclaimed Deana.

A beaming smile crossed Luke's face. He had hoped they would join him and his mum for tea, but didn't want to push it. 'Right, I'll set up her table in front of her chair. She usually eats there, and things are laid out precisely.'

'Good, well, I'll make her a cup of tea and Dante can start putting out the plates.' They all busied themselves intently and went into the lounge. Luke introduced them both again, but his mum already recognised them. 'I know who they are Luke. It's my eyes that don't work, not my ears.' She smiled.

While eating they all chatted like old friends, each in turn telling Luke's mum snippets of their home life, making her laugh in the process. Luke's heart swelled; he was touched by this show of friendship and to be honest, he enjoyed the company as much as his mother did. Normally, they sat alone with him doing most of the talking. This evening was a shared event and one to cherish.

Afterwards, as Luke cleared away and Deana washed up, he told his mum he was popping out for a while but that he would be back in time to put her to bed. 'An hour or so at best Mum.' Seeing her smile, he kissed her on the cheek, as Deana and Dante did likewise.

'Thanks for having us,' said Dante as they left, and Luke switched on the television so she could listen to the news. Looking at the baking tray, they could all see nothing had melted. If anything, it had hardened more. Carefully, Luke put the baking tray containing the meth into a large bag and made their way to Kev's house.

As usual, Kev's place was in full swing, even this early in the evening. It seemed as though his flat was just an ongoing series of party evenings. Kev nodded his head in the direction of the balcony, and opening the French windows, walked out and sat in a deck chair. Luke passed him the bag. 'See for yourself Kev. It's as clear as glass.'

Putting his hand inside the bag, Kev didn't handle it as carefully as the others and took out what resembled an icicle. 'Christ, these pieces are big. It needs crushing more. I can sort that out, if it's any good...' Chipping a piece off the end, Kev grinded it almost into a powder. Putting it on the back of his hand, he sniffed at it. His eyes began to water, and he gave out a loud cry.

Dante's heart sank and he looked towards Deana for support. Kev was rubbing his nose and smacking his lips, coughing loudly.

'Fuck, that is good stuff!' he shouted. 'That's the strongest I've ever sniffed. We're going to have to mix it with something else. Shit Dante, you're a bloody genius! We'll start passing it around the nightclubs first and put it on the menu for our WhatsApp customers. I tell you though' – Kev wagged his finger and gave Dante a warning look – 'you had better have kept this recipe, because you're going to be making an awful lot more.'

'To make more, I'll need more ingredients and as the cook, I'll need a cut of the profits. You can't sell what you don't have.'

Kev was still sniffing the back of his hand but nodded in acceptance. 'Fair point Dante lad. I can get whatever ingredients you need. You just tell me what and when. As for the cut of the profits, that's fair too. You've got yourself a deal Dante the man!'

Dante grinned from ear to ear, even slightly blushing somewhat. 'Is it really okay Kev?' he asked disbelievingly.

'Dante mate, it's incredible. They will bite our hands off for this stuff. I wasn't sure about you, but I always admit when I am wrong, and I've been wrong about you two twice. Sorry folks. So Dante, get your cooking hat on. We need a back-up supply when this stuff starts flying off the shelves.'

Dante nodded. 'Right, well, when it's okay with you Luke, I'll pop by and do some cooking. Although my mum might want to drop me off to meet you to make sure everything is above board, if you know what I mean.' Blushing, he realised he sounded like a school boy.

'That's not a problem, Dante. Bring her, let her have a cuppa with my mum. If it puts her mind at rest and gives you time to cook up more of that stuff, it's okay with me.'

'Thanks mate, I appreciate that. I just feel the best lies are the ones closer to the truth, don't you?' Dante asked.

'My own thoughts exactly.' Luke grinned and held up his hand in a high five. 'Come on, we had better go. I need to sort out Mum.'

'Don't forget, you two have deliveries Friday and Saturday night. Sort out your alibis,' Kev shouted after them as they were leaving. Putting on his sunglasses, Kev lay back in his deck chair and let the drug he had just taken overwhelm him, spacing him out to another plateau.

All the way home, Deana and Dante laughed and joked, pleased at the outcome of Dante's masterpiece. 'We've done good Dante and it's only half past eight. We said we wouldn't be late and so this will appease Mum.'

'It keeps everyone happy, including Grandma. By the way, I've had a thought. When we drop stuff off, why don't we take the foreign approach? We speak Portuguese and pretend we don't quite understand what the customers are saying. That way, we have another alibi because, we'll be known as those foreigners who drop off stuff. That's not me and you Deana. But then when they talk about us, we'll know what they're saying. It covers our tracks.'

Thinking about it for a moment, Deana nodded. 'Actually Dante, that's not a bad idea. It gives us an edge. Come on, let's go and play good school kids for Mum. Christ, all of this juggling and leading two lives is exciting. isn't it?' She laughed.

'I don't know about that, but it certainly keeps you busy.' Just as they were approaching the pub they heard a familiar voice shout their names. Turning, they saw Mark.

'Hey you two.' He wandered over to them. 'I just wanted you to know that I saw your dad today. He looks well,' Mark lied. 'He said he was sorry he hadn't asked you to visit; it was because he couldn't bear to see you both leave. He didn't feel strong enough yet, but he is now. The next visiting order is for you. I just wanted to let you know.'

The stern glare dropped from Deana's face, and was replaced by a frown of concern. 'Is he okay Mark – really?'

'He's fine. Lost a bit of weight, but then he doesn't live in a carvery pub these days and have your mum's cooking, does he?' Mark laughed to lift their spirits.

Looking down at the floor, Deana felt herself blush slightly. 'Thanks Mark, for going to see him I mean. I'm sure it meant a lot to him. I know I acted like a cow, and I am sorry for that – truly.' Without thinking, Deana reached forward and kissed Mark on the cheek. Hearing that her father was well made her feel so much better. 'Thanks for standing by Dad, Mark, I appreciate it. He's been to hell and back, we all have, but this is the time when you find out who your real friends are.'

Touched by Deana's sentiments, Mark blushed a little under his bushy beard. Not knowing what else to say, he gave them both a smile, before walking away.

'I'm glad Dad's okay, I've been so worried about him Dante. I miss him so much,' Deana confessed.

'I know and so do I, Deana. But if we do, think how Mum must feel, eh? Let's try and support her a bit more. She puts on a brave face but she's feeling it.'

'We can't do much more than we are Dante, but I know

what you mean, I hadn't thought of it like that. I suppose I've always been a bit selfish where Dad is concerned. But I don't want you to feel left out. Dad loves us both, you know that. It's just me, possibly my hormones.' She grinned. 'But, at least I have you Dante. You always have my back, don't you? So thank you.'

'You're feeling rather benevolent tonight, Deana. Mark gets a kiss, and I get kind words,' Dante scoffed. 'Come on, Mum will be waiting.'

Deana put her arm around Dante's shoulders as they walked into the pub's back door together. Maggie seemed to greet them instantly and glanced at the clock. Dante caught Deana's eye. 'Sorry we're a bit late Mum. We met Mark outside, and he was telling us he'd seen Dad today and that he's well,' Deana said.

'Did he? Oh well, I'm sure he'll tell you more as the days go on. God knows he's told everyone else. Do you want some supper? How was work, you must be tired.'

Suddenly, Deana remembered her alibi. 'Oh yes, it was good, and they seem like a nice bunch. First step to my driving lessons Mum.' She grinned. 'And we ate on the way home, had some chips. I'm going to have a shower and bed if that's okay.'

Nodding, Maggie kissed them both before they disappeared upstairs. She was pleased that they had come home early as promised, even if they had been stopped by Mark. All afternoon her mother had gone on and on about how late they would be. 'Give them an inch and they will take a yard,' she had warned. 'Especially without their father to keep an eye on them.' It had set Maggie's teeth on edge and she'd been tempted to ring the kids and tell them to come back sooner, but that would mean appeasing her mother. Maggie felt guilty. She had missed her mum so much when they couldn't have contact, but now she wasn't so sure about having her here. She felt it was time to ask her how long she would be staying. Babs had taken over everything and was so used to being a landlady in her own time, she didn't know how to stop being one here. Maggie felt she even treated her like staff, forever bossing her around while Babs sat on a stool at the side of the bar talking to the regulars. It was grating on her. This was her pub, and she had worked bloody hard to get it off the ground. It had been a dump when they moved in and now it was a going concern.

Although Alex's court case didn't help matters, they were back on an even keel now. Some of the stories that had come out had been horrible and she hadn't realised how much of a blind eye she had turned. Maggie had never really thought about it before, but recently, it had overwhelmed her in waves. Could she have changed things? Could Alex have left his life of crime or had she made him carry on? Admittedly, she had enjoyed her lifestyle, but she hadn't really given any thought to what it entailed for Alex. He had been the one doing all of the dirty work, and now he was in prison and she was free to live her life.

Somewhere in the pit of her stomach Maggie felt it wasn't fair. Apart from joining him in hiding under many assumed names, she hadn't really paid any price for her part in all of this. Sometimes, in their darkest moments in hiding, when she'd seen how miserable the kids were, she'd wondered if she should have just kept her mouth shut about the night Matteo had tried to rape her and said nothing. Although, it would have been hard to hide the bruises on her face, where Matteo had hit her. But time and time again, she had wondered if she could have come up with something to prevent all of the misery that had been caused. Besides, maybe she had flirted, or dressed provocatively, giving Matteo the wrong impression?

But no, she knew she hadn't. Why did women always blame themselves for attracting unwanted attention? Matteo had thought he could take whatever liberties he wanted and be protected by his family name. But Alex had killed him and that was why they were in the situation they were now in. It wasn't fair, but then life wasn't fair. And now she had to make the most of it and build a life for Alex to come home to. The last thing she wanted was for him to come to the decision that it had all been for nothing.

He had been ousted, tormented and threatened constantly. Maybe hiding in prison was his way of escape from not only the world but from herself. They had never discussed it properly – Alex wouldn't. Always said he couldn't because it made his blood boil. Night after night since he had gone to prison, these thoughts had her mind in turmoil. And now, on top of all this, she was having to deal with her mum.

Looking up the staircase towards the rooms, she thought of her children. All in all, they had turned out okay. There didn't seem to be too much harm done. Maybe they could all go forward now the dust was settling a little and rebuild their lives. Honest lives, like ordinary people, doing ordinary things. It was a strange sense of freedom. This was their chance to make their own decisions and be on their own without approval from anyone else. It was a whole new world and was taking some getting used to.

'Are you coming Maggie? You've been stood in here for ages. It's getting busy out there and they need help behind the bar.' Babs interrupted her thoughts with more demands.

Sternly, Maggie turned towards her mother. Her mouth

felt dry, but she felt it needed saying and there was no time like the present. 'I was thinking, Mum... I was wondering actually how long you were thinking of staying? I feel I've taken up enough of your time lately.'

Babs' face dropped. 'What do you mean? I thought I would stay a while longer. Help you get over the worst.'

'The thing is Mum, people are tired of your constant bickering and putting yourself in charge of things. I'm the landlady here. You might not rate me much, but it's my name above the door – not yours. I've built up a good relationship with the people here, staff included and truthfully Mum, you're not helping.'

'Well!' Babs stammered, while looking around furtively. 'I've just tried taking charge to take the pressure off you. We're family, Maggie, and these people are strangers. The kids need a firm hand now that Alex isn't around. You need back-up love. That's why I'm here.'

'A firm hand?' Suddenly Maggie's blood boiled. 'What the hell is that supposed to mean? You see, there you go again, presuming and telling me what's for the best. They are good kids, Mum. They've had a rough time of it and they have coped well, so give them some breathing space! They're growing up; they're not babies any more. Let them breathe, and more to the point leave the staff and customers alone and that includes me, Mum!'

'Well, if you don't want me here...' Babs snapped.

'Look, this is not the time and I don't want to say things in the heat of the moment that I am going to live to regret. Stay a little while longer if you wish, but I think it's time I stood on my own feet from now on. I never have. I lived with you, then married Alex and lived with him. I have never had to think for myself, Mum, or stand on my own feet and frankly, I think it's time I did – don't you?'

Babs nodded, making her oversized diamante earrings swing back and forth. 'Fair point love. Maybe I have been a bit full on, but I understand. Give me a few more days and then I'll go home. But promise you'll keep in touch and remember I'll always come back if you need me.'

Tears rolled down Maggie's face and reaching forward, they both held each other and hugged tightly. 'Thanks for understanding, Mum.'

Babs joined her and let her own tears fall. 'Sorry love.' Sniffing hard, she pulled away. 'I need a few more moments with my make-up and a mirror, I think. Thank goodness this mascara is waterproof.' She smiled weakly and walked up the stairs slowly.

Wiping her own tears, Maggie smiled to herself. *She'll need more than a few minutes to repair those tear tracks down her foundation!* Feeling like a weight had been taken off her shoulders now she'd faced up to her mum, Maggie looked at her own reflection in the hall mirror. Taking a brush that she always had on hand there, she brushed her hair tidily. Applying her lipstick, she laughed at herself. Maybe she was more like her mum than she realised!

10

TROUBLEMAKERS

'I've got my provisional licence, Mum. It's here!' Deana shouted excitedly, running into the kitchen. 'I am officially allowed behind the wheel of a car. Look!' Waving the letter and the piece of plastic that held her photo under Maggie's nose, she skipped around the breakfast table. 'Dante, look. I can book my lessons!'

Yawning and walking into the kitchen, Dante squinted at the provisional licence being waved under his nose. 'Well done, Deana,' was all he said, considering they had been out every weekend stealing cars for the last six weeks, dropping off drugs in every unheard neighbourhood they could think of. It had been exhausting. So much so, it was actually being reported that there was car crime in the area.

'Well done love.' Pleased as punch, Maggie hugged her. Taking the driving licence from her, she stared at the photo on it. 'My baby, a driver. I can't believe it. Well now you can book the driving lessons you've been saving up for. You've done so many shifts at that supermarket, you must be worn out.'

Dante almost choked as he sipped his orange juice and stared at Deana. Inwardly he wanted to laugh at the whole charade but kept it in.

Deana glared at him and sarcasm dripped from her mouth. 'Careful Dante, or you will choke, and we wouldn't want that now, would we? Wait until Dad sees this. I can't wait to see him again.'

Deana had been in high spirits since they had been to see Alex. All his wounds had healed, and he had looked well and more than pleased to see them. They had talked about everything. Deana had hogged the visit, filling him in on all the neighbourhood gossip and telling him funny stories. Alex hadn't been able to get a word in. In no time at all, the visit had been over. But it had been a good visit and well worth the wait. Deana was glowing. Maggie had wanted to kiss him, but it wasn't allowed. Instead, she'd blown him a kiss and sat back while Deana and Dante had filled him in on their lives. She thought she would come alone next time. She wanted to speak to him, her Alex. Her husband. She needed to know if he really was okay, but couldn't ask in front of the kids. Instead, she'd sat back and looked lovingly at him, catching his eyes as he looked back at her in the same way. Sometimes, you didn't need words. They knew what each other was thinking. Her heart had pounded in her chest being sat within inches of him and not being able to touch him. They'd had phone calls but there was no privacy with all the prisoners stood in a queue behind him waiting for their turn. And Alex kept his letters short and sweet considering they were all read by the warders. Maggie's heart yearned for him and she wanted to pour out all of the love she felt for him, but life was getting in the way.

Breaking into her thoughts, Deana shook her shoulder.

'Mum, are you listening? I said I'm going to scan it at college and print it out for Dad to see it when I write to him.'

'That's a good idea love. He'll like seeing his little girl with her own driving licence.' Turning towards Dante, Maggie winked and smiled. They were going to hear about this for days. It wouldn't surprise Maggie if Deana mounted it and put it on the mantlepiece! Standing up from the table to go and use the shower, Maggie gave Deana one last thumbs up and left them to their breakfast.

When their mum left the room, Deana pulled her chair closer to Dante's and whispered in his ear, 'What you don't know, brain box, is that I've also applied for my provisional motorbike licence and I'm going to do the CBT course. That licence came the other day. I'll show you later.' She grinned.

'Is this conversation leading somewhere Deana, because I'm knackered. Why do you want a motorbike if you're going to drive a car?'

'Because, after I've done this one-day course, I can ride a bike. Bikes have helmets. No one will see my face when I drop stuff off. It also cuts the time down. You go one way, and I go another. It cuts the drop-offs in half and that means we're home earlier. And Christ do I need it, I'm knackered.' Deana yawned.

'It also leaves you wide open to someone attacking you, Deana. Have you thought of that? Anyway, does that mean I'll be driving a car on my own? What if I'm seen? Surely, we're better off in a pair?'

Scrunching her lips together and pouting, Deana looked at him sternly. 'Why don't we get a licence in Luke's name and details for a bike for you. We could stash them at his mum's place. It would save stealing cars until I get my licence and buy my own. You could do the course in Luke's name, or he could do it. You don't exactly look like the average teenage schoolboy do you Dante? You could easily pass off for eighteen.' Rubbing his cheek with her finger, she grinned. 'You've even started getting a stubble with all the black hair you have and you're tall.'

Dante stopped eating his cereal and rubbed his dark stubbly chin. 'I don't feel like shaving it off yet. Do you think it suits me?'

'What with those dark eyes and swarthy looks of yours, you look more like Dad every day. Definitely, Dante.' She smiled. Sometimes she found it strange looking at a younger mirror image of her dad. Other times when Dante was in his business mood it gave her a warm glow inside. As though her dad was still with her. Dante may be younger than her, but he looked after her in his own way.

Dante thought about Deana's plan. Weighing things up, it made sense, and they wouldn't be out so late if they halved the work, which would be a bonus. 'What about Luke? Do you think he would agree to it – me using his licence?' he asked tentatively.

'Only one way to find out, but I think so.'

'Okay, I'll go with that. It's not a bad plan, Deana. Maybe not fool proof, but it's better than some you've had.' He laughed.

'Anyway, Kev messaged me last night. It's payday today and he has some ingredients for you. Isn't that the third batch you've made for him?'

'Fourth. God knows what he's doing with it, because we haven't had a return yet. To be honest, I'm not sure I trust Kev.'

Deana blushed slightly, and as far as Dante was

concerned, she had a weird, dreamy look on her face. 'Oh, he's okay Dante. A bit on the wild side, but he has charm.'

'Yeah, well he's also got my money, and I want it. Are you sweet on Kev then? I thought you liked Luke?'

'I'm a woman, Dante. We're fickle about these things.' She laughed. Picking up a slice of toast, she walked to the door. 'I'm going to college. I'll meet you at the school gates and we can go straight to Kev's from there.'

Finishing his cereal, Dante let out a sigh. He knew Deana was soft on Kev. She always turned to jelly in his presence and hung on to his every word, although Kev didn't seem to notice or care.

Just then, Maggie came back from her shower. 'Has Deana gone love? Come on, George is downstairs waiting for you. Time for school.' Maggie stopped and stroked Dante's cheek. 'You look tired love, are you sleeping okay? You have dark rings around your eyes.'

'Oh God, Mum, yes, I'm fine. Stop fussing.' Dante brushed her hand away, embarrassed at his mum's attentions.

'I know you're grown up now. But you're still my baby boy. Anyway, I did want a quick word. I know you're spending a lot of time with your friend Luke, but don't forget about George, will you? He's been your friend a lot longer.'

'I know Mum and no, I haven't forgotten about George. I still spend time with him when I can. But him and Luke don't share the same interests so there's no point in taking him with me. Anyway,' Dante snapped, 'I see him all day at school, don't I? I am allowed other friends, aren't I?'

Realising she had touched a nerve, Maggie backed off a little. She just didn't want him ignoring George now that he had another older friend. 'Sorry Dante, I didn't mean to interfere. Yes, you are allowed other friends. But you know what I mean, don't you?'

He nodded and Maggie felt he'd taken what she'd said on board. She knew she couldn't choose her children's friends, but she didn't want Dante to just discard George since he had befriended him when they'd moved in. 'Anyway, on another note, has Deana mentioned her eighteenth birthday? Has she hinted about what she wants?' Maggie whispered.

Stunned, Dante adjusted his glasses and looked up at his mum. He had completely forgotten about Deana's milestone birthday. 'Not really Mum; she doesn't say much to me,' he lied.

'Well, presumably there will be a party on the cards, and I thought about having it here. So can you do some digging for me about what she would like for a present and a party. You're my spy Dante. I'm counting on you.'

Although he knew his mum meant well, Dante couldn't see Deana sharing her excitement at having her eighteenth birthday party at the local village pub with all the neighbours singing happy birthday. But he would enjoy her discomfort, that was for sure!

'I will do my best, Mum.' He grinned and ran downstairs to meet George.

'I don't know how you did it, Silva, but you definitely turned the corner. You were dead meat when you came in here!'

'Fiddler, I thought I *was* dead meat at one point.' Alex smiled. It was that lull of the day after lunch when everyone retreated to their cells and they were both lying on each of their bunk beds. Alex let out a sigh. 'It's much easier serving time without being heckled, snubbed or beaten.'

'Well, you're not exactly on the inner circle, but you're serving your time without hassle and that is something to be grateful for. Everyone just going about their business ignoring you is better than the interest they took in you, eh, son?'

Son? Alex felt a small bubble of laughter rising, but did his best to stifle it. Fiddler had become a good friend, and it was easier for him to spend time with Alex now without feeling threatened.

'I agree Fiddler. I hear and see everything, and that includes Jonesy threatening new inmates and demanding money or cigarettes from their wages.' A few looked like they had been in some form of a fight and as much as Alex felt their pain, he ignored it. He had promised he wouldn't inter-fere with Jonesy and his ruling of the prison, and he wouldn't. Life was calm for the first time in a very long time, even before he'd entered the prison walls.

Fiddler continued to talk about his family and how much he was looking forward to seeing them on the next visit, and while he talked, Alex's mind wandered. He thought about Maggie. He did his best not to think about her too much, especially as there was no privacy, and he was sharing a cell with Fiddler. He could feel an aching in his groin when he thought about her smooth, soft skin and her pert round breasts. How they had lain in each other's arms after being fully satiated by their passionate sex together. When they had spoken, she had said she wanted to come alone on the next visit. Secretly he hoped it was for the same reasons he felt. He was missing her like hell and all kinds of doubts and thoughts went through his mind. The biggest one of all was wondering what Maggie was doing on the outside and who with. Maggie was in full view being a landlady of a pub. She was also lonely and Alex knew she felt betrayed. She hadn't said much on the last visit, although their phone calls were promising.

He realised there was no point in torturing himself in here. No one cared and whatever happened outside happened. The hardship of prison was what everyone feared, but the time was the worst. You had nothing else to do but think. Small things meant a lot. Someone sharing a cigarette with you could be the highlight of your day. You did your chores, you kept your head down, but while doing all of this your mind constantly wandered back home and sent you into turmoil if you let it.

Hearing Fiddler droning on, Alex sat up. 'Come on Fiddler, let's get a cup of tea, even if it is dishwater.' Jumping off the bed, he walked towards the open cell door. 'Well come on!' Fiddler seemed more melancholy than usual today and a little slower. Once Alex looked at him properly, he saw his enlarged pupils. Shutting the door for privacy, Alex confronted him. 'What the fuck are you taking, Fiddler? No wonder you're so bloody depressed.'

'It's just a little pick me up, Silva. I've been doing a few jobs for Jonesy lately. He helps me out when I need it. You know how it is.'

'Jonesy? What, is he letting you go to the cell doors and pass his drugs around?'

'Hey, let it go Silva. It's none of your business. Cell mates don't judge each other.' Fiddler shrugged and Alex realised he was being out of line. It wasn't his business, but he didn't like the idea that Jonesy was using Fiddler. But he was a grown man, and it was his choice.

'Okay, let's have that cup of tea and a game of table tennis. Maybe that will stop you masturbating at night if we tire your hands out,' Alex laughed and led the way.

'Hey Alex, another prisoner shouted from the landing. You up for a game of doubles on the tables? Me and Warren are going to whip your ass, ping pong guy.'

Alex burst out laughing. 'Sure thing. Come on, let's see if you're man enough.' Walking along the landing, Alex looked up towards Jonesy's cell. Making a mental note, he felt he had to do something about Fiddler. And a visit to Jonesy would be what was needed.

* * *

'Hey four eyes, how's life in geeky land?' four boys shouted in the playground during break time towards Dante. George pulled at his jumper sleeve. 'Come on Dante, don't rise to it. They think they're hard nuts and that it's funny to take the piss out of everyone.'

Dante had had enough of the bad jokes and the sarcasm at the hands of these boys and their friends. They were older than him by a year, but they didn't seem to have ambition and staying in school seemed to be a better option for them than getting an apprenticeship or a job.

As Dante spied them over his glasses, an idea popped into his head. These were the sort of customers he'd been dealing with: cocky, bored addicts. It was time to test the water. Ignoring George, Dante wandered over to them, surprising them all.

'Oh my God! Keep your distance mafia boy. Got Daddy's gun stashed away, have you?' They laughed, then pretended to cry and rub their eyes. 'Awe, are you going to cry and tell the teacher?' Although their comments stung a little, Dante ignored them. He had a bone to pick and now was the time to do it.

'Nah, I don't stash guns. I leave that to my dad. Personally, I prefer weed...' Tailing off, Dante turned to walk away.

'Oh, mafia boy, what you talking about?' Turning, Dante could see that he had got the response he'd hoped for. They were taken aback, surprised by his answer. Their puzzled frowns told him what he needed to know.

'I smoke it all the time,' one boasted. 'I bet you've never touched it, geek.'

'Oh, I don't know. The men I get mine off have a different opinion of me than you. My glasses don't seem to bother them. All they're interested in is my forty pounds.' Dante swallowed hard. He had dropped the price into the conversation.

'Is that a gram Dante?' one asked civilly.

'No, two. My bloke only does it by two grams. It's not worth his journey dropping it off otherwise. But, it's relaxing and good for the nerves, so worth the money, don't you think?' Dante's smooth, calm voice drifted towards them, confusing them. Geeky, four-eyed Dante? They cast furtive glances at each other. Dante could see that he'd baited the hook. The worst they would do now was grass him to the teachers. But considering nothing would be found either at school or home and it was known they taunted him, it would just seem like another one of their spiteful games. No one would believe these bitter and twisted boys; their bad reputation preceded them. It was time to dip his toe even further in the water.

'So, who do you get yours off then, Dante the druggie?' They laughed and nudged each other in the ribs. But the conversation, as limited as it was, was proving interesting to Dante. He knew he was playing a dangerous game, boasting about weed, but as a businessman, he felt there was a whole new market of customers out there right under his nose. 'Possibly the same person as you.' He shrugged nonchalantly. 'Anyway, I have to go now. It's the end of the break.' Walking away slowly, Dante waited for their usual sarcasm but none came and for that he was grateful. He knew they would have a lot to talk about once he'd left. But only time would tell if his little plan had worked, and he had a long day ahead of him.

There were no more remarks during the course of the day. 'What did you say to them, Dante? Did you threaten to fight them?' George asked curiously. 'My dad's always reporting them. He said he would sort out their dads if need be or if they picked on me like they do you!' George caught sight of his mum parked at the gates. 'Come on Dante, we'd better hurry. She always parks on the yellow lines.' As George began to run, Dante slowed down. 'I have to meet Deana; she should be here now. College always finishes before school ends.'

'We can give you both a lift,' volunteered George.

'No, you go ahead. We have to run an errand for Mum.' As George waved and ran off, Dante looked around for Deana. Spotting her, he walked faster.

'Hey geeky boy.' Dante turned his head and to the right of the school gates was one of the boys he'd spoken to earlier hanging around, looking almost sheepish.

'That stuff you said you could get. Can you get me some?' The conversation was brief and to the point and Dante was pleased. This was what he had banked on, but now he had to play coy.

'Maybe, but I thought you said you got your own stuff. Mine won't be any different will it?'

'Maybe not, but I think you're bullshitting. So, will you get me some? I have cash.'

Seeing the notes in the boy's hand, Dante nodded. 'I only hear from him now and again. It's not Tesco so you can't just walk in this shop, but I'll do my best. I think he works tonight.' Pausing for a moment, as though deep in thought, Dante nodded. 'I'm sure he does.'

'Well take it, four eyes. Let's see if you're right. And don't fuck with me, four eyes, or I'll kick your skinny arse. Here's your forty pounds. I want forty-five back by the end of the week if you don't manage to get me what I asked for.' With that, the boy scrunched the notes up in his hand and threw them at Dante and walked away.

Feeling a sense of pride in his achievement, Dante picked up the money and walked towards Deana. 'You okay, Dante? What did that prick want and what did he throw at you?' Frowning, Deana felt compelled to run after the kid and punch him. That was until Dante held the money up in his hand. 'New customer, Deana. And more to come if my guess is right.' He smirked.

Puzzled, she looked at the money and then back at Dante. 'What's that for?'

'Cannabis.' Dante grinned and shoved the cash in his pocket.

'What? You're announcing to the school that you're a dealer? Are you crazy? I thought you were the logical one. You might as well shout it from the rooftops you prick!' Her blood boiled as her anger rose.

'Hold fire, Deana, before you fly off the handle. We have

the money, and I never said I supplied it, only that I know a man who can.'

'And, might I ask, are you going to get this stash for that prick? Christ, he's from the shitty estates. He shouldn't even be at that school,' Deana ranted as they walked to the bus stop.

'We're going to Luke's, Deana, and then on to Kev's. If I can't get two grams of cannabis at either place, we're wasting our time.'

'You're doing this just to make you fit in and look like a cool kid. For Christ's sake, don't appease him, Dante. Don't humble yourself in front of him.'

'I'm not, Deana. I'm taking his money. That's what we do isn't it? Take pricks' money, and that's what they are, including your Kev!'

Deana blushed at the mention of Kev's name and lowered her eyes. 'He's not my Kev, Dante. And don't come crying to me when this goes tits up. Do you really think those idiots aren't going to spread the word that Dante smokes and sells cannabis? You could get expelled for this Dante, it's not worth the risk.'

'I'm counting on it, Deana. Word will spread and orders will grow. Word might get to the teachers, but who would believe geeky old Dante could do such a thing? They all think I'm a swat and the teachers know I don't fit in and that lot hate me. It would be bullying, telling horrible lies about me to get me expelled and at the end of the day, they would be admitting they're buying it, wouldn't they?'

Frowning, Deana let Dante's words sink in as they walked. It did make strange sense. Everyone presumed she was the bad lot in the family, but no one ever thought that about Dante. His reputation was impeccable. 'I still think it's risky, but try it this time and see how it goes. Just be careful, okay?'

'I will, but on another note, Mum is hinting about a party for your eighteenth birthday. I'm supposed to find out what you would like for a present. I think she wants to arrange a party at the pub. What have you got in mind?'

A feeling of dread overwhelmed Deana. 'Oh my God, does that mean putting up banners and balloons and having the likes of Mark standing at the bar singing "Happy Birthday"? Oh no Dante, you have to help me.'

'I already have, haven't I? You know she'll want some kind of family party at the pub, including banners. It's up to you to convince her you have other things planned. Have you thought about anything?'

'Not really, well kind of. Some of the girls I hang around with at college have been talking about a new karaoke bar in town. Not the usual stuff, where old blokes pretend to sing like Frank Sinatra. This is nightclub stuff and you can even rent individual rooms for your own party and karaoke. Lots of fancy cocktails and flashing lights on the dance floor. That's the kind of thing I'd like. Grown-up stuff.'

'I take it I'm not invited then?' Dante laughed. 'It sounds more like a hen night!'

'It sounds good doesn't it! And my birthday is on a Tuesday, so we could have Mum's family meal or gathering then, and I could have my party on the Saturday when the Vox is open.'

'Vox?' Dante queried. 'What's that?'

'That's what they call the new nightclub. Voice box, but they call it Vox. That would suit everyone wouldn't it? As for a present, well, paying for that could be my present from Mum and Dad. It's not cheap. Anyway, it's not going to be much of a family party without Dad there, is it? I can't believe he's missing my eighteenth and possibly my nineteenth. I'll be an old lady by the time he gets out.'

'I'll drop it in the conversation but be prepared for the family party Deana and put a smile on your face, for Mum's sake.'

'If I have to sit through a family party to get the party I want, I can stomach it. If it's a private room Dante, you could come too... if you wanted to.' Deana blushed.

'Nah, I think I'll let you and your posse of college mates embarrass yourselves in private. It could be too scary for my young, innocent eyes.' He laughed while Deana elbowed him in the arm.

'Innocent, indeed! But the offer's there if you change your mind.'

11

A NEW WEALTH

Once they arrived at Luke's, he put his finger to his lips, indicating for them to be quiet. 'Mum's asleep upstairs. Come on, we'll go into the kitchen and shut the door. Or we could go down into the basement.'

Deana shook her head. 'Christ, into that sauna? No thanks. It looks like a jungle down there. The kitchen is fine,' she whispered and pushed Dante before her.

Rather than the usual preliminaries as Luke put some cans of cola on the table, Deana blurted out what was on her mind. 'I want to get Dante a motorbike licence. I've got one and it will be a lot speedier dropping stuff off if we both do it separately. But he's too young,' she scoffed. 'Can we use your name and date of birth Luke?'

Shocked at her outburst, both Dante and Luke stared at her wide eyed. 'Well actually, Deana, no,' Luke answered.

'Why? We're all in this together aren't we? And it makes sense.'

'Because, smart arse, I already have a motorbike licence, and I don't need another one!'

'You've got a licence. Why don't you use your motorbike then? You could hide your face under a helmet. Your old enemies would never know,' Deana persisted.

Rolling his eyes to the ceiling, Luke looked at Dante for back-up. 'Because I realised how much safer cars are. Rolling down windows is much easier than sitting on a bike and hoping they won't mug you! As for my bike, I sold it ages ago.'

'And the licence?' Deana almost shouted impatiently. 'Do you still have it?'

'Of course I do, but I don't see what good it will do Dante. I'm older than him and he doesn't look like me.'

'Well, how long have you had it? Two, maybe three years?' Seeing Luke shrug and nod, she grinned. 'Well, nobody ever looks like their photos, Luke.' Drumming her fingers on her chin, she gave them both a cheeky grin and a wink.

'A lot more people get stopped on motorbikes than cars by the police, Deana. And if any bent copper let's my old enemies know that I'm alive and kicking and riding around town with a rucksack full of drugs – what then? Those guys had all kinds of people in their pockets Deana,' Luke stressed.

'Well, I've never seen a motorbike stopped at the side of the road. Anyway, you worry too much. Dante will be careful. He's not stupid. He doesn't want to get caught either. So can he use your licence, Luke?' Pausing for a moment, Luke looked at Dante and let out a huge sigh. 'Could you handle a motorbike, Dante?'

'I think so. Maybe you could give me some tips?' Dante asked hopefully.

'I'll show you. You're not stupid. You can drive a car, look after yourself and point a gun. A motorbike should be pretty easy for a man like you, Dante.'

Dante's chest swelled, and his face widened with a grin. *A man*, he thought to himself. He liked the sound of that.

'Let's go to Kev's place now. From what I've heard, you will be quite surprised.' Luke grinned and stood up.

Deana watched as Dante put his hand in his pocket and pulled out what resembled black goggles. 'What the hell are those and why are you putting them on?' Deana snapped while looking at Dante fastening the sunbed goggles over his eyes. 'Do you know what you look like?'

'Yes, I look like someone entering a drug den full of smoke and fog. It makes my eyes water Deana. These will do the job. Now shut up and let's go. I feel like a marathon runner going from the door to the balcony there. And all that netting is full of dead pigeons who have been drugged to death. Am I the only person who sees them?'

Deana burst out laughing. 'You look like one of the characters out of *Despicable Me*.' Luke burst out laughing, too, much to the annoyance of a disgruntled Dante.

Given that it was still early, there were only a few people milling around Kev's place when they arrived and the smoke wasn't so bad. But still in the corners were people shooting up and passing out while others stepped over them to find their own space. Dante looked on in disgust. This was the other side of his dealing, the junkies. He was providing them with this addiction. He admitted to himself, he didn't like seeing the results of his products. Deana seemed to walk through unbothered by it all, but then again, he thought to himself as she waved to catch Kev's eye, she had something to take her mind off this zombie land.

Pointing his thumb at the window, Kev stood up. 'Balcony

folksies.' He grinned and slid the windows open. Although Dante was glad of the fresh air, he dreaded the images of the dead birds stuck in the netting, but it was better than the alternative. Sitting in his deckchair and adjusting his mirrored sunglasses so that they sat on the top of his head, Kev grinned and pushed a holdall towards Deana. 'That's yours.' Kicking another one towards Dante, his grin widened. 'That's yours, Dante and so is this one. You get two bags. Luke, yours is behind me. Trust me folksies, I will swap holdalls with any of you anytime you like. It's all even stevens, less what we pay the sellers in the clubs for passing the stuff on. They all have to be paid and that means overheads.' Apart from being called 'folksies' which made Dante cringe, he had to admire how quickly Kev stepped up to the mark and became professional about the whole thing.

Out of the corner of his eye, Dante could see Deana unzipping her holdall excitedly. 'What about the other batches?' asked Dante. 'I've made three since the first one. Have they all gone?'

An even bigger grin crossed Kev's face. 'They bloody have, Dante. You just look inside that bag. Your stuff is flying off the shelves.' Suddenly, Kev looked more closely at Dante. 'Is there something wrong with your eyes mate? You have black goggles on underneath your glasses.'

'No. It's my hay fever, that's all,' Dante lied, amidst stifled giggles from Luke and Deana.

'You need to get some shades like mine, Dante,' Kev boasted, although the closer he looked at Dante's glasses the more confused he seemed.

'Get back to the matter in hand, Kev. Never mind my glasses. The stuff is selling... yes?'

'Yes. People love it, Dante.' Without thinking, Kev blew

him a kiss and laughed. 'I don't give a shit what glasses you wear as long as you keep cooking the same shit up.'

Deana gasped out loud. 'Oh my God. Are all those rolls of bills a thousand each?' Dante looked down at the concrete balcony floor to where Deana was crouching down peering into the holdall. Notes of money were folded into a roll, held with an elastic band. Catching Deana's eye, he looked at her. 'There's a thousand pounds in this roll of money, Dante and look, there are loads of them.' Kneeling down further, Deana opened the bag wider and put her hand inside over the many rolls, all tied with elastic bands.

Cockily, Kev lay back in his deck chair and grinned. 'That's right Deana. There is forty grand in your bag. Ours too. Apart from Dante's. He's got his forty grand and an extra twenty grand for his cooking.'

'What?' exclaimed Dante. 'I've got sixty grand?' For a moment they were all silent.

'I'm telling you now,' Kev replied. 'It's good stuff you're making and there is a market for it. Keep it coming and it will soon make us more money than all the other gear we sell. You'll still get your money from the mushrooms, heroin and other stuff, like coke and speed. We share the cannabis, you know that already, cos half of it is your dad's. That the deal.'

Hearing about the cannabis prompted Dante. 'Actually, I want some cannabis. A sample or two. I think I have a new customer, but they want to try it before committing.'

'So, you're rustling up customers, eh? You sure it's not for yourself?' Kev joked and winked at him. 'Your stuff is fifty pound a gram street price Dante my mate. I started charging twenty-five but then realised people were prepared to pay more. Supply and demand. If they want it bad enough, they will pay. But I've had an offer. A bloke I know, well, not know,'

Kev corrected himself. 'He deals here and there but has heard about your stuff and wants a shit load. Three pounds of it in fact.' Kev let out a low whistle.

Confused, Dante looked at him. 'Why sell it to him when we can sell it ourselves? Whatever he pays he will charge double Kev. That's not good business.'

'It is, Dante, because that means he will have the occupational hazard of dealing it. We still sell our own Dante, there's no question of that. My guess is that he doesn't intend selling it here but elsewhere. So that's a lot of cooking you need to do, Dante. His three and another three for us. We need to keep the fires burning now people have got the taste for it.' Reaching in his pocket, Kev took out a few packets of cannabis and threw them towards Dante. 'Take them, see what trade you can drum up.'

Coming out of Kev's flat to the main road, Deana hailed a taxi. 'I don't feel like walking and catching the bus with all this money, and it's so bloody heavy! Let's splash out and get a taxi.'

They all climbed in. 'Can I ask you something Luke? It's personal, but I'm curious,' asked Dante as they were made their way back to Luke's house.

'Anything mate, you know that. Just keep it low key. We are in a taxi.' Giving him a knowing look and glancing towards the back of the cabbie's head, Luke waited.

Clearing his throat, Dante nodded. 'Kev is a good businessman. So why does he wear the same old combat jacket and mirror glasses? Surely, he can afford something better? I don't understand.'

Letting out a deep sigh, Deana rolled her eyes. 'I wondered when you were going to piss on my bit of happiness, Dante. What does it matter to you?'

'Just being nosey, I guess.' He shrugged, and gave a sheepish smile.

'You're still young, Dante, and you don't look close enough.' He grinned. 'Those trainers he wears are a thousand pound a pair. Those jeans might not have seen a washing machine, but when they get too dirty, he doesn't wash them, he just buys another designer pair. Do you get my drift? It wouldn't look very good in his line of work if he wore a suit and tie, would it?' Casting his eyes towards the holdalls on the floor of the taxi to stress his point, Luke looked back up at Dante.

Feeling a flush of embarrassment, Dante nodded. 'I see you what you mean. No offence Luke. Just wondered.'

Sitting back in the taxi, Dante decided to keep quiet for the rest of the journey. Although he wondered just how much money Kev had wasted looking the part. What Kev did with his own money was his business; he earnt it and he enjoyed spending it in whatever way he wanted.

As the taxi drew to a halt, Luke waved them both to get out too. He wanted a word with them both before they went home. Hearing the seriousness in his voice, Deana paid and grinning from ear to ear, she told the cabbie to keep the change.

'Firstly,' Luke asked when they were all sat in the kitchen opening their cans of cola. 'Are you going to take those bags home with you tonight? Have you thought about where you're going to hide them from your mum?'

'Well,' stammered Deana. 'Let's be honest, Luke, we didn't realise it would be so much, did we? This lot isn't going into my knicker drawer, is it?'

'I know, which is why we have things to discuss before

you leave. You can take what you want and leave the rest here if you want. You know it's safe, I'm no thief.'

'For God's sake Luke, that wouldn't even cross our mind. We both trust you, you know that,' Deana stressed.

Luke took a sip of his drink. 'Dante, why don't I use some of your money to buy a motorbike? You can come with me or trust my judgement, but it won't be anything too flash, just something that will do the job and one that you're safe on. Safety first Dante, eh?' Seeing Dante and Deana nod their approval, Luke carried on. Standing up, he opened one of the kitchen cupboards and took out two sleeves of cigarettes with two hundred cigarettes in each and in packets of twenties. 'Dante why don't you take these and see if you can sell them to your new school friends? If not, no harm done. I'll smoke them.' Luke laughed. 'You've an old head on young shoulders, Dante and a brain for business – just be careful, that's all I'm saying.'

'I've got a brain for business too, Luke. What about me? Don't I get any praise? I sell the stuff too, you know.' Deana pouted, not wanting to be left out.

'You,' Luke laughed, 'are the wind up our arses. You're the impulsive go-getter. The chancer. We wouldn't do anything without you, Deana. We don't have the guts.' Luke winked at Dante and grinned. Seeing that Deana was satisfied with that, he carried on. 'Last word, Dante. To cook up that much of your meth is going to take a couple of days. You need to plan and make your excuses, and it needs to be quick, especially as Kev already has a buyer for a huge bulk of it.' They sat in silence for a moment and sipped at their drinks while deep in thought.

'Couldn't I stay the weekend with you here, Luke?' Dante asked hopefully.

'What? Like a sleepover? I suppose that would work if your mum agreed. She has dropped you off here and met my mum. She seemed happy with the set-up.' Luke shrugged.

Dante nodded. Maggie had offered him a lift to Luke's once, on the pretence that she was running an errand anyway, but both he and Deana realised it was a rouse just to meet Dante's new friend. Fortunately, Luke had passed the test with flying colours.

'It will have to be a weekend though Luke. What do you think, Deana?'

Putting her elbows on the table, Deana rested her head in her hands. 'Mum wouldn't let him do it on a school night, but if it's a weekend that's when we're doing our drop-offs. We can't do both, can we?'

'I could do it with you, Deana,' Luke offered. 'Dante can stay here. Talking of that, I have something for you too.' Luke laughed. Opening a draw, he took out a tabard and a fleecy jacket. Each one had the nearby supermarket logo on. 'That should satisfy your mum when she's complaining that your uniform is never in the wash. A friend of mine works there, she gave me them.'

'Bloody hell, Luke, what would we do without you? You always cover our backs. And that' – Dante pointed at the uniform – 'will definitely get Mum off your back – well, for a while, anyway, until she goes in there, shopping of course.'

'I've told her I'm only shelf stacking. I'm not on any checkouts and sometimes I'm just in the warehouses helping them unload the pallets to stack the shelves. That way, if I'm not about when she pops in, there's my excuse. Christ, it's all so cloak and dagger, isn't it?'

Picking up the uniform, Deana stashed it in her rucksack. 'Thanks for these, Luke.' Smiling at them both, Deana stood up. 'We'd better go. And...' She grinned, waving a twenty-pound note in the air. 'I'm going by taxi!'

'Luke, you buy the motorbike, take the money out of my bag. I'll leave all my money here for now. Mum knows I only had my gym bag with me tonight but if I stay overnight, I'll have more bags and I can take some of the cash with me then. I'll give you a call when I sort this weekend out. I've been having a bit of trouble with Mum who thinks I'm ignoring my school mate, George. He was the only friend and neighbour that spoke to me when we moved here and she's friends with his parents. So, I'll have to spend some time with him I suppose.' Dante looked a little down-hearted. He liked George, but these days he had other things on his mind. This was his chance as the only man in the family to bring his family back into the real world and bask in the sunshine. Be it good or bad, he had ambition and soon he would have the college and university of his choice without putting a strain on the family funds. Deana was doing well at college and, for all his misgivings about her, he couldn't deny that. They would both have careers, but they needed money to go that extra yard, and he was damn sure they would have it.

12

CRIMINAL MINDS

'We're back Mum!' they both shouted as they ran into the back of the pub. Maggie was in the bar with Phyllis and Pauline and the pub seemed to be at full capacity with people waiting for tables to eat at. Within a matter of a few months, it seemed Alex and the court case had become a distant memory and now every customer who had deserted them had suddenly turned up again.

'Hello you two. Have you had a good day?' Maggie kissed them both on the cheeks. 'I presume you've stuffed yourself on chips and carbs, so what about ice cream?' Maggie beamed and hugged them both. 'I spoke with your father today. He's well and he's looking forward to seeing you soon.'

'I hope he's remembered my birthday. Eighteen years is a big milestone, Mum.' Deana could have bitten her tongue the moment the words fell out. Dante glared at her defiantly. 'What I mean, Mum,' Deana backtracked, 'is that I hope to see him on or around my birthday – that's all.' Realising what she had said and how bad her mum must be feeling, Deana inwardly cursed herself.

'I'll see what I can do, Deana. I'll speak to your dad and I'm sure he hasn't forgotten, but they don't let you pop out of prison to the shops to buy cards. He'll be sorry to miss it. He would have made such a fuss of you.' Reaching out, Maggie hugged Deana tightly and felt the tears run down her cheeks. 'I'm sorry love. It hasn't been a good year, has it?'

Dante surveyed the scene. Inwardly he felt like strangling Deana and her runaway tongue! Pushing past them at the bottom of the stairs, he ran up to his room and sat on the side of his bed. Opening his bag, he spotted the cigarettes that Luke had given him and took out the cannabis that Kev had given him. Slowly he separated the packets of cigarettes from their sleeve and put a few packets in his bag along with the cannabis. Sniffing at his jumper, he could smell the nicotine and smoke from Kev's opium den on his clothing and hair. He needed a shower, and those clothes needed to be washed. Then, and only then, would he take up the offer of the ice cream, he thought to himself.

'You're all invited. Of course, I will be sending formal invites, but I just want you to make sure you're going to be free on that Saturday night. Make a note of it,' Deana boasted to her girlfriends at college. She was inviting them all to her birthday party at Vox and she could see how impressed and jealous they were. 'Of course, when you come, I'll introduce you to my boyfriend, Kev,' she added. This made the girls even more interested. They hadn't heard about Deana's love interest up until now and they asked all the usual questions. How old he was, how long they had been going out for and whether he was at college or not. As though holding court,

Deana sat in the midst of them in the food hall telling them all about Kev. 'He's older than me and has his own business,' she lied. Although, she wasn't really lying, was she?

'Do you have a photo on your mobile? Let's have a look,' one of her friends asked.

Deana was stumped. Her mouth had run away with her again, only this time she had embarrassed herself. 'No, I don't think so. He usually takes the photos or selfies of us so they are on his phone. I must get him to forward some to me.'

'What about his Facebook? Surely there are photos on there?' asked another girl called Amy. Suddenly, Deana felt foolish. To start with, she hadn't even asked Kev to go to her party, and she had never looked to see if he had a Facebook. How stupid! It had never crossed her mind. What was she going to do now? 'Nope.' She smiled, feeling her face burn with embarrassment. 'You're going to have to wait and see him in the flesh.' She laughed.

Amy nodded and looked around at the others. Sarcasm dripped off her tongue. 'That's if he exists at all.'

'Oh, he does Amy. And I expect a big apology when you see him, or rather *if* you see him, because I don't remember inviting you!' snapped Deana. Her stomach churned. Amy had laid down the challenge and she couldn't backtrack now.

Cockily, Amy grinned. 'I don't care if you don't invite me Deana, I'm sure there will be lots of photos from everyone here on Facebook. So, I will see your boyfriend, one way or another, wont I?'

Deana knew she was being pushed into a corner, and it was all her own doing. Amy and her besties were part of the in crowd. She also knew if she didn't invite Amy, the others wouldn't go either. Or Amy would announce her own party and they would go to Vox for an hour and then disappear to

Amy's party. Either way, Deana knew she was treading a thin line. 'Well, as it happens, Amy, you are invited. Why wouldn't I invite you? We're friends after all. I think it will be a good night, don't you?' Deana noticed all the others almost taking a sigh of relief that they didn't have to choose between. No one wanted to take sides.

Amy nodded her approval, looking pleased that she was invited to the new venue in town that everyone was talking about. As they all parted to go their separate ways, Deana's heart pounded in her chest. She needed Kev to be at her party to prove her point. She wondered how she was going to convince him and Luke to be there. Deana thought how cool it would make her look having older men at her party, unlike the young college boys her friends dated.

They had all asked if they could bring their boyfriends too and Deana, in her moment of excitement had agreed, although as she walked to her class now, she regretted it. Would she be the only girl at her own birthday party without a boyfriend? The very thought of it made her squirm. Firmly, in her mind, Deana decided she needed to have a substitute on hand. She thought about the boys at her college. Some had asked her out before and she had refused or rebuked them in her usual manner. Now, it was her mission to invite a few spares for the evening in case it all went tits up!

* * *

Dante hung around the school yard during his lunch break and he was soon joined by the boy who had given him forty pounds. 'Well geek, have you got my money?' he asked.

Dante walked along to the side of the building, out of sight, surrounded by bushes and flowers. 'You want your money back? Oh, I thought you wanted your order,' Dante answered nonchalantly. 'Never mind, I'll keep it.'

Frowning, the boy spied him curiously. 'What? You've got the weed?'

Dante put his finger to his lips for silence and nodded. Dante had the little plastic packet already in the palm of his hand. Reaching out, he shook the boy's hand and slipped it to him, then walked away. Dante knew it wouldn't be long before he would catch up with him.

'Dante! Hold up. Dante.' Smiling to himself, Dante turned and waited in mock surprise.

'You sure this isn't your mother's mixed herbs from her kitchen?'

'Try it and see. If you don't like it, I'll give you your money back. Oh, actually, as a mark of good faith...' Dante reached in his bag and took out one of the twenty packets of cigarettes. 'Take these, you'll need some tobacco to go with my mother's mixed herbs.' Seeing his customer's face light up when he saw the packet, Dante knew he had done the right thing. This was indeed the sprat to catch the mackerel as he had presumed. Now, the boy looked at Dante in disbelief. Not only could geeky Dante get his hands on cannabis, but he also had spare cigarettes to give away. 'I get them cheap, only seven pounds a packet for twenty.' Dante smiled, but he wanted to laugh. He could see this bully, aptly named Scooter because he went to school on his electric scooter even though the teachers disapproved, which did his reputation as king pin at school no harm. Scooter had constantly jeered at him, especially during the hype of Alex's court case, but now Dante could see Scooter was impressed.

Standing there wide eyed, Scooter couldn't believe his

luck. 'Can you get any more of these?' he asked, holding the packet and staring at it like a jewel.

Dante shrugged. 'Try the herbs first, then we'll talk again. But this is a secret. Keep it to yourself, eh.' Dante knew he was asking the impossible. Word would soon spread. Scooter would want to impress his friends with his cannabis and cigarettes. But he could only impress them as long as his stuff lasted, and then he would come back to Dante asking for more and hopefully, his friends would want some of the same. Now that was good business, Dante decided. He had given away a packet of cigarettes in the hope he could sell the next lot and the next.

Dante noticed that before the end of school other boys who usually totally ignored him, acknowledged him, with a, 'Hi Dante', or just a nod. He knew word was spreading and at least they saw him in a different light now, not just as geeky Dante. For the first time in a very long time, he felt in control of his life. He had a good home, a mum and some good friends. Okay, his father was in prison but, so were a lot of fathers. Even Mark had admitted to being inside prison at some point in his life. He thought about his own birthday. Last year it had come and gone in the blink of an eye, much like Deana's. This year was going to be different. Deana was going to have her party and when it came to it, he was going to have his. He wanted to open a bank account and drip feed some of this money into it, too. Yes, things were definitely looking up.

* * *

Looking at her watch when she heard the door slam, Maggie smiled. 'Well, you two are home at a reasonable hour.'

Maggie beamed. 'It's my night off so how about a movie night with my babies? We'll get some food, sweets and any other junk and lounge in front of some movies. You're so busy these days, I feel like I haven't seen you. Deana's always picking up extra hours at work and you're either with your friends or swotting for your exams in your room. So tonight is our night. No work and no books. That's an order!' Maggie laughed.

'Sounds great; let me get out of these clothes and put my PJs on and get my duvet.' Deana laughed, running up the stairs. 'Me too,' chimed Dante.

'Dante, just a quick word.' As Deana raced up the stairs, Maggie waited until she'd disappeared into her room. 'Have you spoken to Deana about her birthday?'

'Yes.' Dante nodded. 'She's already inviting people to her party at Vox. It's a karaoke club thing she's doing with some of the girls from her college. It's going to cost a few quid but that's what she wants and is boasting about it already. I take it she hasn't sprung this idea on you yet?' Maggie stood wide eyed listening to Dante's revelations; her jaw almost dropped. She was about to speak, but Dante butted in. 'That's what she wants to do on the Saturday and on Tuesday, her actual birthday, she would like some kind of family meal here, if that's okay? As for presents she's not that bothered. She's more interested in the party, and I don't think we're invited.' He laughed.

Dante looked at his mum as the smile appeared on her face. He could see that she was relieved that Deana wanted to spend some time with her family on her birthday, and she was happy with that. 'Well, thanks for that Dante. God knows when she was going to tell me! But you're right, you're too young and I'm way too old to be singing karaoke!' Maggie grinned. 'But I think I'll also give her some money towards those driving lessons. She seems very eager.' Maggie couldn't help smiling as Dante kissed her on the cheek and ran up the stairs to change.

Walking into the bar, Maggie surveyed the busy scene. Mark was at his usual corner drinking with his friends, and everything seemed normal. 'Pauline, can you manage this evening? I'm going to spend the night with the kids while I've got them in the same room at a decent hour, if that's okay?'

'That's more than okay. You haven't had a proper night off in ages. Everything is under control. Old Percy, God help us, is collecting glasses which means a free pint now and again.' She grimaced. 'And the kitchen staff have everything under control, so you have an evening to yourself and forget about this place. Me and Phyllis will clear the bar and lock up and give you a shout before we leave. Now go on missus, raid the kitchen. Get some sweets from the desserts trolley and bugger off!'

Maggie couldn't help laughing and feeling fortunate at having such good friends. Because that was what they were. True, loyal friends. Even if they were bossy.

As Maggie, Deana and Dante all snuggled together with the duvet wrapped around them all, eating cartons of ice cream covered with nuts and sweets, Dante felt this was a good time to mention his own plans.

'Mum, Luke has asked me if I want to stay over at his house at the weekend. You know, just to play some games and stuff. What do you think?'

'I think that should be okay. It's company for him. I don't want to sound horrible, but he's got a lot on his plate looking after his mum and he must get lonely. I know he's older than you, but I still think he should ask his mum before inviting people to stay over – is she okay with you being there? I could bring some plates of food from the carvery over for you all if you want?'

'He wouldn't invite me without talking to her. He already asked his mum before he asked me. I was thinking of asking George as well... don't want to leave him out.'

'Oh, that's lovely Dante. But have you forgot, George is going camping this weekend with Mark and Olivia. That's a lovely idea though Dante and I'll tell Mark you were going to ask him. Maybe next time.'

'Oh, yes,' lied Dante, slapping his head for effect. 'It totally slipped my mind.' Content with the outcome, Dante picked up his tub of ice cream and sat back to enjoy the movie. 'You could come early and bring us a Sunday roast from the carvery if you want before you pick me up. You can come too, Deana. Luke's mum will enjoy that, won't she?'

Maggie beamed her approval and nodded. 'I'd like to help your friend with his mum, if possible. But I don't want to butt in. But Sunday lunch sounds good. What about you, Deana? Do you want to come?' Deana nodded, as Dante cast a glance at her and they both grinned widely.

The next morning over breakfast, Deana frantically searched Facebook, desperately looking for Kev's profile. After ten minutes of searching, she smiled to herself and sat back in her chair.

'What's the secret? You look like the cat that got the cream!'

Almost breathing a sigh of relief, Deana grinned. 'I have, Pauline, today I have. Anyway, apart from working here today, what are your plans?' Glancing at her phone again, Deana smiled, almost chuckling to herself. Kev didn't have a Facebook profile. There was nothing on there so even if her college friends searched for him, they wouldn't find him and they wouldn't see any photos that didn't include herself.

Pauline almost choked at Deana's interest in her plans. 'My God, Deana, if you weren't so young I would say you're going through the menopause.'

Disregarding Pauline's sarcasm, Deana got up and switched on the kettle. 'Maybe I am going through the change of life, Pauline. I'm nearly eighteen and the world is my oyster. I've also been looking at universities close by. I don't want to go too far away from home. Not yet anyway...' She tailed off.

'Well, most people go to London for university, so you're in the right part of England. Which ones were you thinking?'

Taking the tea bags out of the mugs, Deana put one down in front of Pauline. 'I'm still looking, keeping my options open. Anyway, why are you up here at this time? Aren't you normally downstairs sorting out the bar or something?'

'I have things to do, but I'll go down in a moment. It was your mum I was after. But I'll have a cuppa before I bother her. I don't suppose there's any chance of a biscuit is there?' Pauline sipped her tea and spied this new smiling Deana. For now, she was going to milk her kindness.

'Pauline!' Maggie walked into the kitchen. 'I take it they called you when they couldn't contact me last night? It's okay, I've already called the agency.'

'What's this?' Deana asked, as she stood up and placed another mug of tea on the table.

'The chef tried calling last night to say he wouldn't be in

today, and when he couldn't get me, he rang Pauline, and possibly Phyllis.'

'He's off sick again, with another weak excuse,' Pauline muttered. 'If it's not back pain, leg pain or pain in the arse to us pain, it's something else.'

'I know Pauline. I've already called the agency and thank you for coming in.'

'You know what? You should do one of those WhatsApp chat groups. A lot of workplaces have them. You're all included on it but should any of you want to leave a message or anything, you can all see it and can also reply. I'll show you how if you like. You've all got mobiles, haven't you?' Both Maggie and Pauline nodded. Standing up, Pauline picked up her mug of tea. 'That's it, I've had enough of all this niceness, this early in the morning.' Pauline laughed. 'Deana please tell me your usual sarcasm will be resumed soon. Oh, by the way, as it's nearly your birthday, is there anything I can buy you from Poundland? Anything special?' She laughed.

'I'm not rising to it Pauline. You can do your damnedest. But as it is my birthday, you will be pleased to hear Grandma will be visiting with her usual ten suitcases. Nine of them containing her make-up. A bit like yours!'

'That's more like it, Deana. Let the sarcasm drip. Is your grandmother really coming?'

Maggie butted in, 'Well yes of course she is. She wouldn't miss her granddaughter's eighteenth, would she? But it's okay, I'll have her on a tight rein this time.'

'I do hope so, especially after last time.' The grimace on Pauline's face spoke volumes as she remembered Babs' last visit and she walked down the stairs to start work.

'Talking of birthdays, young lady, is there something you

want to tell me about your plans for your birthday – like Vox?' Maggie asked.

'Oh yes, I thought it would be nice to have a big girly party. Kick our heels up. You can rent private rooms. Apparently, they have big screens on the walls, loads of microphones and a million songs to choose from. It's all dim lighting and disco lights. They also do food.' Deana filled her in excitedly. Her face was flushed and her eyes shone.

'And alcohol,' Maggie added. 'Well, you'll be eighteen, I suppose I can't stop you having a drink, but nothing heavy, eh?'

Shocked, Deana frowned. 'You mean it's okay? You don't mind not being there?'

'If that's your way of telling me I'm not invited Deana, I already guessed that.'

Deana put her hands to her mouth. 'Oh Mum, I didn't mean you're not invited. I just thought it wouldn't be your kind of thing.'

'Don't start making excuses and digging that hole deeper love. I won't be there and neither will Grandma!' Maggie laughed. 'But your actual birthday is mine, Deana. Mine and your father's. He said he will call you on your birthday. So, how much is this Vox place going to cost? And how many have you invited?'

Deana cast her eyes down. 'I'm not 100 per cent about cost, given food and stuff. But there will be about twenty or so there. Just girls from college. Some have asked if they can bring their boyfriends, but I'm not sure about that.'

Giving her a sly look, Maggie sipped her tea. 'And what about you, Deana? Is there a boyfriend of yours going to this knees-up?'

'No way. Young, free and single. That's me, Mum. It's just

that life looks good at the moment, doesn't it Mum? I've also been looking at universities...' Deana tailed off.

Taken aback a little, Maggie waited for Deana's words to register. 'Well, good for you. I presume you will be leaving home soon then?' Maggie's heart sank at the prospect. Empty-nest syndrome. Most mums suffered from it, but it wasn't recognised medically!

'Not necessarily. There are plenty of universities in London. It depends on my grades and who will accept me. But it's all moving forward to the future, Mum. At least we know we have a future now. Life's been uncertain lately, but now, everything's coming up roses.'

'Maggie! Maggie are you there? The agency chef is here!' Pauline shouted.

'I'd better go and introduce myself, love. You make the calls to this Vox place and order what you want. I'll go and see our temperamental new chef!'

Quickly showering and getting ready, Deana couldn't wait to go into college today. She would give invites out to a few spare boys to make up the numbers and wallow in her newfound popularity. Running downstairs, she bumped into her mum, Phyllis and Pauline huddled together.

'What's up? Isn't the new chef grumpy enough for you?'

'He's very young. Pauline isn't sure he's up to the job. Some of the kitchen staff are older than him. Poor Sherwin, the kitchen assistant, looks like his father,' Maggie sighed.

'He must be old enough. He works for the agency so this can't be the first job he's had with them, can it? Let me go and have a look at Baby Face. Maybe I can get some information out of him about his experience.' They nodded at each other and agreed with Deana.

Deana walked towards the kitchen and pushed open the

swing doors. Some of the staff were already preparing vegetables and Deana could hear banging and crashing coming from the store cupboard. She walked in, seeing the back of a man dressed in his chef's whites and hat who she presumed was the new chef. 'Morning!' she shouted towards him. Stunned, she stood rooted to the spot as he turned towards her. 'Kev!' she exclaimed. Seeing him standing there almost took her breath away. She thought she was going to faint.

Kev was as stunned as she was and stood there wide eyed. 'Deana, what are you doing here?'

'I live here. This is my mum's pub. Didn't you know?'

'I knew your mum had a pub, but I didn't know which one. The agency called me this morning and only gave me the name of the pub, not the owner. It was a last-minute dash. For Christ's sake, Deana, I don't know what to say. I can't stay now,' he muttered.

'I didn't know you were a chef. I thought, well, you know what I thought. Anyway, you can't leave now, Mum's relying on you.' Deana stood staring at him in awe. He looked totally different dressed head to toe in his chef's whites, and without his sunglasses! 'Does Luke know?' she asked, wanting something to break the ice. She almost bit her tongue once the words left her mouth.

'Of course he does,' Kev snapped, 'but I don't think he knows I still do the odd bit to keep my hand in with the agency. It's legal and keeps the tax man off my back. Anyway, what now?'

Gathering her thoughts, Deana smiled. 'Now, I go to college. And you, Kev, cook three different meats and some desserts.' Almost shyly, she backed away, but as an afterthought, she turned back. 'Although, you do owe me a favour Kev.' Inwardly she smiled. Now she could ask him to her party, and he couldn't refuse! This was their secret, and theirs alone. Kev, a chef, who would have thought it!

Pauline was the first to pull her aside as she walked into the bar. 'Well, has he done this before?' Phyllis and Maggie stood there worriedly frowning, waiting for the gossip.

'Yes, loads of times apparently.' Deana laughed. 'I told you the agency wouldn't take him without a good reference and experience. It's their heads on the chopping block if he fails. He's well busy through there and got it all under control. He's older than he looks. Lucky bugger. He's been blessed with a baby face, Pauline.' Deana hoped she wasn't wrong and that Kev knew what he was doing. She didn't know what Kev was capable of. 'Bye,' she shouted, and kissed Maggie on the cheek.

Walking to the bus stop, Deana felt her heart pounding. This was a very special day. Whatever happened on her birthday wouldn't be as good as seeing Kev in her kitchen. Wow! Dreams really did come true. Quickly taking out her mobile, she texted Dante. He needed to be warned that Kev was in their kitchen, too. Although, she chuckled to herself, he wouldn't believe her. Dante would think she had been smoking something!

13

PARTY NIGHT

'Bye love, have a good weekend.' Maggie left the car running as she dropped Dante off at Luke's house. 'I won't come in, but I'll be here Sunday. If you need me, I'm on the end of the phone. Okay?'

'Sure thing Mum. See you Sunday.' Luke had already opened the door and waved to Maggie, who smiled and waved back. Dante and Deana had gone through this charade meticulously so that everything would look normal for Maggie.

After she drove off, Dante walked into the house and dropped his bag in the hallway. 'Well, that's the worst bit over with. I hate lying to Mum. But needs must. Do you have everything we need?'

'Let's eat first.' Luke grinned. 'I'm going to make some egg and chips, with lots of bread and butter and ketchup. Mum's had hers and is upstairs listening to one of those audiobooks.'

'If you don't mind, I'll go up and say hello while you're

cooking. It's only good manners and I'm sure she's heard Mum's car pull up.'

Cocking his head to one side, Luke smiled. 'She'd like that. And yes, she has the ears of a ferret especially with your mum hooting the horn as she drove off. I'll give you a shout when the food's ready, otherwise she'll have you up there all day.' Luke laughed while busying himself in the kitchen.

Oddly, Dante thought to himself, he felt at home here, in Luke's house. It was quiet with just Luke's music or the radio playing in the background. There was some kind of privacy here, unlike at home were everyone seemed to be rushing around making themselves busy. After a few minutes of chatting to Luke's mum, he heard Luke shout from downstairs and made his excuses to leave.

'She kept you gossiping then. It's nice for her to have company. She doesn't have much.'

'I told her Mum was coming Sunday and bringing Sunday lunch from the pub with her. She liked that.' Dante grinned and sat down to eat. He didn't realise how hungry he was until it was there before him. He hadn't had much chance to eat during his school lunch break as he'd been busy selling his cigarettes and taking orders for cannabis. Thankfully, Kev unexpectedly turning up to work at the pub had made things even easier for him. Once he let Kev know he had orders for both, Kev had brought more supplies in with him in his oversized combat jacket that he hung in the kitchen cloakroom where Dante could rifle through his deep pockets before rushing off to school.

'So, you've found out Kev's secret then?' Luke laughed. 'I don't know who was more shocked, him or Deana. He always liked cooking, did a spell on a cruise ship once, but they kicked him out because of his habit. It's a shame really, because he has a good career at his fingertips, but he messes up every time. I hear he's been at the pub for a few days and your mum gave Kev the thumbs up to stay. Apparently, she's had lots of compliments about his rhubarb crumble.' Luke laughed. 'Makes you wonder what spices he's using.' Looking up, he caught Dante's eye and they both burst out laughing.

'Deana's bribed him into going to her birthday party at Vox. I believe you've been dragged in as well. Good luck with that, because I've heard her singing and it sounds like a cat on heat. She's either tone deaf or totally deluded.'

'I'm only going because Kev has begged me to. I think Deana wants some older guys there to make her look popular amongst her college friends.'

'Either that, or she doesn't have any other friends to ask. Not proper friends anyway. That college lot are all hangers on. They snubbed her when it was Dad's court case and now she's popular because her party is at the hottest place in town.'

'I think she's lonely but covers it well. The pair of you,' Luke said, 'have been through a shit time. I don't know the details, but I can guess it wasn't pleasant. How is your dad anyway? You haven't said much.'

'Apparently okay, well, according to Mum. He calls a lot and it's nice to hear his voice, but it's sad as well. We've been to visit, and Mum's gone on her own to have some together time, but I don't like to think about it. He jokes on the phone with us but it's all an act. I think he's putting a brave face on for us.'

'Prison is no joke whatever you've done, Dante. I've only done a few months here and there for dealing, but Christ I was glad to get out.'

Dante stared at him wide eyed. 'You've been in prison, Luke?'

'Occupational hazard at times, so be warned Dante. It was more worrying leaving Mum. I got her a live in carer. Christ that cost a fortune!' Luke exclaimed. 'Looking at a thousand pound a week. I didn't want to put her in a home, as she knows her way around here. Kev stumped up a lot of the cash and kept an eye on things – thank God.'

Luke's words sunk into Dante's brain. Prison was an occupational hazard. It made him wonder when his and Deana's bubble would burst. He didn't want a prison record. He had ambitions, but the money he was accumulating would pay a lot of his university needs. But Luke had given him something to think about.

Once they had cleared away their plates, Luke laid the large pine table with all the ingredients Dante needed to cook his meth. Between them they rolled up their sleeves and started mixing all the ingredients together. Luke had bought a lot of new baking trays and after a few hours they poured the liquid into them. It was the early hours of the morning, and they were both perspiring. Every window and door was shut, so no fumes could escape. It looked like a science laboratory, with its glass jars and boiling pots. Luke disappeared a couple of times to check up on his mum, leaving Dante to it. 'I've bought a chest freezer and put it in the basement. Took some bloody hard work getting it down there, I can tell you.'

Musing to himself, Dante's brows furrowed. 'It's no good down there Luke. Not with all of those lights on the plants. It's like an inferno down there keeping them warm. The freezer will be working overtime trying to freeze everything. It needs an ambient temperature. Is there anywhere else we could put it?'

'It needs a what?' Mopping his brow with a towel, Luke couldn't believe his ears.

'An ambient temperature. It's made for household. Not that hot house down there. We need to move it and preferably tonight if we're going to freeze this lot overnight.'

Letting out a deep sigh, Luke sat back in his chair. 'I wish I would have known sooner. It half killed me getting it down those steps.' Deep in thought, he looked around the kitchen. 'There's the garage. It's full of crap, and there is something in there for you, which is what I was going to show you tomorrow. I also have one of those trolleys delivery men use. You know,' Luke encouraged, 'to deliver washing machines and stuff. I'm game if you are, and then I am going to collapse into bed.'

They were both tired and drained, but if they didn't move the freezer all of their efforts would go to waste. After a lot of pulling and heaving, they wheeled the medium-sized chest freezer into the garage. Breathless, they switched it on and carefully held the baking trays full of liquid and laid them down into the freezer to set. 'Hopefully, the mixture will set like before and then we can smash it up. I think we'll need to do more in the morning, but for now it's sleep time and fingers crossed, eh?'

Switching off the lights, they both staggered upstairs. Dante was pleasantly surprised at the bedroom's gaily coloured lemon-patterned wallpaper. The double bed and its thick duvet beckoned him and he just threw himself on top of it. Closing his eyes, he felt himself drifting off into a deep sleep.

Hearing banging and crashing, Dante woke with a start. Looking around at the unfamiliar surroundings, he sat up with a start. Many was the time he and his family had been driven off in the middle of the night and he had woken up in unfamiliar surroundings. But this morning after rubbing his face and yawning, he remembered he was at Luke's, safe and sound. Still dressed in last night's clothes, he yawned again and went downstairs. Luke was stood in his pyjama bottoms and a T-shirt. 'Did I wake you mate? Sorry. I still needed to get up and get Mum's breakfast, plus the carer comes early this morning to shower her and stuff. Everything we used last night has been in the dishwasher, so we're good to go once the carer has left.' The smell of bacon wafted towards Dante, and he could feel himself salivating. 'Is any of that going spare?'

'Too right it is. Let me just take up Mum's. You help yourself.' Luke disappeared upstairs and as Dante piled his plate with tomatoes, eggs and bacon, the back door opened and a carer cheerfully popped her head around the corner. 'Morning!' Taken aback, she stopped. 'Oh sorry, I thought you were Luke. Is there any tea in that pot? Always makes a good cuppa does Luke.'

'Hi, I'm Dante. I'm just staying here for the weekend,' he explained, 'and yes, there is tea in the pot. Luke has taken his mum's breakfast up.'

Pouring her tea, she took the mug and walked out of the kitchen. 'It's okay, I know the way,' she shouted back to him.

As he started to tuck into his own plate of food, Luke walked into the kitchen. 'She's a nosey old cow! Considering she's always telling me that she's on a time limit, she always has time to gossip! Mum enjoys it though.' He laughed.

'Does she come every morning, Luke?' Dante enquired between mouthfuls.

'Yeah, don't get me wrong, I love Mum. But I'm not

washing her lady bits!' They both grimaced and burst out laughing.

Once the carer left, Luke beckoned Dante. 'Come on, let's have a peep and I'll share my secret with you.'

As they both walked into the garage, Luke pushed past an old lawn mower. In the corner an old sheet covered something. Confused, Dante looked on in awe as Luke pulled off the sheet, like a magician. 'Ta-dah!'

Dante's jaw fell to his chin. 'A motorbike!' he half shouted. 'Oh my God Luke, you got a motorbike.' Luke stood there grinning from ear to ear and folded his arms. 'Well, are you going to sit on it? It's yours!'

Taking in the black motorbike, Dante looked lovingly at it, then jumped on the leather seat. 'It's fantastic! Absolutely brilliant Luke. I love it.'

'It's not a big engine, but it will do the trick.'

'It's fantastic,' Dante repeated, running his hand along the handlebars. 'I don't know what to say Luke, I really am lost for words.'

'Don't thank me, you paid for it. A copy of my licence is in the glove box at the back along with the helmet.' He grinned. 'Go on, take a look and try the helmet on!' Luke encouraged. His enthusiasm was infectious, and Dante couldn't help grinning and laughing as he tried on the black matching helmet. 'How do I look?' he mumbled as he lifted the visor.

'Like Darth Vader.' Luke laughed as he pulled it off Dante's head and tried it on himself. 'I've already booked in a refresher course, so this morning we take it out and get you familiar with it. You've got a week so come as often as you can after school or whatever and get some practice in. There's a bike track not far from here, we'll go there. I'll ride there and then you can take over. Have you got the balls?' Luke laughed.

'Do I have a choice?'

Luke laughed. 'The sooner we're done here, the sooner we can pop out and try that bike!'

Come the afternoon, all was finished and tidied away before Maggie and Deana turned up. Dante felt his payment for all of his hard work was the fantastic time he had spent riding the motorbike with Luke. He had soon got the hang of it after a few wobbles, and once he gained his confidence, he felt he'd mastered it. He had ridden them both home with Luke on the back, taking his life in their hands!

Luke's mum had thoroughly enjoyed the afternoon with the house full of people and chatter. The colour seemed to have come back into her cheeks as she laughed at some of Maggie's stories about pub life. It had felt like a proper family meal and once Maggie had cleared away and helped Luke settle his mum in her chair, it was time for them to leave. Dante felt a sadness leaving the house. Although it had been a busy weekend, he had thoroughly enjoyed himself.

* * *

'Goodness Deana!' Maggie squealed with delight as she looked at her grown-up daughter. 'Phyllis, Pauline!' she shouted downstairs. 'Come up here.'

Deana stood in the kitchen and did a twirl. 'Well, what do you think?' Deana had curled her long blonde hair, and the waves hung down her back. She had highlighted her face with just a touch of blusher and mascara. Her A-line corn-flower blue dress with a sweetheart neck and matching shoes accentuated her colouring. Pauline and Phyllis stood there wide eyed, with Phyllis the first to speak. 'My God, talk about a silk purse out of a sow's ear. No jeans, no leggings or tracksuit bottoms. I wasn't even sure you had legs, Deana.' She grinned. 'You look beautiful, love.' Leaning forward, she gave Deana a kiss on the cheek. 'Your father would be so proud!'

'Ooh talking of Alex, he's arranged a visit for Tuesday because it's your eighteenth. A big landmark and we're due for a visit anyway. We were supposed to go next Saturday Phyllis, but Alex put in a special request, and they granted it. That is an excellent birthday present – don't you think Deana?' Maggie hugged her daughter.

'Oh, for God's sake, Mum, don't hug her, you will crease something.' Dante laughed. 'You've got more make-up on than Grandma, Deana.'

For a moment, Deana faltered and turned to look in the mirror. A worried look crossed her face. 'Is it too much?'

Maggie gave Dante a playful clip on the back of the head. 'Not at all. He's just being cheeky.'

'Well,' laughed Dante. 'I bet that's how she started out until she had to start filling in the wrinkles. You look okay, Deana.' Dante winked. 'Is it for anyone special?'

'Yes! My friends at my birthday bash, who else?' she snapped.

Maggie, Phyllis and Pauline cast furtive glances at each other and smiled. 'Best form of defence is attack, I say,' muttered Phyllis as she started back down the staircase.

Feeling slightly guilty, Deana hugged Maggie. 'You can come if you want to Mum. Even you Dante.'

'Oh God, no!' Dante spat out in disgust. 'Your mates are horrible. And that one with the glasses and braces on her teeth keeps grinning at me. Nope. What about you Mum?

Are you going to spend the night with a load of eighteen-year-old girls screaming, or should I say, singing?'

'It's a nice thought love, but no. Tonight is your grown-up party with your friends. Have a great time, Deana. Give me a call when you're ready to be picked up. No matter what time – okay?'

Frowning, Deana flashed a look at Dante, and panic rose inside her. She hadn't thought that far ahead. She didn't want Maggie bumping into Kev at her party considering she was supposed to hardly know him. 'Oh, the girls have booked one of those minibuses Mum so that we can all get dropped off together. They've all chipped in because it's cheaper than paying for a taxi each.'

'What a good idea. I never thought of that. Good thinking.' Giving her the thumbs up. 'Well, I'll give you a lift there then.' Seeing Deana's face drop a little, Maggie smiled. 'Don't worry love, I was eighteen once and didn't want people to see my mum with me. I'll park up the road and you can walk down, eh?'

'Actually Mum, I'm getting a taxi there too, so no need to give me a lift, but thank you.' Seeing the beaming smile on her daughter's face, Maggie put down her car keys and smiled to herself. Generations might change, but no teenager on a night out wanted to be seen with their mother waving at them in front of their friends!

As an afterthought, a frown crossed Maggie's brow. 'Did you have enough money to pay for everything Deana? You didn't ask me for any more. I only gave you five hundred pounds. Does that cover food, the venue, those clothes and your ride home?'

Slightly embarrassed, Deana blushed. She hadn't wanted to take any money off Maggie, but had realised she had to to avoid questions. Yet it was an expensive venue and having a private room cost nearly double. Deana tried hard for a credible lie.

Raising his eyes in astonishment, Dante butted in, 'Five hundred pounds? Does that include those free vouchers you were given for the food and the discount because of the party numbers? I thought you said everyone got one of those alcohol-free cocktails with lots of umbrellas and stuff on entry for free,' Dante stressed, helping Deana out in her lie.

'Oh yes,' Deana stammered. Her eyes thanked Dante for his quick thinking. He always seemed to save her and say the right thing.

'Free cocktails, eh, young lady.' Maggie nodded. 'Well, remember you're not eighteen until Tuesday so keep them alcohol free. And it sounds like you've got a real bargain. Good for you, love. But if you need spends...' Maggie picked up her handbag to take out her purse.

'No Mum, I've got enough money and everyone is putting twenty pounds into a kitty.'

Maggie counted out fifty pounds and handed it over. 'Here, take this. Twenty pounds a round doesn't sound much to me. What are you going to get? One bottle of cola and twenty straws?' Maggie laughed. 'Take it love. My mum always gave me "just in case" money.' Hearing a car horn, Maggie went towards the window and looked out. Seeing a taxi, she grinned. 'I presume that's for you, young lady.'

'Do I get fifty quid, "just in case" money Mum?' asked Dante as they both watched Deana through the window get into her cab. Maggie couldn't believe how grown up she looked. Suddenly, over the last year, her little girl had turned into a woman. Turning towards Dante and his request, she grinned. 'Absolutely, when it's your eighteenth.' She laughed and put her arms around his shoulders as they walked downstairs towards the bar. 'Are you helping out tonight, Dante? Or do you have other plans for a Saturday night?'

'I can help out clearing tables and stuff for an hour or so, then I thought I'd either pop and see George or play some games in my room without Deana's interruptions.'

'Well, it just so happens I know the management here and they pay pretty good wages, usually around fifty quid for young, handsome men to clear their tables on a Saturday night.' Maggie winked. Musing to herself, she felt it was only fair. Deana was having two parties and Dante hadn't complained once. She was glad of the close family bond they had. And fifty quid was a small price to pay.

14

THE VOX

As Deana's taxi approached the end of the road, it stopped. The taxi driver gave Deana a strange look as Kev and Luke got into the back seat.

'My mum doesn't approve of my boyfriend,' Deana lied, seeing his confused look.

Kev and Luke looked at each other strangely, both mouthing the word 'boyfriend' to each other and wondering what Deana was playing at.

Deana bubbled over with excitement as she got out of the taxi. Some of her friends were already stood in the foyer waiting for her while they got their wrist bands from the bouncers proving they could come and go during the evening and had paid their fee.

Showing off, Deana linked her arm through Kev's and walked towards the waiting crowd. Her heart was pounding in her chest. She could see all the doubting Thomases, especially Amy, staring at Kev and looking him up and down. In typical Kev fashion, he wore his T-shirt, jeans and trainers, and his mirrored sunglasses, but he had made the effort under Luke's guidance and swapped his combat jacket for a grey leather coat and he cut quite the figure with his fair hair, which looked like it had been washed. All of the girls nudged each other and whispered at this older man with Deana, making her the most popular girl in the room. She relished the attention; for once it was all about her.

The venue was amazing; coloured flashing lights filled their own private club room. One wall was a full screen which showed the karaoke words to the songs and played the music. There were seats, and another wall with a full buffet laid out, including burgers and hot dogs. Deana felt like a princess. Her face flushed with excitement and her head was spinning. Background music started and there were huge catalogues in leather bindings with countless list of songs for them all to choose from.

Their own waiter for the evening arrived with trays full of cocktails, which had been paid for in advance by Deana. This whole evening had cost her a fortune, but at this moment in time and the way she felt, she would have paid double. Everyone surrounded her and chatted with her.

Kev ordered a couple of vodkas for himself, and quickly gulped them back. Being surrounded by a group of college girls wasn't his idea of a good night and he was out of his comfort zone. Luke looked around the amazingly decked-out club room that was full of balloons and banners with Deana's name and age on. Luke watched Deana's friends, and wondered just how many of them would have been at her party if it had been held at the pub rather than here. As they handed Deana cards and presents, he doubted there was a decent friend among them. But it was Deana's money and something she obviously needed to do in order to get some kind of closure on the past, to show she wasn't to be pitied as the mafia man's daughter. She had come out of hiding and was now shining, able to afford the swankiest place in town for her birthday.

Walking into the middle of the room, Luke held up his hands and clapped. 'Okay everyone. Choose your songs and help yourself to food!' He had felt someone should start the proceedings considering the club room was only booked for a few hours and they hadn't started singing yet. It was also aimed at freeing up Kev – Deana's grip on his arm seemed to get tighter and tighter as she beamed at her friends. Luke could see Kev wanted the floor to swallow him up.

Once given the go-ahead, everyone began choosing their songs, ordering more drinks, dancing and laughing. Selfies were taken along with other party photos and some of Deana's friends were already posting on social media about the great time they were having. Luke and Kev steered clear of the photos as much as possible and Kev did his best to hide away in a dark corner until Deana caught up with him again. Luke wanted to laugh; the way Deana and her friends circled him reminded him of a wildlife programme where the lions stalked their prey. Kev was more than happy to grab a microphone and sing the first song that caught his eye, anything to get away from the crowd. There were microphones scattered around the room and Deana picked one up and joined in with Kev. Luke couldn't help but laugh as he realised what Kev was singing. It was an old Frank and Nancy Sinatra song, 'Somethin' Stupid'. Everyone was dancing and cheering at the perfect couple singing to each other. As funny as it was seeing Kev cringing and finishing the song, Luke felt a disappointment inside. Deana looked beautiful, he had always thought so, but her eyes were clearly only for Kev.

Seeing Deana pick up a cocktail and drink it back, Luke walked over to her. 'I hope that was a mocktail, Deana? You're not eighteen yet.'

'Oh, for God's sake Luke, don't be such a party pooper! I'm allowed one drink, aren't I? Christ, you're not my dad,' she snapped.

'No, but this is your first night out as a grown-up. You fuck this up and go home legless and your mum won't let you out again.' Lowering his voice, he pulled her aside. 'And let's face it Deana, if you're to carry on with your business interests, you need to be trusted and able to get out with your mum's blessing.'

Deana felt her face flush. Luke had burst her bubble, but she knew he was right. Nodding her head, she put the cocktail down and headed for the many bottles of lemonade and cola available on the buffet table.

A weak smile crept back on her face. 'Thanks Luke.' Changing the subject, she pointed at the many catalogues. 'So, what are you going to sing?'

'I'm still looking.' He winked. 'I'll leave it to the experts.' Deana followed Luke's eyeline to a couple of girls singing together. Even she had to admit, they sounded awful.

'Now Luke,' she said, 'you realise why I needed alcohol. It softened the blow to my ears.' She laughed.

'This place was your choice, Deana. I'm popping outside for a smoke, won't be long.'

Seeing Luke heading towards the exit, Kev quickly ran behind him. 'Wait for me mate.' Once outside, Kev filled his lungs with air. 'I need some good old-fashioned nicotine. Christ, Luke, how long do we have to put up with this? Those bloody girls are getting on my nerves. They ask more questions than a judge. It's like the Spanish inquisition.'

'Not long. A few hours. You were eighteen once Kev, it wasn't that long ago.'

'Yeah, well, I didn't go around boasting about my older boyfriend, who has his own business. What the fuck has she been saying about me? I've walked straight into this trap, haven't I?'

'You're just a good friend; it's that lot that have made their own assumptions. Just cos she's walked in with two guys that don't go to her college, they've made the rest up,' Luke lied to save Deana's embarrassment. 'Crikey, they probably think we're having a threesome.' He laughed. Seeing the grin appear on Kev's face, he knew he had said the right thing.

Lighting a cigarette, Kev nodded. 'Yeah, no wonder she's popular. They probably think we're all swingers or something. Christ, I hope they don't start throwing their keys into a fishbowl!' Taking out a little plastic packet, Kev turned his back, out of sight and took a sniff of cocaine he had brought with him. Wiping the white powder off his nose, he saw Luke's disapproval.

'For God's sake Kev, you could have done that before we left. What if those bouncers had frisked you or something? You would have really ended the party then!' Luke shouted, louder than he intended to. 'No more, Kev. And don't offer anyone that stuff. Tonight, we're upright citizens playing bodyguard to a young girl who thinks that two-faced lot are her friends. They are fucking spongers, and I doubt she will see any of them after tonight.'

Wide eyed, Kev held up his hands in submission, shocked by Luke's angry outburst. 'Okay, okay. Sorry mate, I didn't mean any harm you know. It's just, this isn't my thing, you know that. I like Deana and Dante but as colleagues and mates.' Kev looked at Luke suspiciously and a wry grin crossed his face. 'Unlike you, who feels he has to be Deana's knight in shining armour. You like her, don't you?' Kev smiled, feeling on safer ground.

'Maybe, but it's pointless and her dad would have me wearing my balls as earrings!' Luke smiled back. 'Plus I don't wear mirrored sunglasses.'

'Oh Christ, Luke, you don't mean she fancies me, do you? Oh my God that is the last thing I need: a lovesick bunny boiler working with us. Sort it out Luke. You know how to say the right things. What if she grasses us up if I refuse to let her have her wicked way with me?'

Luke couldn't help laughing at Kev's panicky state. 'She won't say anything. She won't be happy but she'll get over it. It's a young girl's fancy and it will blow over. Anyway, I've come out to call Dante. I want to see how he's getting on.'

Frowning, Kev nodded. 'Sure, it's his first night on the bike, isn't it? Well, let's hope he's still alive, eh?'

Letting out a huge sigh, Luke couldn't help smiling. 'Christ Kev, when it comes to tact and diplomacy you really are at the back of the queue, aren't you?' Picking up his mobile, Luke called Dante's number.

'If he's driving Luke, he won't answer,' Kev butted in.

'He will; he has an ear pod in. I told him to keep it in in case I needed him, or he needed me. It's easier for him to make the call through his earpiece. Dante mate, is that you? Are you okay?' Luke put his mobile on loud speaker for Kev to listen.

'Yes. All's good here. Nearly finished. This bike is ace, it whips in and out of the traffic. I've got two more to do and we're done. No hassles. How's the party going?'

'Steady on, Dante. No whipping in and out of traffic, eh? I want you back in one piece.'

'Yeah, and I want my money,' Kev said.

'Not taking any chances, Luke. Gotta go, just dropping off. Speak later.' As the call ended, Kev and Luke looked at each other. 'Well, he seems okay, but I don't want him taking silly chances on that bike Kev. He's still getting used to it.'

'He's okay, although I will say he's done that delivery in record time. He's an hour ahead of himself. And with Deana driving and speedway Dante we could double our deliveries.'

'Let's see how it goes first.' Luke flicked his cigarette butt onto the pavement. 'Anyway, let's get back inside shall we and see what's going on.'

The club room was in full flow when they entered. It was obvious some of them had already drunk more than was good for them. Luke surveyed the room and seeing Deana, he walked towards her. 'How's it going Cinders?' He grinned.

'I'm not sure, Luke. It's better than expected, but not as good as I thought it would be. I'm fed up with their karaoke songs. I know this is the hottest new venue in town, but it's starting to get on my nerves. And I'm sick of seeing those guys eat two burgers at a time. It's like feeding time at the zoo. I'm sure I saw them stuffing burgers in their pockets.' Deana smiled. 'Maybe it's because I'm sober under your watchful eye.' She winked. 'And they are all tipsy. You see things differently.'

'Don't worry about it, Deana. It's free food and people always make pigs of themselves for freebies. And drink has a way of bringing out the silliness in us all.' Luke laughed. 'Dante's okay, by the way. I've just spoken to him.'

'Oh, thanks Luke, I should have checked myself. I've been so wrapped up in myself tonight. I hope he misses me and doesn't get too big for his boots! Where's Kev? I get the feeling he's not enjoying himself.'

'Kev's over there with that little group holding court by the looks of things. They're hanging on to every one of his escapades...' Luke laughed. Deana watched Kev comfortably sit down, cross legged with a drink in his hand spinning lie after lie about his escapades around the world, even though, as far as she was aware he hadn't been further than Blackpool. And while everyone seemed to be hanging on his every word, for some reason, Deana didn't feel jealous as her friends smiled at Kev adoringly. If anything, she thought they were pathetic!

Dante was enjoying himself thoroughly, whizzing through the back streets on his motorbike. He felt in control and relished this new taste of freedom. The feeling of power it gave him was incredible, he mused to himself as he sped along. His deliveries had been regular clients that he had been to many times, although him turning up on a motorbike alone seemed to confuse them. 'Where's the two foreigners? Are they not working tonight?' one man had asked as he handed over his money. Dante had kept on his helmet, not even opening the visor, while leaving his engine running and just handed over the small sandwich bag containing whatever drugs had been ordered.

Casting a glance at his watch as he headed for home, he noticed it was just before midnight. Putting the helmet and gloves in the box at the back of the bike, Dante took the keys, knowing that Luke had a spare set. It was easier that way. Once Luke, Kev and Deana were making their way home, Luke would pick up the bike and Kev would carry on home in the taxi.

Opening the back door, Dante popped his head around the corner towards the bar. The last few customers were leaving. Percy walked around filling the bar with empty glasses he'd collected while Maggie, Phyllis and Pauline filled the glass washers. 'Any chance of a free Coke, Mum?' Dante grinned. Maggie smiled. Taking a glass, she filled it full of cola and ice. 'There you go young man. Have you come to help us clean up?'

'Yeah, sure. I'll give Percy a hand and wipe down the tables if you like.'

Pauline picked up a cloth and threw it at him. 'Never say no to a spare pair of hands.'

Fitting in well after his absence, Dante helped put the chairs on top of the tables, so it was ready for the cleaner to hoover. Once Pauline and Phyllis's taxi arrived to take them home, Maggie sighed and sat down. Putting her own cloth on the bar, she brushed her hair back. 'Crikey Dante, I'm shattered. It's been one of those nights, busy, busy, busy. I wonder how Deana's night's going?' Maggie looked at her watch; it was nearly 1 a.m. 'I presume she'll be a while yet, especially if they are dropping off the others on the way.' Suddenly, they heard a shout, and both of them got up from their seats and looked down the hallway to the back door. 'Deana!' Maggie shouted, almost running towards her, hugging her. 'You're earlier than I expected.'

'Mine was the third drop off,' Deana lied. 'Look, I've got lots of presents. The bar staff let me have this bin liner to put them in. I never thought about taking a bag or getting presents off them all. But it's a nice thought, isn't it?'

Opening the bin liner, Maggie looked inside. 'Wow! Who's a popular young woman? So, tell us about your night. Did you enjoy yourself?'

'Oh yes, it was good fun, and everyone enjoyed themselves. Although, to be fair, the venue isn't as great as it's said to be. After the tenth karaoke song it became a bit boring. I enjoyed it, but I wouldn't go again. Everyone had a great time though, thanks Mum. But I'm bushed and I need my bed.'

Inwardly, Deana felt the night had been disappointing. She'd paid a lot of money, and she knew she had just been showing off to these so-called friends. She had wanted to be the centre of attention, but it hadn't felt like she'd expected it to. It had served her right when, during the course of the evening, they all seemed to end up in their own little cliques and she'd felt like the outsider again. She'd been glad that Luke had been there, and he seemed to be the only person she really talked to. She was glad she would be leaving college soon and going to university. She wanted that fresh start now. New beginnings. A future. Wearily, she stood up. 'Well, my presents can wait, I need to sleep. All this excitement isn't good for me.' She laughed.

Maggie yawned and put her arms around Dante and Deana's shoulders. Dante reached up and, switching off the bar lights, they all went wearily upstairs.

15

HAPPY BIRTHDAY DEANA

'Dad!' Deana squealed and waved as they walked into the prison visiting room.

Alex stood up but couldn't hug his wife or children, which broke his heart. They were in reaching distance, but he couldn't hold his wife's hand or touch the softness of her fair skin. It was agonising. He'd looked forward to this visit, but also dreaded it.

'Happy birthday Deana. You're a woman now.' He smiled and blew a kiss across the table. 'Where has my little girl gone, eh?'

'I'm here, Dad. Always your little girl.' Tears welled up in her eyes and she looked down at the table.

'Yeah, well, I personally think she looks more like Grandma now with that lipstick on. How many layers is that lip gloss, Deana? If anyone tried kissing you, they would slide off,' Dante butted in as Alex laughed. Maggie glanced at Dante and smiled. He had done the right thing. This was to be a happy visit, one to keep Alex going until the next one.

There could be no sadness, even though she knew his heart ached as much as her own.

'Christ, don't turn into Babs. That's everyone's worst nightmare!' Alex grinned.

Maggie smiled. 'We're having a small party at the pub for Deana tonight. Some kind of... get together dinner.' She'd been about to say 'a family dinner' but had stopped herself in time.

'It's okay, Maggie. I know you're having a family dinner and I can only imagine it. When I get out, we'll have our own family dinner. Don't walk on eggshells around me, Maggie.'

'Well, it doesn't sound right, does it? How can we have a family dinner without you, love? But we're having a little bash to celebrate Deana's eighteenth.' For a moment they held each other's gazes. They both knew how they felt about each other.

'So, tell me, Deana. How did your fancy party with your friends go? Karaoke and cocktails, eh?'

'It was good Dad, although the place is hyped up a bit. It's not as good as it sounds, but I've been there, done that and got the T-shirt!' She laughed, and went on to tell him funny stories of the evening, all the while omitting to tell him about Kev.

'Hey, don't I get a drink and some chocolate?' Alex grinned. 'You two go and get them. I want a quick word with Dante here.'

Alex leaned over the table a little and lowered his voice as he saw Maggie and Deana walk towards a vending machine. Clearing his throat, Alex looked at Dante. He seemed to have grown in the short time he'd been away from him. 'I hear you've been spending a lot of time with a new friend. Luke, is it?'

Blushing slightly, Dante looked down at the table. 'Yes Dad. And I'm not going to lie to you. It's the same Luke you know.'

'I know that by the description your mother gave me. Are you working for him? Please tell me you're not going down his pitiful road.'

'No Dad. I've been selling cheap cigarettes to the kids at school – that's all,' Dante lied. 'Luke gets cheap cigarettes, and the kids at school smoke at break times. It's just a money-making scheme. Apart from that, Luke is a good friend. I'm surrounded by women and women's gossip. With Luke, I get man's talk. It makes a change – that's all.'

For a moment, Alex listened to his son and realised how lonely he must be. All the women, including Phyllis and Pauline, had each other to talk to, but a young teenage boy wasn't going to pour his heart out to two old women. 'What about Mark and George? You have them, don't you?'

'I do, but to be honest, George and me don't have a lot in common. It's just convenient for us to hang around with each other when there's nothing else. Mark, well, what can I say? He's just Mark, but I'm not going to hang around with him, am I? Luke listens and his house is quiet, unlike the pub,' Dante explained.

'Sorry Dante. I really am. I've left you to be the man of the house and yet, you have no one to confide in, man to man, I mean.' Alex had an idea. 'Do you remember John, a family friend from the old country?'

Dante rolled his eyes to the ceiling. 'Yes, of course, Dad. I remember him. He came to the pub, didn't he?'

'Yes, he did. If you ever need anything while I'm in here and feel there is no one to turn to, you can speak to him. You know where my private mobile phone is or was? Well, his number is in there. If it ever gets too much for you, John will listen and help. As for Luke, just don't disappoint me Dante and get swallowed up in his other life, eh?' Alex gave him a knowing look. He wanted to believe his son, but his gut instinct told him otherwise. But there was nothing he could do stuck in here. 'Just be careful son. You don't want to end up in here like me.' Seeing his son blush to the roots, Alex decided to dismiss it and go no further. He felt he had said enough. It was supposed to be a happy visit – not a lecture, although he hoped Dante had got the message.

Embarrassed and humbled, Dante averted his eyes and welcomed the return of his Mum and Deana carrying cans of Coke, crisps and chocolate. Flashing a glance at Deana, he smiled, although part of him resented Deana. He was taking all of the blame for befriending Luke and Alex hadn't even asked about Deana's part in it. She'd been the instigator in their business dealings, but in their dad's eyes she was innocent of course. Daddy's little girl! Wasn't that what his father had said?

'So, tell me about your job, Deana. Are you enjoying it?' Alex kept the conversation light.

'It's good Dad and paying a lot towards my driving lessons. My instructor feels I'm ready for my test, so I've put in for a cancellation. The sooner the better, eh?' She smiled. She hated lying to her dad, but she had to carry it through.

He laughed. 'Well, that's good. It's all part of responsibility and being a grown-up.'

'It will come in handy for when I go to university, and I can also help Mum by popping to the wholesalers when she's busy and stuff.'

'Of course, university. Have you chosen any? You have to get in quick, places are snapped up and you have to have the grades they want. What about you Dante and your exams? My little boy is soon to be sixteen.'

'Oh, he's a swot!' Deana laughed. 'He's never got his nose out of books. He will get straight As for everything. It's me who will have to work at it.'

'Then don't let this job of yours distract you from your learning, Deana. See the bigger picture. If university is what you want, take the time out to get the grades you need.'

Dante gave a little cough, and looked at Deana. 'I believe Dad asked about me, Deana. Any chance I can get a word in? There are three of us here,' he snapped.

Taking her reprimand on the chin and realising she had taken over the visit, she apologised and picked up her can of Coke.

'I'm doing well, Dad. My mock exams were good and so I'm pretty confident. If not, I know how to wipe tables and serve carvery meals.' Dante grinned.

As Alex bit into his chocolate bar and savoured the taste of something so simple and so taken for granted on the outside, he watched his children. They were not children any more, he could see that. Maggie chattered on about life at the pub and looking at the huge clock on the wall, Alex realised it was nearly time for the visit to end. 'Hey, you two, would you give me and your mum a few moments together? It's been great seeing you and I will see you soon, but...'

Standing up, Deana and Dante grinned and patted Maggie on the shoulders. 'We understand, Dad. Speak soon.' Deana blew him a kiss and walked out with Dante. 'We'll see you at the car, Mum,' she shouted after her.

Alex's tone softened. 'You look tired darling. Are you okay and not working too hard?'

A weak smile crossed Maggie's face. 'I'm fine Alex. I may

be on the outside of this place, but I am living every day in here with you. I'm not going to lie to you, you can always see right through me. It's hard being without you and the nights are the worst. The emptiness of the bed and the time when it was our time alone to discuss our day in private. I miss the intimacy, but I'm sure you do too. At least I'm not having to share a room with a stranger.'

'My cell mate is okay, although he's up to his neck in debt to someone else. He has depression and needs things that can lift his spirits,' he whispered.

Maggie knew exactly what he meant – drugs. 'Don't get involved, Alex. It's not your business,' she warned. 'Grown men can look after themselves.'

When Alex didn't say anything, she added, 'Do you hear me, Alex? Don't be a hero. We need you. Your family needs you. You're not in the protection business any more.'

Holding his hands up in submission, Alex grinned. 'Okay woman, I hear you.' He laughed. Hearing the warder shout, 'Time,' Alex looked at Maggie. 'I wish I could kiss you, but it's not allowed. Instead, I will imagine kissing those rosy lips of yours and blow you one instead. Forever thine, forever mine, forever ours.'

Maggie, half closed her eyes, hearing his words of love, and breathed in the scent of her husband she loved so much. 'Thank you, Alex, you have given me strength already. I love you,' she mouthed as they both stood up to go their separate ways. 'Alex!' she called after him, craning her neck for one last glimpse, not wanting to let him out of her sight. 'Call me when you can.' Seeing Alex nod as he was lined up to leave, she smiled. As much as she liked seeing Alex, she knew seeing the family was hard for him. Leaving the prison walls behind her and walking to the car, a cold chill ran through her and Maggie couldn't stop the tears from falling.

Dante saw her first and slowly walked up to her and put his arms around her. 'I know Mum. It's hard for all of us keeping up that happy, smiling pretence that everything is okay, when it definitely isn't. Come on, let's organise Deana's party. Grandma should be here by now, so that's something to look forward to.' Wiping her eyes, Maggie looked at Dante and burst out laughing. 'Your sarcasm does you credit, Dante. Yeah, come on, let's see what the birthday girl has in store for the rest of the day.'

* * *

Fiddler shut the cell door behind them as Alex sat on his bunk. 'Your visit looked good, Alex. All the family laughing and talking. I hear your daughter's got a job at a supermarket?'

'You don't miss much, do you?' Fiddler had just confirmed Alex's suspicions that there were eyes and ears everywhere.

'Your son is the spitting image of you. Mini me,' laughed Fiddler. 'And that daughter of yours is pretty. How come she's so blonde? Is that how your wife paid the milk man?' Fiddler laughed again, jokingly. 'At least my wife is going to put more money on my phone card.'

Confused and frowning, Alex looked up. 'I didn't know you made any calls. I've never seen you in the queue for the phone.'

'I don't, well, not often. But I hand my phone card over to Jonesy in return for… well you know what. Don't judge me mate, I don't need a lecture.'

Shaking his head, Alex ran his hands through his dark wavy hair, which seemed to be growing and have a life of its own. 'Christ, Fiddler, how much do you owe him?'

'About a hundred, but I'm working it off so don't worry about that. Let's have a cup of tea, eh?'

'That's a lot of money Fiddler, but, as you say, it's not my business.' Remembering Maggie's warning, Alex ended the line of conversation. 'I've always got room for tea, Fiddler, if you're offering.' Alex grinned.

Handing Alex a plastic mug of tea, Fiddler said, 'I'm not the only one in here that takes Jonesy's help Alex, or the only one who owes him. And at least I'm only giving him my phone card as payment and not sex like some of the others.'

Alex's eyes widened with horror. 'You're telling me he takes sexual favours?' Alex knew that kind of thing went on, he wasn't stupid, but it surprised him that Jonesy did it. Or was it more a power thing to humble his victims? Either way, Alex found it sickening. Seeing Fiddler's face redden as he cast his eyes down to the floor, Alex bit his tongue. 'Well, I can see why he would want your phone card instead, you ugly bugger.' Giving a false laugh, Alex looked at his cell mate and his gut instinct told him that Fiddler was doing the same. He obviously didn't like it, which was why he was doing his best to pay him off in other ways, but he was hooked and was clearly in a desperate situation. Again, he remembered Maggie's words: 'It's none of your business, Alex,' but still it angered him to think that Jonesy was preying on the weak. Bullies like him were cowards.

'Let's just leave it and drink our tea. Maybe, just maybe you will actually get a word right on that crossword in the newspaper. Your spelling's awful. Go on, read out the clues and we'll find the answers together.'

* * *

'Grandma! What have you done? People will think I'm five years old. And what is it with the baby photo of me stuck in the front window of the pub?' Deana was horrified as she looked around the pub, decorated with balloons and banners with 'Birthday Girl' written across them.

'I think it looks lovely dear. Mark helped me hang the banners and I thought the baby photo would be a nice touch – don't you think?'

'No, I don't. You can take the bloody lot down, especially that photo.'

Dante couldn't contain his laughter as he watched Deana strut around examining all of their grandmother's hard work.

As though on cue, Mark came walking in with his step ladders. 'I've put some banners outside in the beer garden. It gives the place a real sense of occasion. What do you think, Deana?' He beamed.

'How old do you think I am, Mark? I have periods, I have breasts. I am not five years old. Christ, you will be putting out party hats soon!' Immediately, Babs and Mark looked at each other guiltily. 'You have, haven't you? I bet there are party bags with sweets in, too.'

'It's your eighteenth, Deana! We have to make an occasion of it. You've already had your grown-up party, now it's our turn. This is just family.' Babs flashed a glance at Mark and changed her statement. 'This is your family and friends,' she corrected herself. 'We want to make a fuss of you. We'll take down the baby photo, but this is your last birthday of being our little girl and I've missed so many birthdays.' Tears brimmed on Babs' eyelashes, and she sniffed hard to keep them at bay.

Maggie felt it was about time to step in and stop this argument before it got out of hand. Babs was right, she had missed the last couple of birthdays and now wanted to go over the top to make up for it. Giving Deana a harsh look, Maggie looked around. 'Well, I think you two have been working really hard.' Seeing Pauline and Phyllis standing behind the bar looking sheepish, Maggie realised that they had also helped decorate the pub. 'Thank you, all of you!' Maggie looked at them and smiled. 'Don't be so ungrateful, Deana. If your father was here, he would be having everyone wearing T-shirts with that baby photo on, so you've had a lucky escape. You're eighteen today so act like a grown-up then and thank everyone for their hard work and not like some spoilt brat having a tantrum,' Maggie snapped. She could see everyone had gone to a lot of trouble to make the occasion special. Maybe they had gone a little over the top, but they were only trying to make up for Alex's absence.

Blushing to her roots, Deana felt her face almost burning. 'Sorry everyone, sorry Grandma. I didn't mean to sound ungrateful. You've all worked hard.' As she walked up to the long set of tables pushed together, she thought about the genuine friendship behind this display. They hadn't done it on the promise of a good venue and cocktails like her college mates. They had done it out of love and stupidly, she had overlooked that. Yet again, her mouth had run away with her. 'Thanks everyone. Really, I'm sorry. It's been an emotional day seeing Dad. Thank you for making it special.' Walking up to her grandmother, she put her arms around her. 'Thanks Grandma.' Then, she cast a glance at Mark. 'I'm not hugging you with that beard. It's like a scouring pad when it hits me in the face.'

'Had no complaints from the wife Deana. In fact...' Mark

grabbed hold of Deana and lifted her off her feet while rubbing his long bushy beard in her face and landing a smacker of a kiss on her lips. 'Your dad asked me to give you this.' He laughed as Deana struggled and did her best to push him off.

'That's disgusting. Get off me you oaf!' Deana dramatically rubbed at her lips. 'I doubt my father said you could molest his young daughter!'

'You're a woman now with periods and I can confirm, you definitely have breasts,' he bellowed with laughter, which was infectious and made everyone else in the room laugh as well. 'Here, talking of presents, ladies, Olivia took a parcel in for you while you were out. Olivia also took a parcel in yesterday for that Steph next door. She didn't realise it was for her at first and opened it by accident. Inside was a luminous pink vibrator! Olivia texted me and wanted to know why I'd bought it. After a bit of argy bargy, she looked at the box properly and realised it was for her next door. Shoving it back in the box, she knocked on Steph's door. Weird woman, never talks to anyone, thinks she's better than everyone. Anyways,' Mark bellowed. 'Once Olivia had apologised for opening the box and not letting on that she'd looked inside, that Steph said, "Oh, it must be my new whisk, I've been waiting for it."' Mark burst out laughing. For a moment he couldn't speak and was almost red in the face. 'That is what I call multi-tasking. A vibrator that whisks your scrambled eggs at the same time! There you are, Deana. Maybe your mates have bought you a whisk!' Mark was beside himself with laughter, almost choking in the process.

'Why luminous pink?' Phyllis asked without thinking.

Puzzled, Mark looked at Phyllis curiously. 'How the hell should I know? Maybe it's so she can find it in the dark!'

* * *

Dante was staying well out of the day's preparations. Their mum and grandmother wanted this and everyone was doing their best to make it a good day for Deana, considering she had just left the prison. Making a mental note to himself, Dante decided not to go and see his father on his birthday. It didn't set you up for the rest of the day, leaving your dad in prison while you were organising a party. Out of curiosity, Dante looked for his dad's mobile. Once he'd switched it on and waited for it to kick into life, he scrolled down the names and found John's number. Taking out his own mobile, he copied and saved it. Friends with influence like John were few and far between. This was a number he would keep to himself for now.

'Dante, Dante, where are you?' Deana knocked on Dante's bedroom door. 'Are you in there?'

'Yes, I am. Where's the fire?' Opening the door slightly, he waited.

'Let me in for God's sake! Anyone would think you had a woman stashed away in here.' Pushing her way in, she sat on the edge of Dante's bed. 'You did the deliveries Saturday night, so today is pay day. Plus, don't you want to know about all that cooking you did at Luke's? Come on Dante screw your head on the right way,' Deana snapped.

'Dad knows,' interrupted Dante. 'Well, he knows something's going on. He's not stupid.'

'He knows nothing. It's just your guilty conscience, Dante. Stop overthinking things. Come on, we should get going.'

Stunned, Dante cast her a glance. 'You want to go now?

On your birthday? For God's sake Deana, where are you supposedly going to? Your party starts soon.'

'We're just popping out, that's all. Give them all a chance to do some more embarrassing balloons.'

'Are you that desperate for the money? Did your college friends wipe you out with their sponging? Strange you haven't heard anything from any of them since Saturday. I can't wait to see those presents. I bet it's all a load of rubbish. Admit it, Deana. You spent a lot of money on your vanity and you didn't even get a quick snog off Kev in the back of the taxi, did you?' Dante expected Deana's quick temper to fly off into a rage, but, instead, she just sat calmly on the edge of the bed.

'No Dante. I haven't heard anything from anyone. You're right, as always. Nobody gives a fuck about me apart from you and Mum, plus Dad of course, but at the moment he doesn't count.'

Realising he had touched a nerve, Dante linked his arm through hers. 'All those people and their stupid balloons, as you put it, care about you, Deana. Grandma, Phyllis, Pauline and Mark have worked hard to make this place look good for your party. And I've just found out, everyone has chipped in for your birthday present. Christ, it even surprised me. That's all I'm saying.'

Dante saw the excitement flash in Deana's eyes. 'They are your real friends, Deana. Those people downstairs love you in their own way when you're not being a bitch. We can pop to Luke's if you want, but we are telling Mum the truth. We're going to Luke's because he wants to give you your birthday present and doesn't want to leave his mum. So, come on, let's go, but we're not going to Kev's and we're not going to be late back – okay? In fact, Mum can drop us off and pick us up. That will give them time to finish off.'

'Yeah, come on, let's tell Mum and go see Luke so I can pick up my card. It's not often you get a day off in the week so we might as well make the most of it.'

Luke was pleased to see them when they turned up. Once inside, Deana beamed with delight. There was a tiny birthday cake with a candle in it, next to a gaily wrapped parcel and a card. 'Come on, Deana. Mum wants to wish you a happy birthday, too.' He took her through to the lounge and Luke's mum wished her a happy birthday while Luke made tea and brought in the cake with the candle lit. 'Come on, Deana. Blow out your candle.'

Excitedly, she clapped her hands and blew out the candle. 'Thank you. Really, I mean it. Thank you.'

'Go on then, open your present and cut the cake so Mum can have a slice. Jam sponge is her favourite.'

Doing as she was told, Deana ripped the paper off her present. Inside was a square box and she looked at Luke and then at Dante shyly. Opening the box, she saw a gold bracelet. Taking it out, she saw that it had three charms already on it. One was a key, another was the number eighteen in a circular-shaped mount and the last one was a house. Deana looked up at Luke inquisitively.

'There's your age. The key to the door now that you're eighteen, and your first proper home. Happy birthday, Deana.' Without thinking, Deana flung her arms around him and hugged him and then hugged his mum. 'Thank you. Thank you both of you,' she said. Although she knew it was all Luke's doing, she didn't want to leave his mum out.

Luke's mum beamed a smile. 'I may be blind Deana but I'm glad you like the present.' Immediately, Deana got Luke to put it on and held up her wrist to admire it. It was lovely. After their tea and cake, Luke proposed that they take the cups into the kitchen and wash up. This was to give them all a little privacy to talk.

'Luke, how did Dante's last batch get on? Have you heard anything yet?'

'Really? I thought you just wanted your money.' He laughed.

'No, that can wait. I also wondered if you're coming to the family dinner at the pub. You and your mum of course.'

Shocked, Luke hung his head. 'I didn't realise I was invited. Mum can't come and I think I should stay here too, but thanks for asking Deana. It means a lot – to both of us.' Seeing that Deana's invite was genuine touched Luke. He hadn't thought of himself as a family friend.

'As for Dante's amazing cooking, well, Kev wanted to hug and kiss you Dante and give you the good news. But, yeah, it's fantastic. That buyer he was talking about has bought the lot. Apart from the stuff we made for ourselves. He liked it, tested it and bought it. Kev has the money for that though. I've got the money from your Saturday night deliveries, Dante. How did you get on with the bike? Everything go okay?'

'Brilliant, Luke. I loved it. Thanks for getting it for me. So, we did it, bro. We cooked up a pot of gold, eh?' Dante reached out and hugged Luke, patting him on the back as they parted.

'Bro? What is this brotherly love?' Deana laughed.

'He's the closest thing I have to a brother, or ever will have, Deana. Who else watches our backs as closely as does?'

Nodding, Deana agreed with him. Luke was always there for support in one form or another, she had to agree with that. 'You're right Dante of course. And Luke, you're an honorary Silva now.' She laughed. 'Are you sure you can't come to the party later, Luke? You're welcome, you know that.'

'I know, Deana. But I don't want to openly bump into that Percy bloke from down your street. It was his house I was trapped in and the one your dad blew up. That's where you found me that night and I don't want him exposing me to his drug dealer mates that I'm still alive. They think I'm dead, Deana, and it's better that way, but thank you.' Impulsively, Luke leaned forward and kissed her on the cheek. For a moment, they both looked at each other, then the sound of a car horn beeped outside.

Blushing slightly, Deana smiled at Luke. 'I doubt he would even recognise you now, Luke. It's been a while.'

'Have a good time, Deana.' Luke grinned.

Deana was full of chatter during the drive home. She kept holding her wrist in the air and showing Maggie her bracelet. When Maggie pulled up outside the pub there was a red Citroen with a large bow on the roof, and a banner along the side saying 'Happy Birthday Deana'.

Gobsmacked, Deana leaned forward towards the windscreen and read the banner again. 'A car. You've bought me a car?'

'Everyone has chipped in for you, Deana. Mark found it going cheap. It's about ten years old, but he said it had to be an older one for the insurance. He's done some maintenance on it and everyone, including the bar and kitchen staff, have all put money in towards it for you. Even Percy opened his wallet and put twenty pounds in the kitty. It's taxed and insured and ready to go. So, fingers crossed you pass your test, eh, love? Me and your dad have paid the lion share and oh yes, Olivia bought the pink fluffy dice for the rear-view mirror, but that can't be helped.' Maggie laughed.

Dumbstruck, Deana got out of the car and walked around it. By now, Mark had shouted everyone out of the pub to stand on the pavement to sing 'Happy Birthday', while he videoed it for Alex. Instantly, Deana burst into tears. Mark threw her the keys. 'Well, sit inside it then, let's have a picture for your dad.' Mark came forward and showed her where the indicators were and how to switch the lights on.

'Let's hope it bloody works, Mum, if he's fixed it,' Dante muttered to Maggie under his breath.

'Fingers crossed, here goes. Start it up, Deana!' Maggie shouted. 'Get in with her Mark, let her take it up the street and back.' Doing as she was told, Deana got in. As it started, both Maggie and Dante breathed a sigh of relief. Driving up and down the street confidently, Deana even surprised Mark. 'You're really good, Deana. I didn't realise you could drive that well. She'll pass Maggie, deffo.'

Giving everyone the thumbs up, Mark got out of the car and headed towards the pub doors. 'Come on everyone, let the party begin! I'm buying Deana her first legal grown-up drink. What's it to be, Deana?' Shrugging, she didn't know what to say and looked at Maggie. She couldn't take her eyes off the car and for once she was lost for words.

'Why don't we have some wine with dinner?' Maggie interrupted. 'You order the white wine Mark, while she comes down to earth. It's a lot to take in getting a car on your birthday. I think I got a watch for my eighteenth, didn't I Mum?' Maggie turned to Babs inquisitively.

'An expensive watch, I might add,' Babs answered snottily.

'Well, I got my first blow job,' Mark shouted to everyone and laughed. Everyone cringed at the thought, including George, his son. 'Too much information, Dad. But did you really have to wait until you were eighteen? Oh, well, I've beaten that.' He grinned. 'Milly at school does it in your lunch break for a fiver!'

'So that's why you're losing weight. You're not eating lunch and you're handing over your dinner money. Cheeky bugger. That's my boy,' Mark boasted.

As everyone ate and laughed, Deana felt a real sense of belonging. Even ordinary customers having their own meal in the pub got caught up in the festivities and wished her a happy birthday. Then Deana started unwrapping her presents, mainly from her friends from college. Cheap perfume and cheap bubble bath. After the fifth try, Deana gave up and put the black bin liner containing another dozen or so presents back on the floor. 'I'll open the rest later.'

'Just as I said, Deana, Poundland did a roaring trade. How many baths do they think you take?'

'Who cares? This is my family, Dante. The street. This pub and everyone at this table.' Shaking her wrist in the air, she winked at Dante. 'And him.' she grinned. As the chef wheeled in a large square birthday cake with candles and sparklers lighting the way, everyone sang.

Deana felt her heart would burst. What a fantastic day. She had seen her father, got a beautiful present off Luke and now the neighbourhood had bought her her first car. What a memorable eighteenth, she thought to herself, so different to last year in comparison. She couldn't remember the last time she'd been surrounded by real friends while having a birthday party. Happy birthday Deana, she said to herself and took a sip of her wine.

16

THE WAY FORWARD

'Deana, I've hired us a storage container. You have to sign for it though because you're eighteen and then we're going to have to come up with some other ways of legalising our money.'

'Why do we need a storage container? What are you on about, Dante?'

Lowering his voice, Dante explained. 'Have you seen the amounts of money we have stashed away? There aren't enough cupboards or wardrobe space left. We can't keep putting it in the cellar; other people go down there – including Mum. We can put our money in a storage container away from anyone's eyes. Then we have to open bank accounts. We have to drip feed that money in; no one goes to banks with lump sums unless they are dealers or sex workers.'

'I do have one thing I would like to do if possible. I'd like to buy the pub for Mum. Not sure how, but I would like to contact the brewery and find out how much they would like for it. That is, if they're willing to sell.'

'What the fuck?' Raising his voice, Dante couldn't believe his ears. He looked around at the other passengers on the bus who were all giving him frowning looks of disapproval. A schoolboy swearing on a bus! Lowering his voice again, he sat closer to Deana. 'You're not going to get a mortgage and no one takes a holdall full of cash to a brewery.'

'I knew what you'd say and yeah, I know I have no credit history, but it's a lovely thought, isn't it? Think about it, Dante. There has to be a way. How do dealers buy stuff if they can't ever reveal how much cash they've got and don't want it going through the books?'

'Well, gangsters launder it through businesses they already have, which we don't have. Some, I presume can get crooked lawyers to help them out, but we don't know any.'

'This is my stop, Dante, but there has to be a way we can launder our own money or make it look like we are making money legally. Couldn't we buy a whole heap of stuff then sell it online? That money would be legal income, wouldn't it?'

As Deana got off and waved through the window of the bus, Dante's mind began to whirl. For Deana, that wasn't a bad idea, he thought to himself. They could buy all kinds of things and sell them online and that would be money coming from legitimate accounts into their own accounts. It needed a little thought, he mused, but ideas were forming in his mind. Although, there was another option, he thought to himself. There was maybe someone who could launder his money for him. John. His dad had told him that if he needed anything then he just had to ask John. Well, he needed financial advice, and he couldn't ask a bank advisor, could he? Dante took out his mobile and searched for John's name. He was tempted to call it but thought better of it. Maybe a text?

Or was he being too impulsive? Either way, he knew he would have some explaining to do.

> Hello John. Dante Silva here. Dad said if I ever needed advice I could ask you. Can I call you sometime? Dad's okay, no problems there. Just advice I'm looking for man to man.

Letting out a huge sigh, Dante felt nervous. He'd sent the text and didn't know if he'd done right or wrong. Putting his mobile back into his pocket, he rubbed his sweaty hands on his trousers and ran his tongue over his lips to moisten them. John was a high-ranking gangster and was now a big gangland boss. Dante bit his bottom lip. Maybe, given the circumstances, he shouldn't have called him 'John'. It sounded too informal given his status. Suddenly, his phone burst into life and started ringing. He was waiting to get off the bus now it had reached his school and he quickly scrambled in his pocket, while holding on to the handrails as the bus came to a halt. 'Hello, is that you Uncle John?' Dante asked down the phone and gave the added respect of uncle, not knowing what else to call him.

'That depends young man. How do I know you are who you say you are? And how did you get my private mobile number? Tell me amigo, *qual é o nome do seu pai*?'

Confused for a moment, Dante realised John was testing him. Of course he was. That text could have been from any one of his enemies.

'My father's name is Alex Silva. Or *o nome do meu pai é Alex*, or as he was known, *a bala de prata*.' Dante felt, if he mentioned that Alex was also known as the Silva Bullet, it might cut some ice.

The voice on the other end of the phone was steady and calm as though thinking. '*O nome de solteira da sua mãe?*' John asked.

Dante had to think for a moment. Trying to gather his thoughts at such an important call, stupidly he realised it was the same as Babs, his grandma. 'White or Branca,' Dante blurted out, almost kicking himself for stammering stupidly over such a simple question.

'Very well, Dante. Not a lot of people know that and so I will take your word for it. Describe Babs to me?'

As Dante walked and talked at the same time he was nearly out of breath and hoped to God that his signal wouldn't give out. 'Do you want me to be polite Uncle John or tell you the truth? Well, here goes. She's a very nice grandmother but she knocks you out every time she turns her head with those long dangly earrings of hers. Her make-up is put on with a trowel, matching that peroxide bleached hair of hers and she's a nosey cow!'

Instantly, Dante heard belly laughter down the phone and had to wait until it stopped. He realised he'd said the right thing, or John wouldn't be howling down the phone. Looking across the road at his school, Dante stopped and stood in a shop doorway to finish the rest of the conversation.

'Okay Dante, I believe you. I couldn't have described her better myself, nor could your father. We will meet up. Today. I will meet you at London Bridge in two hours. Can you afford it? Do you have any money?'

'Yes, I can. I'll have to skip school, but I'll see you in two hours. I'll wait outside the front of the station for you.' Dante wasn't sure if his signal had died, or John had just ended the call because there was no reply. Thankful that his school was near the bus station, he realised he needed an excuse to get out of school or they would call his mother. Quickly, he dialled Deana's number. Once she answered, Dante filled her in quickly on his plans and he asked her to ring the school and say he wasn't well.

'What the hell are you playing at Dante? For Christ's sake, yeah, I will make the call but, I'm coming with you. Meet me at the train station and don't leave without me!' The bus terminus was near the train station and so Dante went in and waited for Deana. Checking out the train times, he saw that it was only a forty-minute journey approximately.

Breathing heavily and red faced, Deana ran through the station and shouted Dante's name. 'Dante, Dante!' she bellowed, making all the other travellers turn and look at her.

Sitting on a bench outside of the ticket office, Dante waved at her. 'Christ Deana, I could hear you above the tannoy. You look puffed out, you okay? Did you ring the school?'

'Yes, I did. I was Maggie Silva. You've got diarrhoea and vomiting. No need for a doctor's note. They said it's usually forty-eight hours before you can return. So when we're finished with whatever you've come up with, go home and tell Mum you've got stomach-ache and that you had to go home from school. Anyway, how come John wants to see you? Tell me what mad scheme you've got up your sleeve?'

Dante filled Deana in on all the facts during the train journey, and now they both stood outside the station waiting. They had no idea what car they were looking for, or indeed if John was walking. Why London Bridge? Deana had asked, only to be met with a shrug of the shoulders from Dante.

From nowhere a black Jaguar pulled up in front of them and the window slid down. 'Get in.' Seeing that it was John, they opened the car door and both got into the back seat. 'I didn't think you were coming. You said two hours, it's been nearly three,' said Dante.

'I know. I've been watching you from over the road. Just in case anyone was with you or you'd been set up as bait by your police friends.'

Casting a furtive glance at Deana, Dante spoke first. 'We haven't had anything to do with the police for ages now. They don't take much interest now the court case is over. Although, I presume they will always take an interest in us.'

'You're not wrong, Dante. You will always be on their radar. I got the impression I would be meeting you alone. Man to man. Isn't that what you said? Why are you here, Deana? A change of sex or just being nosey?' John grinned through the rear-view mirror at them both as he turned in to the railway station car park.

'Neither,' she snapped. 'It concerns us both and Dante's jumped in and contacted you without speaking to me first.'

'The mystery deepens.' John parked the car up, turning off the engine, and turned to face them both. 'So, what's the problem?'

Deana's blue eyes flashed, and her face flushed. 'What? Here? You want us to have a conversation with you in a car park. Aren't you taking us to your office or a café or something?' Seeing John shake his head, she stopped.

'This is private, discreet without being overheard. Now, I am a busy man. What's the problem?'

Shyly, they both looked at each other and then at John who sat waiting patiently. His diamond stud earrings sparkled in his ears and the warm scent of his aftershave wafted around the car. Swallowing hard, Dante felt he should take the lead. He had set this meeting up and couldn't bottle it now. His heart was pounding in his chest as he tried forming the words he wanted to say.

'We have acquired a lot of money Uncle John. We have no proof of earnings, which means we can't spend it or put in the bank without questions. I wondered, erm,' Dante stammered. 'We wondered if it would be possible for you to put the money into a new bank account for us and we could pay you the money in cash. That way, the money would come from a legitimate account – yours. And it would be legal,' he blurted out.

They could both see that this wasn't the kind of request John was expecting. Frowning at them both, he searched their faces as his eyes bore into them. 'Before anything else, lift up your shirts and blouses. I want to see if you're wired.'

'Wired? For fuck's sake. You think we're wired for the police? Is that it, John? Once a Silva super grass, always a super grass. Well, if you want to see my pair of tits you pervert, take a good look!' Without a second thought, Deana pulled her blouse over her head and sat there in her bra. 'Do you want me to take my bra off too? You've watched too many gangster movies,' she spat out, disgusted at his request.

Dante put his hand on hers. 'Shut up, Deana. He's just being careful. After everything that's gone on, who can blame him? Our request isn't a small one and he barely knows us.' Dante undid his shirt and took it off under John's close scrutiny. 'God knows what people in this car park are going to be thinking. Us two stripping off in the back of your car.' Dante grinned.

Calmly, John lit a cigar and opened the window slightly to let the smoke out. 'Firstly, no one can see in. The windows are tinted, you can see out, but no one can see inside.' Reaching forward, he pulled Dante towards him and half turned him to see his back. Indicating for Deana to turn, he felt satisfied that this was all above board. 'How much are we talking about?' he asked, ignoring Deana's outburst.

Again, Dante swallowed hard. This was the bit he'd dreaded. Explanations would be needed. His throat felt dry as he spoke and the cigar smoke wasn't helping. 'About three hundred thousand approximately.'

Smugly, Deana sat back in her seat. 'Are you wired, John? Are you going to strip for us? How do we know you're not a super grass?'

'Shut the fuck up lady, your smart mouth isn't the way to get a favour out of me. Dante, repeat that amount to me again.' Scrutinising them closely, John listened and stubbed out his cigar as Dante repeated the amount.

'And just where did you two get your hands on that kind of money? I presume your mother doesn't know anything about this little windfall of yours, let alone your father. What have you two troublemakers been up to? And I want the truth, if you want my help.'

'We sold some cannabis,' Dante blurted out. 'We had some plants and we sold them.'

'Bollocks! Get out of the car if you're going to lie and take me for a fool. You haven't made that out of a few plants.'

'No wait, John. Sorry. I've been cooking meth and selling it plus the cannabis. That's the truth.'

'You're a young boy, Dante. How can you cook meth? How are you distributing it? Who are your contacts? Definitely no one I know has a teenage boy for a cook. And what's your part in all of this Mrs Big Mouth? You have your mother's looks and your father's hot temper.'

John sat there while both Deana and Dante confessed everything. How their father knew of a man with cannabis plants. How Deana had carried on what their father had started and about Dante's gift with chemistry. How, on occasions, they all worked together and delivered the drugs, mainly at weekends. John's jaw almost dropped when they told him how they stole cars and how Dante now had a motorbike.

John shook his head, his face flushed. Once they'd both finished they sat back waiting for his response, their eyes lowered like two naughty children in front of the headteacher. 'You know what? I seriously wish I hadn't asked now. You do realise by confessing all of this you're involving me?' Inhaling a huge breath, John continued. 'To start with, your father is my friend, and I promised him I would look after you in his absence. What do I tell him about this? Secondly, you've been selling, here, there and everywhere, which means you're pissing on everyone's parade. Everyone has their own turf. You don't just cook meth and sell it willy nilly. If you sell on other people's turf you pay commission. Christ, you two are going to start a turf war! Every dealer up and down the country is going to get blamed for this and it's you two! Two fucking kids living in a pub in Kent!' he half shouted. 'There will be blood wars. Do you understand that? As you have found out, there is a lot of money to be made and you're cutting in on someone's business. Have you ever thought of that? Drug dealing isn't a game, you fucking idiots. It stops and it stops now! You will either get yourselves killed or other dealers will be killed because of you.'

As they both sat there red faced, they contemplated John's words. They had never thought about it seriously before. Deana reached out and held Dante's hand for comfort. 'We didn't mean any harm. It was just money to pay for our university fees. We don't have a pot to piss in, John.

We lost everything – you know that. We would like to buy Mum the pub too. A bit of security with Dad being away.'

Calmly, John put his emotions to one side and contemplated their proposal. 'Three hundred thousand you say. I don't know if that would be enough to buy the pub *and* pay for university.'

'Three hundred thousand... each,' Deana muttered under her breath, casting a furtive look at John. A weak smile crossed her face, and from under her lashes, she looked at John again. They both knew they were on rocky ground and in trouble. For a moment, Dante regretted contacting John; it had been impulsive and stupid and he hadn't really thought this through.

John raised his head slowly and looked them both square in the face. 'Each? By that, do you mean that you have six hundred thousand pounds stashed away in cash?' Seeing them both nod their heads, John put his head in his hands and rubbed his face. They had totally taken the wind out of his sails and he didn't know what to say. He knew Alex would go bonkers if he helped them and be angry if he didn't get them out of this scrape. He was damned if he did and damned if he didn't.

Suddenly he had a sick feeling in the pit of his stomach. Only a week ago there had been talk that some supplier had 'acquired' three pounds of pure meth and was selling it and undercutting other people's prices. It had caused arguments and suspicion. At one point one gang had burst into a pub of one of their opponents shouting accusations and waving a gun around. They had asked for his help to find the culprit and dispose of them. And here they were sitting in his car confessing. Narrowing his eyes, he looked at them curiously. 'Are you selling it yourselves and for how much?'

'Oh yeah, it's flying off the shelves! We're asking for fifty pounds a gram, cos Dante can always make more. We already have orders!' Deana's face was flushed with excitement as she boasted about their success.

John's eyes widened with horror. 'You sound like you're on an episode of *MasterChef*. Dante can cook some more for fuck's sake. Can you hear yourselves? And you're giving pure meth. You're not cutting it with anything else?' Disbelieving, he waited for the answer, although he felt he knew what was coming.

'No, it's all good stuff. Nothing dodgy about Dante's magic potions.'

'Do you realise how much you're undercutting yourself? Pure meth sold in the right circles and cut properly could make you millionaires. And you're selling it for pennies. You're ripping an awful lot of people off. Who else are you in league with?' John felt he had to tell them that already there was word on the streets and that people were angry.

'Are we really hurting anyone?' Dante swallowed hard; his heart was pounding in his chest. In his own circle, with Luke and Deana, stupidly he had thought it was just between them, but now people were talking. The jungle drums were out and without knowing it they were famous, but for all of the wrong reasons. 'Surely our small outfit doesn't affect the big guns?'

'Dante, you're pissing down people's backs and telling them that it's raining. People have taken years to build up their own turf and custom. Stealing people's money and undercutting their empire makes them angry. Fortunately, at the moment they are arguing amongst themselves, but they will follow the trail to your door, Dante. Believe me. Are these others that you're in league with forcing you to do this?

Are they blackmailing you or something?' Inwardly, John hoped someone was because he could then dispose of them and help Alex's children, but deep down, and looking at their faces, he knew this was their own doing. Part of him wanted to laugh. It was unbelievable. Two kids wanting to pay their university fees and one could cook meth! No one would believe this story. Turf wars were one thing, but how did you start a war against two teenage kids?

Letting out a huge sigh, he tried to think positively. 'If I did as you ask and put the money into accounts for you, that could also look suspicious. Why am I giving you that kind of money? Could it be that I am bribing Alex or paying him off for not dragging me into his sordid mess? Have you thought of that?' Shaking his head and running his hands through his thick hair, he said, 'No, of course you bloody haven't. Let me think about this. I can't make a decision now. You're both on dangerous ground. People get killed for what you're doing. Christ, who was it that said ignorance was bliss. Because that sums you both up in one sentence. It's not a game, drug dealing. It can be a death sentence or a prison sentence. Have you thought about that?'

John was totally amazed that they hadn't taken any of this into consideration. They lived in a deluded bubble. What he needed now, was a stiff drink and to think about what they had told him.

'Would you buy the pub?' Deana butted in. 'That wouldn't be for us. You're just buying a property. Is that so unbelievable?'

'It's your father's pub!' John shouted at her. 'Why would I buy Alex Silva's pub?'

Angrily, Deana glared at John; she was fed up with his lectures. 'Because you said you were a businessman and it's a going concern! Fuck Alex Silva. We're Deana and Dante Silva. Dad is in prison, he's not involved. Mum doesn't know, we've covered our arses on that one. We're not totally stupid. We've done this for a while now and all we need is to legalise the money. Maybe we could get a solicitor to buy it for us if you haven't got the balls,' Deana shouted.

On impulse, John reached out and slapped Deana across the face hard, knocking her backwards. He felt angry at their stupidity. 'Mind your manners girlie.' Hearing her cry out in pain, Dante was about to intervene when John held up his hand to stop him. 'Don't even think about retaliating. By rights, I should shoot the pair of you! Now get out of the car, I have things to do and so have you, busy little bees. Your work stops now. Let me think about the money, but, as you say, I'm a businessman and you're desperate. I want a 10 per cent commission for saving your arses. It's a one-time offer. Now get out!' he shouted and turning forward in his seat, started the engine up. Avoiding their looks, he heard the door slam and drove off leaving them stood on the pavement.

As he drove along thinking about their story, he found himself laughing out loud. In different circumstances, he knew Alex would find it funny, but not where his own children were concerned. These two kids had found an opportunity and taken it without a care in the world. It was a bit of pocket money that had got out of hand. Shaking his head, he laughed again. 'You pair of cheeky bastards!'

17

FORBIDDEN TERRITORY

As two men sat huddled together whispering in the pub, emotions and suspicions were high. 'Titch, have you found anything out? You usually have a nose like a ferret. What about your regulars not texting for their orders? Can't you ask them?'

Titch, standing well over six feet, had been given the name since school as he'd never stopped growing. 'I already have. Word is, it's a young foreign man and woman. They don't speak English. They take the call and drop off the gear. That's all I know.' Titch took a large gulp of his pint of lager and put the glass down on the table. 'I can't stay in south London long. This isn't my outfit, it's yours. How do I know that you're not ripping off my bosses?'

'For God's sake, it's me, Titch, Billy. We were at school together until you moved north and got in with your own crowd. There's something big going down. Someone has moved in on all of us, but I want you to know, whether you believe me or not, it's not me and it's not my lot. We're as puzzled as anyone. There have been no threats, and no one has tried fighting for our turf. I don't understand it. Surely someone would want a meeting by now or there would be violence?'

'I know what you're saying, Billy. Everyone is shouting about this great new drug on the market but no one has offered to cut us in on anything. They don't need protection, and they have no respect which usually means they want a war! I think you're right. Your lot and mine should have our own meeting. Maybe we could join forces on this one. This is dangerous ground. Whoever this is comes from outside London. That I do know. Apart from that the trail ends.' Titch shrugged. 'Are you buying me a whisky chaser to wash down this already watered-down beer?' Titch grinned.

As Billy walked to the bar, Titch spied him closely. They had known each other for years, but life had got in the way, and they had moved on and now worked for different gangs. There had been occasions when they had been at war with each other, but they had tried tipping each other off, when possible, before things got too hot. Titch had warned Billy to arrive somewhere late or not turn up at all to save him from being shot or beaten. Titch's gut instinct told him that Billy had been told by his bosses to have this meet up with his old friend and sound him out, so to speak. The rival gangs all had a common interest – who was muscling in on their business? Well, Titch thought to himself, it wasn't Billy's lot and it definitely wasn't his. But they wanted blood, that was for sure. They had already accused some rival gang and run in with shotguns shooting the place up. It had been madness. But gangs were getting twitchy and nervous, and it was causing unrest.

Billy sat down and put Titch's whisky in front of him. Moving closer and resting his elbows on the table while glancing around at the customers, he dropped his voice to a whisper. 'I believe someone made an appointment to see the "big boss" to see if he knew anything. After all, that's what he gets paid for, isn't it? Keeping the peace.'

Shocked, Titch sat there wide eyed. 'Well, they've got balls. They must be desperate. Do we know what was said?' Billy just shook his head and shrugged. 'I was hoping you would fill me in on that conversation.'

Gulping back his whisky, Titch stood up and looked at his watch. 'I've got to go. See you Billy mate.' Slapping him on the shoulders, he left the pub and walked around the corner to his car. Once he got in, two men in suits were sat in the back. 'Well, what does he know?'

'Same as us – nothing. He's trying to get information out of me and I'm doing likewise. Whoever these bastards are, it's not his lot. I tell you, Boss, this new lot are not in London. They are outsiders. No one else would dare cross you.'

About to drive off, Titch looked in the rear-view mirror and a cold chill ran though him. His boss was holding a gun to the back of his head. 'Well, Titch, let's hope your loyalties lie with us and not your old school chum or Titch will definitely be your name, because I will get the boys to cut your fucking legs off.'

Not daring to move his head, he looked again into the rear-view mirror, which was the only eye contact he had. 'Hey Boss,' he stammered, 'I only did this for you. You've no reason to doubt me.'

'Keep it that way. Let's just hope you and silly Billy haven't decided to cream it off the top as partners. You looked so friendly, sat there together like a pair of old women gossiping.' With that the two suited men in the back opened the doors and got out of the car. One carefully put his gun in the waistband of his trouser near his back. 'We'll see ourselves home.'

Titch watched them hail a taxi and suddenly a sense of foreboding came over him. Why didn't they want him to drive them? What was wrong with the car? Looking at the keys in the ignition, he felt nervous and afraid. A cold sweat broke out on his brow, and he wiped it away with his arm. Getting out of the car, he hailed his own taxi. He couldn't be sure if the car had been tampered with and he wasn't prepared to take the risk. Calling a local garage, he asked the mechanic to pick up his car, lying that it wouldn't start, and that something was wrong. He wasn't putting himself on the line for a one-off meeting with a rival. He'd been accused of creaming it off the top before and to be fair he had. He also had a habit, but now it was down to just smoking dope. Remembering how they had hung him upside down in an old warehouse and put the wires of a car battery to his balls made him feel sick. He could still feel the pain and the horrible singe smell in his nostrils. They didn't trust him and this was his test. The only person that might help him would be that fat bitch who loaned monies for extortionate interest. She always had her ear to the ground. He had to come up with a name or some kind of lead for his bosses to look kindly upon him once more.

* * *

'Well, that was a waste of time, Dante. Why do we need him? Fucking waste of space!' Deana was angry, and still smarting from John's comments and the harsh slap he'd given her.

'Because we have to have some kind of explanation in order to start depositing regular huge sums of cash into a bank account.' Full of remorse, Dante sat opposite Deana on the train. She wasn't happy and he felt his confession to John had not only been pointless, but dangerous too. Now he knew what they were up to, Dante felt sure he would be watching them. Maybe it was time to take the money and run.

'Maybe if the heat is on us, we should stop. We've got a lot of money, much more than we bargained for. Maybe we should quit while we're ahead, eh?'

'Bollocks. That's just his scare tactics. No one knows about us. No one gives a shit about a small outfit like ours. We're not exactly the Cartel, are we? John's just trying to scare us and it hasn't worked on me. Come on, man up!'

Dante wondered if maybe Deana had a point. John had warned them to stop but maybe it was just a scare tactic.

'Right, we're nearly home. You go in and look ill and don't forget to run to the loo. I'll come in an hour or so.'

As expected, Maggie fussed over Dante. 'You do look pale love and you're hot. Crikey, you haven't been running have you? Go to bed. Let me get you a bucket in case you need to be sick. I'll bring you a hot drink, too.'

Dante felt pale. It had been one hell of a day, and he felt drained. He wanted a lie down. Giving Maggie a weak smile, he turned and almost crawled up the staircase to bed. Once in his room, he opened his wardrobe door and looked inside. From the floor upwards there were carefully counted out thousand-pound bundles of money piled on top of each other. While looking at it all, he felt sick for real. What the hell were they going to do with it all? They needed to get the money out of there.

An hour or so later, Deana opened his bedroom door and winked. 'How you feeling, Dante?' Giving him another wink and a knowing look meant that Maggie was hot on her heels. 'Are you awake, Dante love? I've brought you something to settle your stomach. Pauline popped to the pharmacy, and they advised these sachets.' Sitting up in bed, Dante looked up at Maggie as she handed him a glass of water, obviously containing some kind of diarrhoea sachet. 'Well, drink it, love. It will do you good.' Reluctantly, Dante took the glass and drank the mixture as Deana and Maggie looked on. It tasted awful, but he had no choice. 'I'd better go downstairs, Dante. If you need me shout. Don't wear him out Deana. Let him sleep.' Dante waited until Maggie left the room and closed the door behind her.

'Oh my God, I am so glad that wasn't me. Was it as disgusting as it looked?'

Dante nodded. 'It serves me right for lying, Deana. There's the address of the storage unit. You need to sign the documents and we need to fill the boot of your car and start emptying this place.'

'I can't drive the car yet on my own, you know that. It's going to take a lot of carrying and journeys to this unit of yours getting this lot out. Why don't we just put the wardrobes in the unit. That would be easier.'

Dante's jaw dropped. 'How the hell are you going to get two wardrobes out of here without Mum or anyone seeing you? I presume you're going to leave the money inside them and let some poor furniture removal man carry them down.'

'Why not? That's their job and what's a little more weight? As for when, well I have an idea. Mum said Mark was due to visit Dad again soon and I think we should convince her to take some time out and have a day out with Grandma. Either that or she should go with Mark to see Dad. Either way we get her out of the way. When she asks where the wardrobes are, that's not a problem. She wants to redecorate, and I don't want old furniture in my room!'

'Or we could just say we're going to give our old wardrobes to Luke's brother, sister or aunty. Luke could hire a van and take them away for us. We'll put so much tape around them no one will get inside the doors, then we tell Mum we've seen some new bedroom furniture that will look better after she's redecorated. That's makes much more sense.'

'Actually, that's not bad. In fact, it's very good. Okay, I'll sort out this unit and I also want to sort your bank account and my own. I want a current account and a savings account. We have passports, so we have proof of identity. That should be enough. That's it then, we're sorted. As long as we have each other Dante, we don't need anyone else. The Silva family stick together through thick and thin.'

'Don't get sentimental, Deana. But I agree. Being cooped up with each other these last few years we haven't killed each other, so there's hope for us yet, eh?'

So there it was, their plan was hatched.

'Hey Bernie mate, how are you?' Titch had done his best to hang around this crappy estate for hours. He knew if anyone around here would know something about these new dealers on the block, Bernie would.

'Fuck off Titch I'm busy, and definitely too busy with arseholes who have problems. I know that because that's the only time I hear from you. Just like you're always at the back of the queue when it's your turn to buy a drink.'

Bernie frightened Titch a little. She was a huge woman,

but it was all muscle. Her huge melon-like breasts seemed to hang below her naval and there wasn't much space in between her sleeve of tattoos. Her short dark hair was shaved at the sides, showing another row of tattoos down the side of her neck, plus a load of piercings around her ears. Bernie worked for the big guns and so Titch knew she was fearless and liked nothing more than to beat some poor unsuspecting victim up. She was a loan shark and collector, and most people paid up.

'Nice little unit you have here Bernie. I didn't know you sold used goods, furniture and stuff. Nice sideline.' He nodded and lit a cigarette. 'I've brought you a bacon sandwich, lots of brown sauce. Just how you like it.'

'Well, put that fucking thing out, laddie. As you say, it's furniture and stuff and you're there with a ciggie in your mouth. You must be fucking desperate for something, dipping into your pockets, to buy me something. Don't flirt with me Titch, you're not my taste.' Bernie let out a huge belly laugh as she walked around the unit putting price tickets on things. Doing as he was told; Titch took the cigarette out of his mouth and threw it towards the kerb. Bernie's unit was quite big inside, and he strolled around looking at the many televisions, sofas, gaming software and laptops. You name it, Bernie had it all for sale.

'So, what do you do, go to auctions or something? Lot of decent gear here.'

'Keep your clammy hands off the goods, Titch. This stuff is what I've taken in lieu of money people owe me. I take it out, bring it here and if they want it back, they have to buy it back at a higher price of course. If they haven't paid anything off in a week it's all for sale. More than one way to skin a cat, Titch. You just carry on playing small-time gangsters with the little boys. I wouldn't piss on them if they were on fire. Well, you might as well put the kettle on then and get it over with,' she sighed and lit a cigarette while standing in the doorway of the unit.

'I thought you said no smoking,' Titch shouted and laughed.

'I said you can't smoke, you prick. I don't remember saying anything about me. Two sugars in my tea, lapdog, then you can tell me your sob story.'

Handing her a mug of tea, and taking a sip of his own, Titch's stomach turned as he watched Bernie gnaw on the bacon sandwich. Brown sauce ran down her chin and she just wiped it away with her hand. He appreciated she was a woman but felt that was just a technicality of nature. 'How's the wife, she okay?'

Still chewing, Bernie raised one eyebrow and stared at him. 'She's okay, the cat's okay and I believe my neighbours aren't dead. So, that's the small talk over with. Spit it out for God's sake.'

Trying to gather his thoughts and wondering how to put his query to Bernie, he looked at her. He felt nervous as she stood there still chewing with her arms folded. He could see she was bored already.

'Have you heard about these new dealers on the streets? They're undercutting everyone and stealing customers. Everyone is twitchy and nervous. All the bosses are suspicious of everyone including myself. And hey, before you start, Bernie, I am innocent on this one.'

Bernie stopped what she was doing and listened to him. 'It wouldn't be the first time you've creamed it off the top, Titch. Your bosses getting wise to you?'

'It's nothing to do with me, Bernie. Couple of foreigners, I heard, but then a lot are in that line of business.'

'Foreigners! Foreigners! You're always pointing the finger at someone else. Well, I'm Scottish, so I presume I'm a foreigner, eh, laddie? Have you tried looking into the Liverpudlians? They've been very quiet lately. Even their contact has gone to ground. And I presume you would call them foreigners, too! They could be getting some kids to do it, that's usually the case, isn't it? Get a boy to do a man's job, isn't that what your bosses do?' Bernie laughed and gave Titch a sharp dig in the ribs with her elbow.

'What about your boss? Aren't they worried? Have they said anything?'

'This is too small for my boss. She deals in kilos not ounces. The Liverpudlians used to use some sweaty old bloke in Kent to hide some of their stash. He'll do anything to top up his pension. Not a bad man to know, though. But anyway, I'm digressing. He works for Argos and when people send stuff back, cos its broken or something, he picks it up. And seven out of ten times it finds its way into my little unit. Everyone's a winner, Titch. That is apart from you, you sad bastard. You've always been a loser...' Bernie looked at him. 'Check out the Blue Parrot nightclub, off the Old Kent Road. It's full of druggies and they are always selling in there. It's usually crap gear, but there was talk about some decent meth. Someone in there might be able to tip you off.'

Relieved at this information, Titch let out a huge sigh. 'Thanks Bernie. You've given me a couple of leads there. If nothing else, I need to come up with something, just to clear my own name.'

Holding out her fist at arm's length, Bernie waited while Titch did the same and then tapped them against each other.

'Might need a favour of my own one day Titch. Hope it helps. Don't come back soon!' Bernie laughed and carried on pricing her electrical goods up. 'Hey! One more tip loser... don't rush in. Sit back, see who they are selling to, and what they're selling at what price. Slowly, slowly, catchy monkey, eh?'

Giving her the thumbs up, Titch hailed another cab and left. He couldn't wait to get back to his boss's headquarters and offer some information. It was a small peace offering, but it might just save his skin. Titch wondered about his car. He hadn't heard of any explosions in the area, so hopefully, it was just his imagination working overtime. Men like the ones he worked for were temperamental, especially when things weren't going their way. Their moods could change like the flick of a switch. And when they did, someone was in for a real beating – or worse. Titch couldn't remember how many bodies were buried under London Bridge. They were possibly the only things holding it up!

'Mark! Over here mate,' Alex shouted in the visitor's room. He'd been looking forward to seeing Mark whose visits were like a tonic. Even the other prisoners looked forward to it, because of his entertaining conversation. It was all bravado and bullshit, but it was all good listening.

'Brought you some magazines and stuff. Some with tits in. Unless you've decided to bat for the other side since you've been in here?' Mark's infectious laugh caused a lot of smiles among the inmates and the warders. 'I've sorted some cash out to put some money on your phone card, too, then you can give us a call when you can. I'm keeping my eye on

Maggie and the kids, although I've kept out of the way lately. Your mother-in-law, Babs, has been hanging around. Christ she's scary, and what a gob on her. She's making herself scarce though, now Maggie's talking about decorating. Although, if it was plastering, she'd be an expert. Can be as hot as a jungle out there but her make-up never moves. I told Maggie to get in touch with the brewery if she's decorating. After all, it's in their interest to keep the place up to scratch, isn't it?'

'Good idea. They might put something towards it, although I doubt it.' Alex shrugged.

'Sorry Alex, here I am gabbing on like an old woman. I'll get us some drinks and stuff. Christ I've so much change in my pockets for those vending machines, I'm bloody jangling when I walk. As long as you lot don't think I'm farting!' he shouted to the room causing a great guffaw amongst everyone.

Mark bought cups of teas, chocolates and cigarettes, the stuff that dreams are made of when you're in prison.

'Your Maggie's been busy. She's got wallpaper charts, and all kinds of things planned for your return. Says she's going to decorate the whole house. I helped your kids get rid of those old wardrobes in their bedrooms, too. Bloody hell, Alex, my back is still killing me!' While talking, Mark looked around and spotted Jonesy in the far corner of the room and immediately diverted his eyes. Alex picked up on this instantly. 'What's the beef there, Mark?' he whispered.

Mark cast another furtive look to the corner of the room where Jonesy was sat. 'I know that geezer. Did a bit of dealing here and there. Well in with the coppers. I went to pick up some stuff from his gaff once, he had a few copper mates around there having a few drinks. That's where he gets his stuff from,' Mark whispered. 'When the coppers take it off people, they don't declare all of it and some of it gets lost, if you know what I mean.' Mark winked. 'Watch him, he's a bad lot. Mean bastard too, because he has the back-up. No one likes him and I haven't used him in ages. The way I saw it was, he sells it to you but then his copper mates know you're a druggie. So, if you change suppliers or don't want to pay his extortionate prices, he gets them to investigate your drug habit, and you end up in court with a fine or whatever. He let me get away with it, which surprised me, but I only bought now and again. I wasn't worth anything to him, and even then, I used to fix his car in return. Never paid in cash,' Mark mused.

'He also demands sexual favours off the inmates he's handing out drugs to. He's in with one of the warders and he's handing out gear to my cellmate. He's a pathetic guy, manic depressive, but he's okay and means well, but he's being used, and I don't like it. Anyway, enough of that, how's Deana's driving coming along? I've seen the pictures of the car everyone got her. It's amazing and thank you for checking it over, Mark. Your valuable, mechanic experience makes all the difference.' Alex couldn't help the sarcasm of his double-sided compliment. But he crossed his fingers and hoped that Maggie had actually taken it to a garage at some point, given Mark's history.

'Deana's taken to driving like a duck to water. You'd think she'd been doing it for years. Got her test sometime soon, then she'll be off. I've told her, when she's going out in the car, let me know so that I will stay in. Christ, your Deana in a bad mood on the road, that's all we need. Dante's doing well, too! Really clever lad you got there. He will go far in life. As for your cellmate, Alex, leave well alone. He's old enough to make his own choices, just as long as he doesn't creep up into your bunk at night!' Mark laughed, breaking the tension in the conversation.

The rest of the time whizzed by, and Mark hardly took a breath because he had so much to say. In no time at all the visiting time was up and Alex felt sad. He enjoyed Mark's visits and loved hearing about all the neighbourhood gossip. He was a great mate and Alex felt lucky to have him.

18

CHANGES

'It's been a couple of months now Dante and we haven't heard anything from John, so that was a waste of space. But we're okay. We keep doing what we do. Your bank account is looking healthy and so is mine. We've got accounts now and I've got a debit card so I don't have to carry cash all the time. Good idea of yours though, saying your estranged father sent you some money in cash cos he didn't want your mum to know about it. Estranged father! Where do you get these ideas from, Dante? Plus telling them that it would be a regular thing because your dad wants to pay university fees when the time comes for you.'

'It's a start, Deana, and now you've passed your test, we need to go to another bank and do the same.'

'Oh, stop being so sensible, Dante. Everything is looking up for us, especially as I've just heard I've been accepted at that university I applied to. It's pending my results, but it looks like I'm in.' Deana grinned. 'Are you at Luke's this weekend?'

'Yeah, business as usual, eh? Especially now that you're

legal on the roads and you can drop me off there. I can pick up my bike and we can deliver to our hearts' content.'

'Oh God, more bad news.' Holding a letter in her hand, Maggie entered the kitchen and sat down at the kitchen table. 'Look at this.' Handing over the letter to Dante and Deana, she picked up her cup and took a sip. 'The brewery is selling the pub to an anonymous buyer. We could be homeless kids. I can't believe it.'

'*What*?' Deana shouted. 'They can't just throw us out, not after everything you've done. What do they say about us? Have they given you notice?'

Dante had the letter in his hand and his gut instinct told him John was behind this. The conditions were too lax for a new anonymous buyer. 'Listen to this bit, Mum. It says you are to stay on as manager in complete charge. You will have to end your contract with the brewery if you wish to stay here because you will no longer be working for them. I presume that means you would have to sign another one with this anonymous person.' Before Deana could vent her anger, Dante cast a glance at her and slowly shook his head without Maggie seeing him.

Tears brimmed on Maggie's lashes, and one was about to fall when she held her hand out for the letter. 'Let me see, I didn't know there was another page. Maybe I should call them.'

Comfortingly, Dante put his hand on Maggie's. 'I would, Mum. It's better to talk things like this out. Look, it also says that, if you don't want to stay here, they would happily find you another one of their pubs to manage. So, there you go, Mum. You must have done well, because they are offering you a job.'

Once the initial panic had died down, Maggie read the

letter again. 'Oh, I see, yes. Well, that's good. I'm going to ring them this morning when they open. Anonymous buyer?' Maggie mused. 'That doesn't sound very stable, does it? At least if you work for a brewery, it's an established company. We don't know anything about this new buyer.'

Taking Dante's lead, Deana smiled. 'Which is why you should talk to them, Mum. Just because they're anonymous doesn't mean they aren't a known company. It could be anyone. They just don't want to make it public yet.'

'Fair point, love. Maybe they're not allowed to say without permission. My heart skipped a beat though, when I read the first lines. I thought we were going to be homeless – again! Are you at work today, Deana?'

'Yes, Mum, I'm going to do some extra shifts. I need to earn some extra cash because wonder boy here is nearly sixteen, unless you'd forgotten.'

Maggie reached over the table and ran her hands through Dante's dark hair. 'Absolutely not. My baby, sixteen. I can't believe it. And it's nearly Christmas. So, we're going to be busy here too. Dante, have you decided what you want for your birthday? Any mad weekends like Deana?'

'Nothing so grand, Mum. Just a few mates, a takeaway maybe. Luke was talking about having a weekend away. Him and his brother are going to Amsterdam for a weekend. Well, overnight really. That's an idea I suppose.'

'Luke's going to Amsterdam?' Deana butted in. 'Isn't that all prostitutes and drugs? Isn't that why all men go there?' she snapped.

'Oh, I do hope so, Deana. It sounds better every time I hear about it.' Dante laughed.

'Well, I'll think about it. I know Luke is a sensible lad, but it will be near Christmas time and prices will skyrocket. Anyway, do you really want to be away from home?'

'It's only overnight, Mum. I stay at Luke's most weekends anyway, so what difference does it make? It might be good fun; lads weekend and all that. And the way Deana describes it, it sounds great!'

Maggie burst into laughter. 'I suppose so. If that's what you want to do. Have a think about it and let me know how much. But I want you home for your birthday treat. Anyway, I'm going to ring the brewery; you get ready for work. What about you, Dante? Are you in school today?'

'Of course, not like those college kids who break up early. Lightweights. I'm showering first. I don't take as long as you two... oh, Deana, I've got that book you wanted. I'll give it to you now before I forget.' Dante winked and cocked his head for Deana to follow him.

As Deana left the room, they could both hear Maggie on the phone to the brewery. 'It's John, I tell you,' Dante whispered as soon as they were out of earshot.

'What is?' whispered Deana. 'I don't understand what you're saying.'

Pulling her into his bedroom quickly, Dante rolled his eyes at the ceiling. 'The anonymous buyer, Deana. John is doing what we asked him to! Okay, it's taken a couple of months, but you can't buy property in a day. Solicitors need to be involved, paperwork and stuff. I wonder if the brewery even wanted to sell. They have a going concern here. Why would they want to sell, if it's making money? It's John, I tell you. We will be hearing from him soon because he will want his money.'

'Oh my God, Dante. Really? Check your phone or ring him. Do you really think he's bought this place for Mum?

That means we've bought this place for Mum. Oh, Dante.' Impulsively, Deana wrapped her arms around her brother and hugged him tight. 'That would be fantastic,' she squealed.

'Let go, for God's sake.' Dante wrestled himself from Deana's grip. 'I'm not ringing anyone. If it is John and he wants his money, then he will contact us when he's ready and not before. And stop bloody hugging me. Yuk!'

'Never mind. That's the closest you've been to a woman with wobbly bits and probably always will be.' Laughing out loud, she left, ducking to avoid the pillow Dante threw at her.

Ready for school, Dante took out the black bin liner from under his bed. Checking inside, he saw the cigarettes and cannabis for today's sales. It was becoming quite a good side-line. Even to the point that a teacher had seen Dante handing out a packet and asked where he got them from. With his heart pounding in his chest, he'd confessed he got them cheap off a friend. He was waiting for the tell-tale letter to pop through the letter box informing Maggie and had been surprised when there hadn't even been a phone call. Instead, one day the very same teacher had asked to speak to him and slightly red faced had asked Dante if he could get him some, no questions asked. Dante had been elated. This was music to his ears. The teacher gave his order, and they met during lunch to exchange money and cigarettes.

Also, word had spread, and the teacher had told some of his mates, hence the orders went up. The money was rolling in, and even when Dante informed his teacher that the cigarettes had gone up by another pound, they didn't care. It was still a lot less than the shop prices. Dante had set up a PayPal account and gave the teacher the details. It worked like a dream and the teacher preferred it, because it meant he didn't have to run out for cash and couldn't be seen handing money over to a pupil. This way, he could just mobile bank it. It was a very lucrative business.

'I'll give you a lift if you like,' Deana shouted to Dante. 'I'm going your way.'

Knowing she wanted a private chat, he took his stash and stuffed it in his rucksack. Getting in beside her in the car, Dante waited for the conversation to carry on about John. Instead, it was all about Kev. 'When did Kev say he was going to Amsterdam? He never told me!'

'Why should he? It was Luke who mentioned it to me. He asked if I wanted to go along because Kev always takes a friend, and Luke feels like the odd one out.'

Sticking her chin out in a stubborn stance, Deana asked, 'What friend? Who is she?'

'Deana, will you watch the road? It's not she, it's he. But he drinks and parties with Kev when Luke doesn't. This is a respite weekend for Luke and they've paid for the carer to stay all weekend. She can stay sometimes and Luke makes the most of it and always has a weekend away. He just asked me if I would be interested. Apparently, Kev likes to go and suss out any new cannabis and stuff. Let's be honest, that is something Amsterdam is famous for.'

'Oh, I see. I thought Kev was taking his girlfriend or something.' Deana blushed. 'It's just that you never mentioned it before. Amsterdam is also the diamond centre, so I thought he could have been buying a diamond ring for someone.' She smiled.

'Why should he? Or has your crush on him raised its ugly head again? Deana Silva jealous. I never thought I'd see the day.' Dante laughed.

'I'm not jealous. I just don't like being left out. I could

come with you. That would be nice, and Mum would like it because I'm older than you and I could keep an eye on you, couldn't I?'

'No! This is a lads' weekend. That doesn't include some nosey, lovesick older sister. Who takes their bloody sister to babysit them for a holiday? For fuck's sake Deana, back off.'

'All right, shirty pants. It was just an idea. We're all friends, aren't we? I'll say no more about it. Anyway, do you want to see what I've bought?'

Intrigued by the sudden turn of conversation, Dante turned towards her. When Deana had some kind of idea, it usually meant trouble.

'It's at Luke's. Come on, you'll love it. I do.'

Turning up at Luke's, Deana got out of the car and went around the back way to the garage. Using her own key, Deana opened it. 'Ta-Dah!'

Dante's jaw dropped. Stunned, he looked at Deana, who was grinning from ear to ear with her hands pointing at the object before him.

'That's a Triumph Spitfire. A classic car and it's pink! What the hell is it doing here?'

'It's mine, all mine. A pink sports car just for me! It even has a lipstick holder on the dashboard. I think it was custom made, but when I saw it, I just had to have it. I got a discount for cash.'

'Are you fucking crazy?' Dante couldn't believe his eyes, let alone his ears. Deana had bought – in cash – a classic car and it looked like a Barbie car. 'You can't drive around in that. How much did it cost?'

'I can drive around in it, and I will. I'm not being ungrateful, but that old shipwreck I've currently got has broken down three times, Dante. So, I can leave the house in it and swap cars here. Luke said it was okay. Don't you love the white tyres? I think it's gorgeous.'

'I think it's tacky. Oh my God, Deana, I can't believe you've done this. What if people see you and they tell Mum?'

'That's the beauty of it, she won't believe them. Because I'll be driving shipwreck around just praying that it gets me to the top of the street! I'm not telling you how much I paid, because you will go bonkers. The insurance isn't cheap either, but I expected that. It's brilliant, Dante. Absolutely brilliant and I love it. I only got it yesterday and I wanted you to see it, rather than just tell you. Oh, go on Dante, say you love it too.'

Luke walked into the garage, via the kitchen door. 'She's told you then,' was all he said.

'Didn't you tell her she can't have it? People will wonder where she gets the kind of money to buy a classic car like this. She's supposed to be shelf stacking for Christ's sake!'

Yawning, Luke nodded and rubbed his eyes. 'Said it all, Dante. But it's her money and she can do what she likes with it. Though, I totally agree with you.'

'Listen to the engine, Dante. Shall I drive you to school in it?'

'Absolutely not! Apart from anything else, if you think I'm turning up at school in a Barbie car, you're bloody wrong! I really cannot believe your stupidity, Deana.' Dante turned towards Luke. 'By the way, I've dropped Amsterdam to Mum and I think she's okay with it, if your invite is still open?'

'That's great. I'll make the arrangements and let you know. What dates do you break up for the Christmas holidays?'

'I was thinking of coming,' Deana butted in hopefully. 'We could take my car on the ferry?'

Together the boys both looked at her and grinned. 'No!' they shouted in unison and burst out laughing. 'And unless you haven't noticed, its only got two seats. Where do the rest of us sit?'

'Please yourself. I'll go on my own road trip. Me and my Barbie car! Come on schoolboy, teacher's waiting. I will be back in ten minutes Luke, put the kettle on and then I'll take you for a spin.'

Seeing Luke's face drop, Dante laughed. 'It looks like I have the better option, Luke. Good luck with that.'

Hearing his mobile buzz, Dante looked at it. 'Deana, it's a text from John. All it says is £300,000 plus £4,000 legal fees and 60 per cent commission. Call when free. I told you Deana. He's done it. It's taken a couple of months, but we're home and dry!'

'When does he want the money? Do we get the deeds to the pub? Oh Dante, we could give it to Mum for Christmas.'

Rolling his eyes to the ceiling, Dante shook his head. 'Are you totally insane? How can two kids hand over the deeds to a pub for Christmas? Who are you, Santa Claus? How did you get the money for that then? We need to meet John, or at least speak with him. If it can remain anonymous, let's leave it that way. Mum will just work for someone else, but she'll get a pay rise and the plus side is, she can order from any brewery she likes. Okay, there will be insurances and stuff to pay, but that should come out of the accounts. Mum needs a proper accountant now, because the brewery has sorted all of that out before. Maybe we have bitten off more than we can chew...' Dante thought there was a lot more to it than buying a pub. Now it was down to Mum to make it work and pay for itself. Inwardly, Dante crossed his fingers and could only hope for the best.

'Excuse me.' Deana cleared her throat. 'I'm a bloody accountant. Well, I will be when I qualify. I can do the books.'

'No, let's leave it to an outsider. Then our names are not involved. You can always check it, but I think that's for the best.'

'You're right, I just get carried away sometimes. Sorry, Dante. I'm just so excited about buying the pub for Mum and Dad.'

'Hold that thought, and your excitement, for when you eventually tell them together!' A sick feeling overwhelmed Dante. How on earth were they ever going to be able to confess this to their parents? Would they accept the pub, considering how they'd acquired the money to buy it? Their dad would be furious, and they would be nothing but a disappointment to Maggie. To tell them would mean to tell them everything and he, for one, wasn't looking forward to that one little bit.

* * *

'I've been coming to this shithole these kids call a nightclub for weeks now. Look at them all, it's disgusting. Watered-down overpriced drinks, music that doesn't have any words or rhythm and a sleazy dance floor that's more like a skating rink. The men smell and the women are worse. The Blue Parrot nightclub is a joke in itself. I'd call it the shithole of London.'

'You wanted to come Titch. You knew it was full of drug-gies. Christ, even the police don't come in here. And look at him, he's like something out of the dark ages.' Titch followed Mike's eyeline, where he was looking at a youngish man, wearing a combat jacket and mirrored sunglasses. He was dancing around, holding court and shaking hands with his friends. 'So, what's the big deal about him? Apart from the fact that every circus needs a clown.'

'You're looking Titch, but you're not seeing. He's not shaking hands, he's handing them something, and my guess is that it's little plastic packets of dope. He's the club dealer, that clown of yours.' Titch was just about to take a sip of his watered-down beer when he looked up and scrutinised the man waltzing around, shaking hands and laughing and joking with groups of people.

'Fuck! You're right. I can't believe I never spotted that. That clown is a dealer and he's doing it right under my nose. Do you know him?'

'No, not really. I think he's small time. But he could be just the lead you're looking for. If he's dealing, he's getting it from somewhere, isn't he? Maybe we should make ourselves acquainted with him.'

Making their way to the bar, they purposely stood near the guy and his group of friends. Holding his pint of beer in his hand, Titch purposely tripped and spilt some over them. 'Hey, watch out mate!' the guy shouted, while rubbing himself down, although it was only a little drop on his combat jacket.

'Oh, sorry mate. Someone nudged me. It's manic in here, isn't it? I can barely see. Those strobe lights distort things, don't they?' Titch smiled. 'Let me buy you a drink, in a way of an apology.' A smarmy grin crossed his face, and he winked at Mike.

'No worries, mate, happens all the time in here. But the drink will pay for the dry cleaning.' The guy laughed, and then looked at his group of friends, who joined in laughing.

'Hey barman, give us three whiskies over here please,'

shouted Titch. 'You look like a whisky man, and this beer is like dishwater.' He winked.

'Sure thing, erm what's your name again?' the kid asked tentatively. 'I haven't seen you in here before, have I?'

'My friends call me Titch, but that's another story. I've been coming here for a few weeks now. I was told this was the place to be if you wanted a little fun and action. It's a bit overpriced though, and to be fair, I feel a bit old. Here, take your drink.'

Titch was pleased now that he'd patrolled this place for a few weeks. He felt certain his story would be checked out. If this kid was dealing, he wouldn't be a fool. 'What's your name then?'

'Kev, just Kev. Everyone knows me here. Don't get in much these days, which is why I haven't seen you.' Taking his drink, Kev took a sip and then held up his glass to chink against Titch's. 'Cheers mate. Nice meeting you.'

'Drink up Kev! Mike here has ordered us another. Always nice to meet new friends.'

Kev grinned, full of bravado in front of his friends. 'For a moment, we thought you were coppers. So, what do you do?'

'We're travelling salesmen. We sell stationery.' Titch winked at Mike. 'Places like this just take the boredom away. And believe me, it's boring travelling up and down the motorway all the time and living in digs, eh Mike?'

'Well, let me and my friends give you the guided tour.' Kev laughed. As he was drinking his whisky, Titch put his hand to the bottom of the glass and gently raised it, so Kev took a bigger gulp than intended.

Like a gift from God, two young men walked up to Kev, and stood there aimlessly. 'Can I have a word, Kev?' It was blatant that they wanted to speak to Kev alone, and this intrigued Titch more than ever. This was what they had waited for; someone wanted whatever Kev was selling.

'Sorry folksies, business calls.' Titch and Mike watched Kev walk towards the toilets. A few minutes later he returned. 'Trouble?' Titch asked innocently.

'Nah, just a bit of business. I think I owe you two a drink. Don't want you to think I'm skipping my round.' Kev grinned.

'What business are you in, Kev? You seem like a really popular guy in here. Crikey, I don't see anyone wanting to speak to two stationery salesmen! Although, I could do with a little pick me up. Finished my last spliff this afternoon and I don't know anyone in this area.' Mike passed Kev another drink. By now he was getting a little tipsy.

Just like magic, Kev's mouth was running away with him. 'Maybe I know a man, who knows a man who can get you what you need. Spliff, you say. Cannabis?' Kev muttered. Although by now, his lips felt numb.

Ignoring Kev's swaying and the faraway look in his eyes, Titch carried on. 'I like a spliff, calms me down but my real passion is meth. Do you know a man who knows a man for that?'

Surprised at the request, Kev sobered up a little and frowned. 'I wouldn't have put you two down for that kind of stuff.'

'Why, just cos we look like old fuddy duddies? We weren't back in the day Kev mate. These young kids don't know what real pick-me-ups are.' Titch nudged Mike in the ribs and together they both laughed. 'Got you there, Kev. Never mind, we go home in a couple of days anyway. Got some good stuff coming our way.'

Stammering, and not wanting to look a fool, Kev blurted out, before his brain connected with his tongue, 'I can maybe help you both out, at a price. But how do I know you're not coppers?' Kev laughed. In front of his friends, who were listening in on the conversation, Kev wanted to save face. 'Anyway, the coppers get their cut from this place. They get the landlord to charge twenty quid to come in here, but a tenner is for them. They make a packet here. Just look at how crowded it is.' Picking up his drink, Kev turned his head to the overcrowded club, packed to the hilt.

'Well, if you could introduce us to someone who could meet our needs...' Titch moved forward and put three twenty-pound notes down the neck of Kev's T-shirt and winked at him. They both saw Kev's eyes light up at the money and instantly he snatched it from his neck and pushed it in his pocket. 'Meth, you say?' Seeing Mike and Titch nod, Kev cocked his head and walked towards the toilets.

The queue inside was nearly out of the door and it stank to high heaven of piss and vomit. The black walls were covered in graffiti of all colours. Squirming, Titch turned to Mike and shrugged. 'In for a penny,' he whispered in his ear. Two or three men were all urinating in the same urinal. It was hot and they could barely breathe. 'This one,' said Kev and pushed past the queue. At the end of the three cubicles, was one that had an 'out of order' sign on the door. Following him in, they saw a smashed toilet bowl, which was still slightly leaking. Titch looked down at his wet feet, and inwardly cursed. 'This is my office, Titch,' Kev boasted. 'No one can use this as you can see.'

The toilet cistern was very old fashioned and was high on the wall with a chain to flush it. Kev held on to the walls and unsteadily put his hand into the top of the cistern and pulled out a small, waterproof, polythene freezer bag. Jumping down from the broken toilet, Kev opened the bag. 'I think I might have what you're looking for. Let me just check my magic bag.' Kev grinned, full of intrigue and mystery. He pulled out a tiny plastic bag and waved it around in the air. 'Pure as driven snow this. Yours for fifty pounds.'

'Do we get to sample some before we buy? No offence, Kev, but we've been ripped off before.'

'I expected that. Go on, fill your boots lads. Dip in one little finger and taste it, you'll like it. Trust me.'

Titch looked at the packet, then, wetting his finger with his tongue, he dipped it into the powder and tasted it. Instantly, he coughed and shook his head. 'Jeez.' He coughed again. 'That stuff is strong! Fuck Mike, it's the real thing – taste it.' Kev stood there beaming, like the cat who had got the cream. He had obviously impressed these men, which meant more custom as far as he was concerned. Mike took out his wallet. 'We'll have two packets if you have it Kev mate,' and handed him one hundred pounds. Flattering Kev's ego, he grinned and took the packets Kev gave him. 'Nice doing business with you. You really are a man to know. I don't think I've ever known anything so pure as this.'

'Trust me, you won't find anything as pure as that, even if you walk to the ends of the earth. Sorted it myself,' Kev lied. 'I've got magic fingers.'

Surprised, Mike and Titch looked at each other and frowned. 'You make this?' they questioned.

'Maybe I do and maybe I don't.' Kev laughed. The stench of the place was making Titch want to vomit. He could hear other customers banging on the cubicle doors, shouting for them to hurry up. 'Do you live around here, Kev? Maybe next time we're in town we could pop and see you again.'

Kev reached inside his jacket pocket and took out a pen

and scribbled his address on the inside of a torn cigarette packet. 'You guys like that kind of thing, then I reckon you will love my digs. Be sure to pop round when you're in town again.' Kev was doing his best to talk business, even though his sight was slightly blurred, and his speech was slurring. His head throbbed and he could feel the sweat pouring down the sides of his face.

'You okay, Kev?' Titch asked as he took his address off him. 'We'll be seeing you real soon. But let's get one last drink to seal the deal.' Titch could see the spiked drinks were working their magic, although it had taken longer than usual on an old druggie like Kev. Swiftly, Titch pulled Mike's arm and walked quickly through the crowd, pushing them aside arrogantly.

Rooted to the spot, Kev watched them leave, but his feet felt like lead, and he couldn't move. He tried to shout out, but only a dribble of spit dripped down the side of his mouth. Overwhelmed by dizziness, he felt himself slump to the ground and didn't have the strength to stand up or shout out. Closing his eyes, he lay there on the wet floor on his back, unconscious.

Outside, Titch and Mike got into the car. 'That bastard idiot is cooking this pure meth. Can you believe it? He hasn't got two brain cells to rub together, and his mouth is a runaway train. What do you think, Mike?'

'Personally, I think he wrote the book of bullshit. He likes to make out he's the local Fagin, the man to go to, but he's nothing.' Waving the small packet of meth in the air, Mike continued. 'I want to know the man behind this little packet and when we find him, I'm going to fucking shoot him. What we have here, is Brownie points. We've gone to a lot of trouble trying to sort this out and now our bosses will definitely show their gratitude for this information. Now open the fucking windows. I want the smell of that place out of my nostrils, and I need a shower. Christ, it stank in there.'

Titch opened the car windows and lit a cigarette. Offering Mike the packet and his lighter, he nodded. 'I don't think I'll ever get rid of the stench. Come on, I'll drop you off.'

Later and alone, Titch made his way to Bernie's unit. It was a chance, but he thought she might still be in there. When he arrived, the shutter was a quarter up from the pavement and he could see a light on inside. 'Bernie, you in there?'

The shutter rattled and quaked as it rolled up. 'What are you doing here at this time of night?'

Titch grinned. 'Thought I'd grab an early bargain. So, why are you here, Bernie?'

'Been collecting, just putting the stuff away that I've taken from the homes. Christ, sometimes I feel like a rag and bone man. Look at some of this shit. Although these medals look okay to me, I think I'll get those priced up.'

Without saying a word, Titch waved the small packet in the air. 'Thank you for the tip off at that Blue Parrot. I found Father Christmas and look what he brought me.'

Frowning, Bernie took the packet out of his hands. 'What is it?'

'Meth, and it's bloody pure Bernie – believe me. You helped me and now I am helping you. You might want to pass it on. Either way, I've got two packets of the stuff. One is for my boss and the other I thought you might be interested in?'

Curiosity got the better of Bernie. 'Come in and sit down. I've got a flask of tea here. Do you want one?'

'Is this a date Bernie?' Titch laughed and nodded, while

following her as she weaved in and out of the piled-up stock she had acquired. 'You going to give it to your boss, Bernie?'

'I don't have a boss, laddie, and even if I did it's none of your business.'

'You've never said who you work for. You have your fingers in everything, and everyone respects you or fears you, which amounts to the same thing. But who do you collect for? Maybe you could find me a job. You know,' Titch prompted. 'Put a good word in for me.'

Pouring the tea from the flask into a mug, Bernie eyed him suspiciously. Inwardly she wanted to laugh. Idiots like him always wanted to muscle in on the action. 'Always after a free ride aren't you, Titch? Have you burnt your boats with all your other friends? That's if you ever had any friends.' Bernie wagged a warning finger at him. 'Now you know, I never divulge anything about my evil ways, and I don't intend starting now. So why don't you just tell me about that packet of meth and how you came by it.' She sighed. 'In fact, hang on a minute, Titch. You help yourselves to some biscuits, I just need the ladies. Except, there's no toilet here so I just piss at the kerbside.' Seeing the look of disgust on Titch's face, she grinned and walked outside.

Dropping her jeans, she squatted near Titch's car, but instead of relieving herself, she put a tracker she had picked up on the way out of the unit and put it under Titch's car. Musing to herself, Bernie felt that would do the trick. Titch would want to track this golden goose that had fallen into the palm of his hands and now she would know where that was, too. Walking back into the unit, she rubbed her hands together and picked up her mug of tea. 'That's better, now where were we?'

Bernie listened carefully to Titch's story. She already

knew some of it, but Titch had just filled in all the missing pieces. People were talking and it needed investigating, but Titch had taken the bait and done her investigating for her. Someone was selling pure meth, which meant the users didn't buy as much. One small ounce would last longer than usual because of its strength, unlike the stuff she pedalled which was always cut with something. A sly grin crossed her face, as she raised her mug to her lips. Stupidly, Titch showed Bernie the cigarette packet with Kev's address on it, which made her want to laugh. How stupid was that! She knew of the block of flats and that some small-time druggies used a flat there. That was all part of her job, keeping her ears to the ground. Yes, she had a boss, but a decent one who didn't mind Bernie running her business and who wanted no cut of her earnings. All her boss was interested in was her collection money and to see that things were running nicely and that was exactly what she got!

Looking down at the packet of meth Titch had handed her, Bernie realised this was just what she needed and so was that address. And Bernie knew she had to get there first.

19

HARSH REALITY

'I paid the money, Dante, just as you instructed. It was kind of weird though, because I felt like I was being watched and probably was. I found the key to the locker at King's Cross, just as you said, taped to the side of one of the bins outside. People must have thought I was scrambling around for old cigarette ends on my hands and knees on the floor. Then I found the locker which was more than big enough for my wheelie case and left it in there. I didn't know what else to do with the key, so I taped it back to where I found it. Do you think that was silly?'

'Yes, but no doubt the minute you left the station whoever was watching you would have emptied the locker anyway. Don't worry about it, Deana. We've paid our dues and now I want the deeds.' Picking up his mobile, they both watched as Dante typed, 'Deeds,' and sent the text to John.

Dante's phone buzzed and with bated breath, Deana waited while he opened the message.

'In the post along with land registry.'

Their hearts pounding in their chests, they stared at each

other. Deana was the first to speak. 'Is that it? Have we bought the pub?'

'It looks like it, although I will feel better when we have the deeds. How do we know he hasn't ripped us off? But I guess we'll find out soon enough. Come on, Mum wants us to help her put up the Christmas decorations. She's already taking Christmas bookings and sorting Christmas menus.'

'Yeah, I know. You haven't mentioned your trip to Amsterdam with the boys lately.'

'It's more likely going to be New Year time rather than Christmas. Everywhere has been booked up for months and Luke's carer, the one that's going to look after his mum, prefers to have Christmas at home. So we're looking at that. And no, before you ask, you're still not invited.'

'I know, I was only asking. What about your birthday, have you got any plans? Mum's asked me to find out what you want.'

'I presume we'll have a family party, much the same as yours and I will have my lad's party in the New Year. As for presents, nothing major, although I would like a smart watch. But that's going to be pricey, so I could always buy my own.'

As Deana turned into the road near home, she smiled. 'Come on, Dante. You can't say that. Mum wants to get you a present from her and Dad. She wants to make us equal. She gave me money towards my party and a new car, so I'll need to give her an idea of something she can buy you.' Raising an eyebrow, Deana turned to him.

'Okay, well I'd also like a Kindle. So, there you are. Give her those hints. I wish I could ride my motorbike properly, but at least I can now apply for a licence.'

'I can tell Mum that as well, that you want a licence for a motorbike. Anyway, you think you've got it bad, I'm still driving around in shipwreck, when I have my pink sports car just waiting for me. I hate all this cloak and dagger still! Although this week I'm going delivering in it. That will be my trademark – Lady Penelope!'

'We're back, Mum!' Deana shouted as they got in. As usual, Maggie was behind the bar serving. For a moment, Deana saw her through different eyes. Suddenly she felt sorry for her mum. All she ever did was work her fingers to the bone and bide her time until their dad came home. She rarely sat down. Deana presumed that was because that gave her time to think and dwell on things and so she kept herself busy.

'Where's Dante? Is he with you? You've been gone ages.'

'He's gone upstairs. I just wanted you to know, our little outing gave me time to suss him out for his birthday and I've got a couple of ideas for you. That's why I've been a while. He's still talking about going to Amsterdam with Luke, but not until the New Year now so maybe you could pay for him to go?'

'Thanks, Deana love. He just shrugs when I ask him and says he doesn't mind. Of course, we'll have another party with our friends and he can invite Luke and George and well, whoever.' Maggie laughed and hugged Deana. 'Thank you, love. Are you working tonight? I presume the supermarket will be busy getting near Christmas.'

'I'm not working tonight, I thought we could all do the Christmas tree for the pub, although I thought you would get a real one, not one of those plastic things.'

'Apparently due to health and safety, it has to be fire-proof or something, so a real one isn't what's called for. Although I don't know where I stand with any of it. I'm sick of surveyors walking around the place and men from the brewery calling in. I still don't know who the new owner is. The solicitor won't say but he has given me a watertight contract that the job is mine for as long as I want. Although, I have to see that the insurances and bills are all paid. The buyer wants nothing else, but their profits. I have a business bank account number and that is what I pay the profits into once everything else is paid. Anything else I need, I go through the solicitor. I did ask if everything was legal and above board and apparently it is. It was nice though, the brewery said they would be sorry I wouldn't be working for them any more. I thought that was sweet, it means I've done a good job. I wish your dad had been here to hear it.' Maggie's eyes glistened, and a tear nestled on her lashes. Sniffing, she brushed it away. 'Don't mind me, it's that time of year.'

'Dad will be home soon, Mum. Months have already whizzed by. We've just got to keep positive.'

Frowning, Maggie bit her bottom lip. 'Deana, do you think I'm doing the right thing staying here? Do you think I should leave and take another pub with the brewery? Why would the new owner want to be anonymous? I've spoken to your father about it and he says it's my choice. But we're settled here and I really don't want to leave, but I don't understand it.'

A feeling of dread overwhelmed Deana. She couldn't believe that after everything they'd been through, Maggie would consider moving again. She felt like telling her mum the truth, but now wasn't the time. 'You stay put, Mum. If it's a watertight contract then it's all above board. And if you don't like it, you said yourself the brewery like you and would employ you again at the drop of a hat.'

'I never thought of it like that. Nothing ventured nothing

gained, eh? Thanks Deana. You're getting quite a wise old head on those young shoulders of yours.'

'Stay put, Mum. This anonymous person will make themselves known soon and the brewery wouldn't sell out to a crook. Just carry on as you have been. You said yourself, you're doing a good job. What difference does it make if it's the brewery or a rival brewery.' Deana purposely dropped the hint that it could be another brewery to make Maggie feel better. Suddenly, Maggie's face lit up. 'Crikey, I never thought of that. Yeah, it could be another brewery who doesn't want to be known to this brewery yet. Deana, you're a genius.'

Deana smiled and breathed a sigh of relief.

* * *

'Silva!' the warder shouted. 'You're working in the kitchens today. They have a delivery coming and they are rushed off their feet. Hop to it now.'

Surprised, Alex did as he was told and walked to the kitchen area. Working in the kitchens was a much sought after job and only long-term prisoners with a good record got assigned them.

'It looks like I'm working with you today.' Alex stood behind the kitchen serving area near the doorway. The chef, another inmate, was already stirring an enormous pot of liquid. 'You're on potatoes and believe me there's loads of them. But you can make yourself a cup of tea while you work. I'm Alfred – Alfie – and this is my kingdom.' He laughed, waving his wooden spoon in the air. 'And today, we're having a casserole. Pass me those big tins of meat in gravy.'

Looking around, Alex spotted some large tins with yellow

labels on. The label said simply, 'stewing meat'. 'What meat is it?' Alex asked.

'Dunno, I just presume it's edible. Go on, fill that kettle, I'm parched.' He laughed. Alex reached for the tin opener and then the kettle. As Alex made a drink and the other kitchen assistants came in, he began to enjoy his morning sharing light-hearted banter with the others. Suddenly he heard a loud horn from outside the fire exit doors. 'That'll be the delivery,' Alfred shouted. 'Don't worry, we just do the carrying. The warders will be here in a minute and they check the boxes against the order.'

No sooner had he spoken, the doors flung open, and two warders came in. Alex instantly recognised one of them as Jonesy's friend. Alex didn't like him. He hadn't done anything to Alex, but it was a gut instinct.

Alex and the other assistants were given their orders to stand outside and form a chain for the many boxes they were to unload from the food delivery van. Puffing and panting after two hours, they all made their way back into the kitchen. 'Get me some flour out of the pantry over there will you Alex,' Alfred shouted. Finding his way into the pantry, Alex noticed two cardboard boxes. He remembered unloading them, but now noticed they each had one black circular dot in the corner. Finding the flour bucket, Alex took it out to Alfred. 'Here you go. By the way, there's two boxes in the pantry. It looks like they haven't been checked off as they're not with the others.'

Alfred shook his head slowly. 'What boxes, Alex? I don't know what you mean.' Quickly he cast a furtive glance to the left and following his lead, Alex noticed the warder, Jonesy's friend, walk towards them. 'What boxes are you talking about Silva?'

Seeing Alfred's warning stare, Alex stammered, while trying to think. 'I just wondered if there were any more to bring in? It's my first time in here, so I don't know the routine.'

'No, that's the lot. We were only expecting twenty boxes today and that's what we've got. Twenty boxes!' the warder emphasised. 'Let's hope it's not your last day in the kitchen, Silva.' And with that the warder walked out. Alex looked at Alfred. 'Not my business and definitely not yours if you want to carry on working here.' Alfred winked and carried on, checking the food and what the other assistants were doing.

The rest of the morning passed in a haze, and it was nearly lunchtime. Alfred went out the front where the serving counter was and put out the many dishes, mainly compiled of mashed potatoes, carrots and stewed meat in gravy with many more frozen vegetables thrown in. Alex had stirred the rice pudding so much it had become lumpy. It reminded him of school dinners.

While everyone was busy out the front, Alex walked back into the pantry. Slowly, he peeled a little bit of the tape from the end of the box and peered inside. Sliding his fingers in, it confirmed his suspicions. This was how Jonesy had his drugs brought in. The warder was his outside man and obviously on a generous cut of the earnings for all his hard work. Sliding his hand out, Alex saw that there were plastic bags containing all kinds of pills and potions. Carefully, without being seen, he stuck the tape back over the box and walked out to the front where Alfred was setting up.

Once the hustle and bustle of lunch was over, Alex was bushed. It had been a mad dash of running back and forth with pans. After they had finished, the kitchen staff all sat around a table in the kitchen area to eat their own lunch.

Impulsively, Alex walked past the pantry and noticed the two boxes had miraculously disappeared while they had all been rushed off their feet.

Once everything was put away and the kitchen cleaned, Alfred told them all to go back to their cells for a break before it all started again for the evening meal.

'Do you want me to come back, Alfred?' Alex asked tentatively. He had enjoyed his morning, even though it had been hectic. The time had passed quickly.

'Sure do Alex. Smithy, the one you're replacing, left yesterday which means we're short-handed. You've worked hard and given no trouble. Not even with the deliveries,' Alfred added as a cautionary warning.

'See you later then. I could do with a lie down.'

Pleased with himself, Alex walked back to his cell. Fiddler was lying on his bunk as normal, reading the newspaper. 'You're a cushy bastard, Silva. Getting a job in the kitchens. Make sure I get extra portions. After all, we're mates.' He laughed and carried on reading.

'They just needed an extra pair of hands because their old kitchen assistant has left.' These days, knowing how friendly Fiddler was with Jonesy, Alex kept his conversation to a minimum. He didn't want anything passing on which may make him vulnerable or could be used against him.

Deana loved driving around in her pink car making deliveries. She carried on the pretence of not speaking English, even though she could hear the people she delivered to mocking her car and laughing at her. She didn't care; she loved it. It was much more up to her own standards than old shipwreck, which had broken down again while she was on the way to the wholesalers for Maggie. Mark had fixed it, which meant there was no hope of it ever working properly again.

Dante was doing his rounds on his motorbike, and en route he needed to pop into Kev's place and pick up some more ingredients. This weekend he was staying at Luke's house to do some more cooking. Luke had said they needed to double up because Christmas was a busy time when people partied and made merry, and they always wanted something to give the party a bit of a kick.

After a long night, Dante headed over to Kev's but was greeted by an eerie silence. There was no music playing and the door to Kev's flat was slightly ajar. Pushing it open, Dante saw that the usual opium den he was used to seemed bare. He walked in stealthily, his heart pounding in his chest, and his throat dry. Looking around the entrance of the flat, he could see things had been thrown around and there were broken cabinets on the floor. He knew it wasn't the tidiest of places but this looked like it had been burgled. But no one would burgle Kev's flat, would they? It was known for what it was and apart from the drugs there was nothing worth taking. Not even a television. From the bedroom, Dante could hear men's voices and banging and crashing. Without thinking, Dante took out his gun. He always carried it on his deliveries, especially when he was alone. He hadn't had to use it, thank goodness but it was back-up if he ever did.

His gun gave him the courage he needed to walk in further. Now, he could hear screams and he recognised Kev's voice, howling in pain and begging for mercy. Instantly, Dante made haste and saw Kev. His face was covered in so much blood Dante hardly recognised him. Even his once green combat jacket had now turned crimson as he lay on the floorboards in the empty room. A tall man Dante didn't recognise turned around, his fist covered in blood. 'Get the fuck out, you druggie. You haven't seen this.'

Stunned and rooted to the spot, Dante looked at Kev's limp body. His arm hung at an awkward angle and Dante could see it was broken. Swallowing hard and moistening his lips, Dante summoned up all of his courage. His first instinct was to do as he was told and run, but Kev had been good to him and how could he explain to Luke that he had left his brother at the mercy of these men who were most certainly intent on killing him.

'These your fucking cooking hands, Kev? Well, let's see what you can cook with no hands.' The other man shouted. Dante hadn't noticed at first, but now he saw the man pull the chord of a chainsaw to start it up. Shocked, Dante realised these men, whoever they were, were going to cut off Kev's hands! Without thinking, Dante raised his gun and fired at the man with the chainsaw and then quickly turned and shot the larger man who had been punching Kev. Dante was a pot shot and had shot both of them in the head. Both men slumped to the ground and Dante made his way over to Kev. Putting his head to his chest, he could see that Kev was still breathing. Though only just. Picking up the edge of Kev's jacket, Dante wiped the blood from Kev's eyes. 'Kev! Kev, can you hear me?' Dante shouted. He looked around the room and seeing the two dead men on the floor, Dante started to shake. The realisation that he'd murdered two men suddenly hit him, even if it had been in self-defence, or rather saving Kev. He didn't know what he was going to do with two dead bodies. How could he call an ambulance for Kev with these two in the room? He took out his mobile and called Luke.

'Luke, get over to Kev's place now. I think he's dying.' Dante's voice was shaking as he shouted down the phone.

'What's wrong, Dante? Who else is there?' Luke replied in a panicked voice.

'No one! The place is empty, but two men were here, and they've beaten Kev up. He's covered in blood. Just get here!' Dante felt tears rolling down his face. His body was shaking so badly he couldn't hold his mobile. He wished to God that his father was here and not in prison. He would know what to do. Picking up his mobile again, he called Deana and shouted at her to come to Kev's, too.

Hearing the panic in his voice, Deana shouted back, 'Stay on the phone, Dante. Don't end the call. Keep talking to me.'

Dante sat in the blood-stained room with his back to the wall looking at Kev's chest rise and fall. The eerie silence in the usually noisy room frightened him and he felt cold. Eventually, Luke came running through the door spotting Kev first, then the two men on the floor. Dante was sat on the floor with the gun at his side.

Kneeling down to Dante's level, Luke surveyed the murder scene. 'What the fuck have you done, Dante?' Luke shouted and shook him to wake him from his dazed state. Leaning over to Kev, Luke shook him too. 'Kev, are you alive? Give me a sign, you prick, that are you alive.' Hearing a murmur, Luke felt satisfied and turned back to Dante who reached out and hugged Luke and burst into tears. Spit dribbled from his mouth as he blurted out what had happened. Hearing the door burst open, Luke swiftly turned, expecting it to be some druggie coming for a parcel. Instead, he let out a sigh of relief when he saw Deana.

'Thank God it's you. Look at this lot. I need to get Kev an ambulance. The police will come and we have two dead bodies and Dante's in shock. We need to act fast; Kev's breathing is laboured.'

For a moment Deana stood rooted to the spot. 'Do you know these men, Luke? Have you seen them before?'

Luke shook his head. 'No. But then I don't know everyone who comes here.'

'They've raided this place. Look at the state of it. Stuff is scattered everywhere. Whoever they were, they were looking for something, Luke. And I think I can guess what. Don't you?' Deana remembered John's warning about turf wars. 'Dante! You're the brains. Get a grip, you. You started this, now finish it. Stand up!' Although Dante's legs felt like jelly, he did as he was told.

'Open the French windows. We'll throw them out of the window.'

Amazed, Luke looked at each of them in turn. 'With two fucking bullet holes in their heads? they haven't tripped over the balcony, have they? That's ridiculous.'

'Look! Do you have a better idea? Then we leave and call an ambulance. We can't be here, Luke. We can't be,' Deana pleaded. 'We have to get out of here and fast.'

They all stood rooted to the spot, when the door opened and a woman walked in. 'My, my, what a party gathering. Three dead bodies and three live ones.'

'Who are you? What do you want?' Luke shouted. Looking at Deana, he let out a deep sigh. The game was over. They had been caught in the act. Luke stood with his back to the wall and letting out a huge sigh, slowly slid to the ground and sat on his bottom. 'Get it over with. Call the police. I didn't want to spend Christmas at home anyway,' he muttered and put his head in his hands.

'Don't look so glum, laddie. I ain't the coppers.' Walking over to Kev, she looked down at him. 'He's still alive, yeah?'

Deana nodded. 'Yes, he's breathing. Those two broke in and raided the place. Dante' – she pointed to her brother who still sat shaking – 'came looking for Kev. That's Kev.' Deana pointed to the bleeding pulp that was once Kev. 'He's Luke's brother.' She pointed her finger at Luke, and sniffing, she wiped her nose with the back of her sleeve.

Turning towards Deana, Bernie looked her up and down. 'Who shot them – you, wee lassie?'

'No, I've just got here. Dante found Kev beaten to a pulp and shot them both. Look, they have a chainsaw. Do you realise what they were going to do?' Deana stressed.

'Well, as there are no trees in here, I think I can hazard a guess.' Bernie turned towards Dante and slapped him across the face. 'Stop snivelling, Dante. If you're old enough to carry a gun, you're old enough to man up and face the consequences.' Instantly, Dante wiped the snot from his nose and tears with his sleeve, while Bernie grimaced.

'Don't they have handkerchiefs in your house? Christ, at least I buy kitchen roll. Anyway, back to business. What do you plan on doing with these dead bodies, Dante?'

'Throwing them out of the window. We need to call an ambulance for Kev. We need to save him. They were going to cut his hands off!'

'Or possibly his balls laddie.' Bernie chuckled. 'Mm, not bad, especially around here. People expect that kind of thing.' Bernie looked around at the bare floorboards. 'Do you have any plastic sheeting?'

For once, Luke felt it was his turn to speak. 'I have in the boot of my car. Why?'

'Go and get it,' Bernie ordered and Luke ran from the room, half glad to be out of there.

'Do you think Luke will come back?' Bernie asked Deana and Dante. 'Or do you think he'll run for the hills and leave you to face the music?' Seeing them both nod, she felt satisfied. Bernie stood with her arms folded. 'Tell me what happened, Dante. Just the outline, I don't want your life story.'

Dante began telling her and before they knew it, Luke ran back into the room with his tarpaulin sheet. 'This is all I have.'

Bernie nodded. 'Roll Kev on it and carry him out of here. The sheeting will stop the blood smearing all over the floor. We don't want to leave a trail, do we?'

Puzzled, Deana frowned at her. 'You're going to help us?' Seeing Bernie nod, Deana looked at Luke. 'Well, come on then. Let's get on with it.'

Luke laid the sheeting on the floor and between them they rolled an unconscious Kev on to it. Then they each took a corner and slowly carried Kev out of the room and into the corridor while Bernie fired instructions at them.

'Put him in the lift. You three go with him. When you get to the bottom, leave him in the foyer and fuck off! Where do I find you, Dante? Who are you?' Bernie had done her homework and knew exactly who these three kids were. She had even visited the pub they lived at and had a drink, passing the time of day with their mother at the bar. It confirmed her suspicions that she wasn't aware of her kids' business dealings. Now, she thought to herself, were they going to lie their heads off to get out of this scrape? Because as far as she was concerned, Titch had got what he deserved. Looking around the room, she could see that it had been ransacked. He knew what he was looking for and he knew how much it was worth. Greedy bastard!

'I'm Dante Silva. This is my sister, Deana.'

Bernie was surprised at their honesty, and admired them both, considering they were facing murder charges. 'Silva? I know that name.' Drumming her finger on her chin, pondering, Bernie was trying to recall the name when Deana put her out of her turmoil. 'Our father is Alex Silva. You've probably seen him on the news lately.'

'The mafia man?'

Deana nodded and hung her head. 'Yes, that's him.'

'So, that's how you know about guns and possibly how you got one. Am I right?'

'Yes.' Dante nodded. 'Dad taught us how to defend ourselves. People didn't want to just kill him, they wanted to wipe out our entire family...'

'Well, you two certainly have balls, I grant you that.'

Bernie looked at Kev's lifeless body and even she realised time wasn't on their side. Titch and his mate had done a real makeover job on the poor bastard. 'Right, do as you're told and get out of here. I'll be in touch.' Wagging a finger at the three of them, she narrowed her eyes. 'You three owe me favours and big ones! Don't ever forget that.'

'Who are you?' Deana asked. 'Are we allowed to know? And why are you helping us? You don't know us.' Deana looked at the obese Scottish woman, and suddenly her suspicions rose. This was an odd situation, and yet this woman was very calm about it all. It all felt a bit random that some strange woman had calmly walked into the flat and taken over the situation.

'Your fucking fairy godmother, lassie. Now do you want me to help or not? Makes no difference to me. Don't forget, I haven't shot anyone!' Bernie emphasised. 'In fact, I could easily call the police and tell them I dropped by for a bit of weed and found three kids over two dead bodies with a gun matching those bullets still in those losers' heads upstairs. Now scoot!' Bernie barked. 'Or I might just change my mind and leave you to it to throw these two out of the window.' Bernie laughed. 'Now, empty Kev's pockets for anything that might incriminate you or him. And while you're at it, Luke, is it? I want your mobile number. I know who Bonnie and Clyde are here, but I don't know you.' Luke read out his number while Bernie typed it in. Then she rang the number and waited for Luke's phone to ring. 'Just checking, laddie.'

Luke meticulously went through Kev's pockets, as the sticky red blood covered his hands. Then Luke, Dante and Deana carried Kev into the foyer and checking no one was around, they ran outside and hid.

'Deana, call an ambulance and the police and tell them there is a body in the foyer of the flats. Go on! Tell them you were out walking and have spotted a body, and you think he's bleeding to death. Then you can come back to my place and get showered. We need to get our acts together.'

Doing as she was told, Deana made the call. Once done, they took one last look through the glass doors of the entrance to the flats at Kev lying on the floor and each went to their vehicles to meet at Luke's house.

20

A SPIRAL STAIRCASE

In the early hours of the morning, Luke stood at the front door of his house while two policemen politely asked him to confirm his name and asked if they could come in. With a puzzled look, Luke had given them the information they required, while asking them to go into the kitchen where they could speak in private, explaining about his mum. Doing his best to hold his nerve, and with his heart in his mouth, he listened as the police told him about Kev and how he had been found badly beaten.

Feigning shock, Luke had asked where Kev was and if he was still alive. The police had looked at each other before replying. 'Well, let's say it's been close. But the doctors are doing everything they can. He doesn't live here with you, does he?' one policeman asked, although Luke felt they already knew the answer, so there was no point in lying.

'No, he doesn't. He has his own flat, and as you probably already know, some dodgy friends, but all I'm concerned about is my brother. I can't come to the hospital now; I don't want to wake Mum and worry her. But I'll call her carer who can maybe come and sit with her for a while.'

Understanding the situation, the police nodded. 'There's no need for that. We can get another police officer to sit with your mum. She'll be well cared for. We do need you to confirm your brother's identity. He's a bit of a mess, but if the worst comes to the worst we'll need a formal identification.'

Luke's heart sank and he felt sick. He realised that they were expecting Kev to die. Without realising it, his hands were shaking as he broke out in a cold sweat, whether it be the aftershock of the evening's events or this latest news. Kev was his brother, and he had left him at the flats bleeding to death, while he had gone home and waited for this visit from the police. As he'd waited, his mind had raced with what had happened as he'd paced the floors. The house had been in darkness, and the silence had been deafening. Only the clock ticking on the wall had kept him from collapsing out of complete exhaustion. He had cried and fretted while wondering about Kev and how he would tell his mum about what had happened to him. What this would do to her worried him more. She was in no state to face a shock like this.

Now, hearing the police say they feared the worst for Kev, consumed Luke with guilt. Bile rose in his throat and he ran to the sink and vomited.

The policeman stood beside him and put his hand on his shoulder comfortingly. 'It's all right Luke, let it out. We know this must have come as a bit of a shock.' The other police officer, wanting to make himself useful, stood up and put the kettle on. 'I'll make you a cup of tea with plenty of sugar. That's good for shock. I've radioed through to the station and they are sending another officer to look after your mum. I know it's early, but do you want to let your mum know about the situation? It might be easier coming from you, than our officers.'

'No, it's way too early to wake Mum. I'll explain the situation to her when I get back. I just want to get to the hospital now.'

The officers nodded and when the support officer arrived, Luke and the other officers made their way solemnly to see Kev. Luke just hoped he wasn't too late.

* * *

Walking into the side room at the hospital, Luke saw a policeman stood at the door and gave a puzzled look at the officers escorting him.

'We need someone here in case he wakes up. We need to know what happened and if he knows who did this.'

Horrified, Luke looked at the machines surrounding Kev's bedside. Lights flashed and beeping noises filled the room. Walking forward, he could see that Kev's battered face had been cleaned of the blood, but he was still hardly recognisable. A huge bandage was wrapped around his head. Tubes were down his throat and he had an oxygen mask on.

'Kev, it's me Luke.' Tears rolled unexpectedly down his cheeks as he reached out and held his brother's limp hand. Luke's legs shook and he could barely stand. Noticing this, the policeman pulled up a chair and told him to sit down. 'It's okay Luke, take your time. Do you want us to leave you for a minute? We'll get the doctor and he can fill you in more on the situation.'

Luke nodded and waited while they left the room. Luke leaned closer to Kev's ear. 'I'm sorry I left you Kev. I really am.

We didn't know what to do,' he whispered. 'Please Kev, wake up. For God's sake, wake up!' he pleaded while his own tears spilt on to Kev's face. Suddenly the door opened and the doctor walked in with a clipboard containing pages and pages of notes.

'Well Luke, it would be easier for me to tell you what bones aren't broken. Whoever did this meant business. There has been some bleeding on the brain and we won't know any more until the swelling goes down. He's had scans and x-rays and we also took him for an emergency operation to relieve the pressure on his brain. We will know more in the next twenty-four hours.' Luke listened as the doctor outlined what Kev had been through and how, although he was still alive, his future was still hanging in the balance. Thanking him, Luke watched him walk to the door, then stopped him. 'Excuse me, doctor, will he live? You haven't said anything about that.'

'As I said, we will know more in the next twenty-four hours. If he survives the night, then there's a good chance.'

Standing in the room looking at Kev, Luke had never felt so alone in his life. He wished he could call Deana and Dante. He would have valued their friendship on a night such as this. But he knew he couldn't. For the time being, they all had to stay away from each other without contact. That was what they had agreed, even though Deana had argued against it. She had wanted to stay with Luke and neither of them had wanted Luke to be left alone tonight, but they understood what they needed to do.

Luke turned now and saw the policeman standing outside the glass door. A thought about the flat occurred to him; he wondered if the police had been there, or what the state of it was.

'I should go back to his flat and get him some things. He might need them if and when he wakes up. Yes,' Luke repeated, 'when he wakes up.' Surprisingly enough, the police didn't say he couldn't go to Kev's flat. Surely, if they had been inside it and seen it, they would have stopped him and told him it was currently a crime scene? But they merely dropped Luke off and offered to wait for him, which Luke declined. Thanking them for their kindness, Luke watched them leave and then hastily ran up to Kev's flat. Nervously opening the door, unsure of what he would find, Luke stood rooted to the spot as he looked at the room in front of him. The flat was spotless! Unlike Kev's usually empty flat with odd deck chairs scattered around, it now had an old three-piece suite in the lounge area and a coffee table in the middle. Scattered around were the usual bits of furniture that most flats had, but definitely not Kev's. Curiously, Luke stepped outside into the corridor and looked at the number on the door again. Seeing it was definitely the right address, he walked back in amazed, half dazed and weary, and looked around. He couldn't believe his eyes. It looked scruffy, like the usual bachelor flat, but it was a far cry from how it used to look.

Tentatively, he walked into the bedroom. His mouth felt dry, and he was afraid to turn the handle. Keeping his eyes tightly shut, he turned the handle and pushed the door wide open. Luke's jaw almost dropped. There was no sign of the previous evening's events. The dead men had gone and the place had been cleaned to within an inch of its life. Luke felt so tired, he thought he was dreaming. Rubbing his face with his hands, he walked around the bedroom and looked around. Suddenly, his mobile burst into life. Not recognising the number, he presumed it was the police and answered it.

'I will be sending you the bill for the furniture, laddie. How is he?'

Luke instantly recognised the woman's voice from last night. 'He's in a bad way, but we won't know anything for twenty-four hours. How did you do all of this?' Luke asked, while still looking around the room amazed.

'The ambulance came pretty quickly and once they'd left, I waved my magic wand. Not a word now. Trust is on both sides here. How are the other two?'

Luke looked out of the bedroom window but couldn't see much as he squinted to look at the car park below. 'They're as well as can be expected. It must be torture for them. They had to go home to their mum and brazen it out. They must be wondering what's going on, but we've agreed to stay away from each other and not make contact that could cause suspicion.'

'They are Silvas, and I think they have had enough police scrutiny so that's maybe for the best. But remember, your brother was beaten up in his own flat by two strangers and would probably be dead anyway now. You and those two had nothing to do with that. You didn't harm Kev – those two men did. That young Silva did what anyone would have if they had been in possession of a gun.'

'You're right, but can I ask – what do you get out of all of this? Why were you here? What made you turn up out of the blue? Sorry, it's just that I've had all night to think about this and I don't understand.'

'You overthink things, laddie. Just accept a good Samaritan when it passes you by. Call it three hundred for the furniture. I'll keep in touch.'

Breaking out in a cold sweat, Luke stared blankly at his mobile and looked around the room. It was unrecognisable.

But he also knew there was no such thing as a free lunch, and as much as this woman had offered a helping hand, his gut instinct told him that he would pay more than three hundred pounds for it!

* * *

'Are you awake Deana?' Quietly creeping into Deana's bedroom without being overheard, Dante sat on the edge of her bed.

'Of course I am,' she whispered. Deana was lying on her side, facing the door, her head under her hands in the darkness.

'I can't stop thinking about Luke and what's happening. Do you think Kev is still alive? Oh, Deana.' Dante's voice was choked with emotion. 'What have I done? For Christ's sake, what have I done?' Dante buried his head in his hands and stifled a sob.

'Shush, Mum will hear you. I think we should text Luke, at least to let him know we're thinking about him. It's the not knowing that's torturing me. And that woman... I wonder if she's a friend of Dad's or John's. That could be the answer.'

'That woman can't be a friend of Dad's. She didn't know who we were, so that's a dead-end lead. I don't know about John, but I'm a bit hesitant about contacting him again, especially after last time. Do you think I'm going to prison, Deana?' Frightened, Dante reached for her hand and squeezed it tightly.

'Come here and have a hug.' Deana pulled him on to the bed and laid him beside her. They looked like two spoons in a drawer. 'You're not going anywhere little brother. If that was the case, I'm sure the police would have been hammering the door down by now. Luke won't say anything; after all, you were fighting for his brother. You tried protecting him, even if it did go pear-shaped. Try and get some sleep.' Deana stroked his hair soothingly like he was a small child.

She didn't know what fate had in store for them, and she inwardly cursed herself for encouraging Dante to carry a gun for protection. Dad always used to say: 'Don't carry a gun unless you intend using it.' Well, she sighed, the worst had happened now. A tear rolled down her cheek; how she wished and prayed that their dad was here now. She needed him – they both needed him. Then she thought about Luke and the worry he must be going through. He was alone, when at least she had Dante and they could talk about what had happened. *Fuck it*, she thought to herself, *I'm going to text him*. Reaching under her pillow, she felt for her mobile and without disturbing Dante, who by now, under her soothing, comforting words seemed to be sleeping.

> Are you okay, Luke?

She felt this wasn't too intrusive, but showed she cared. Instantly, her mobile buzzed, which surprised her.

> Not sure really. Feel a bit numb. Police have been and took me to the hospital where Kev is. In a bad way. Even the doctors don't know if he's going to pull through. I'm at his flat now. I can't explain it. You really need to see it for yourself. I will tell you more when I see you. All is okay though. Thanks for texting.

Puzzled, Deana read the message again. Why did he think she should see Kev's flat? Looking at the back of

Dante's head, she couldn't help but think how small he looked, almost childlike. He was her little brother, and she intended to look after him no matter what. Her mind wandered back to Kev. It sounded as though he was in a bad way. A part of her wanted to tell Maggie about what had happened; after all, their mum wasn't naïve about guns and killing. Christ, Deana thought to herself, she had lived with their dad for years and been surrounded by his dodgy friends. But lying on her back and looking at the ceiling, she thought better of it – what good would it do now? No, Deana decided to herself, it was better to say nothing for the time being. Slowly hearing the sound of Dante's breathing, she felt her own eyelids drooping and closed her eyes.

* * *

'Visitor for you, Silva. Governor wants you. Come on man, be quick about it!' the warder shouted. Raising his eyebrows, Alex looked at Alfred who had stopped his stirring of another culinary delight and turned to see what the warder wanted. Alex took off his white kitchen apron and hat and cast them aside on the work top. Intrigued, he followed the warder, wondering what this was all about. His mind raced as he wondered what kind of trouble he was in. He was enjoying his time working in the kitchens, but a sick feeling in the pit of his stomach made him fear it was all about to come crashing down.

'Who is it? My wife?' he asked as he was more or less frog marched out of the kitchen. A few prisoners looked up, surprised, at Alex being escorted by a warder, but most bowed their heads and ignored it.

'Well, I believe it's a woman, but that's all I know. The

sooner we get there, the sooner you will find out who it is, won't you?'

'Oh God, I hope my kids are okay. That would be a reason for the governor wanting to see me, wouldn't it?' Alex did his best to question the warder, whom he felt knew more than he was letting on, but he said nothing and just led Alex towards the governor's office.

Standing outside the door, the warder knocked. After a few moments the door was opened slightly and the governor popped his head around the door. Looking up at him, Alex felt he looked nervous and pale. 'It's okay warden. I can take it from here. Come in Alex.' Waiting until he saw the warden walk away, the governor opened the door wider. 'Come in.' He beckoned swiftly.

Stepping inside, Alex looked around the room. Sat with his back to him, facing the governor's desk, was indeed a woman. But this was no ordinary woman. Alex spied the long, calf-length mink coat and the dark hair. It definitely wasn't Maggie, he thought to himself. His curiosity was getting the better of him. This was indeed a mystery, and he had no idea what it entailed.

Wearing large black sunglasses, the woman half turned. 'Thank you, governor. I won't take up too much of your time, you can leave us now,' she purred through her bright red lips. 'Come Alex, take a seat.' She smiled.

Nervously, Alex looked at the governor, who mopped his brow with his handkerchief, opened the door, and left the room.

Encouraged by the woman patting the wooden chair beside her with her long red fingernails and smiling, Alex stepped forward and did as he was told. His mouth felt suddenly dry, and he didn't know what to expect. 'I'm afraid you have the advantage. Who are you and what do you want?' he asked nervously.

'That's a lot of questions, Alex. Let me speak first. I've come about your children, and what little minxes they are.' She grinned. Alex opened his mouth to speak, but the woman held up her hand. 'Let me finish, please. Your children have had quite a party at a lot of people's expense, pedalling and making drugs to sell. They've also been undercutting other dealers' prices, which has caused a lot of bad feeling, as you can imagine. These bosses have their own turfs and as long as each keeps to their own there is peace on the streets. But I'm afraid they have lost patience, and these men now want war. In fact, they are already waging war against each other. People have been threatened and beaten up. Pubs have had shoot-outs, all because of your two kids.' The woman paused as her words sunk into Alex's brain. The blood had drained from his face, and his jaw almost touched his chest.

'My kids?' was all he could muster as a response.

'Exactly so. The other night, they really did reach their peak when your son shot two men dead and that is where I come in.'

Alex stood up and walked towards the barred window. 'Do you realise what you're saying? My kids don't peddle drugs!' he heard himself shout. It felt surreal, like an out of body experience.

The woman didn't flinch. Instead, she sat there grinning.

'I'm a parent, Alex, and I daresay I would feel the same as you do now if someone told me this.'

Narrowing his eyes, and gathering his thoughts, Alex spied her closely. 'Why are you telling me this? It's bollocks and you know it. So what do you want missus? Everyone knows who I am and why I am in here. I have no money, so if it's money you're looking for, I have nothing to satisfy your greed. And why are you in the governor's office? How come he's even left the room. Just who the fuck are you lady?'

The woman ignored Alex's outburst, almost as though she expected it. Opening the Chanel handbag on her knee, she undid the clasp and put her perfectly manicured hand inside. Taking out a see-through polythene bag, she waved it in the air. Peering closely, Alex saw that it was a gun. 'Nice little trinket this.' She smiled. 'And it just so happens to have your son's fingerprints all over it. He hasn't grown up enough yet to have your foresight, Alex. He abandoned the gun when he fled from the flat with his sister and their friend and left the murder weapon behind,' she drawled. Alex snatched the bag out of her hand and looked at the gun closely through the plastic. Instantly, he recognised it as one of his own. Panic rose within him.

'Where did you get this?' Alex heart was pounding in his chest, and he felt almost dizzy.

Letting out a deep sigh, the woman smiled again. 'I take it you recognise it. It's an assassin's gun, not the usual kind of thing you find in Tesco, and I take it it's yours.' Seeing him nod his head while not daring to take his eyes off the gun, she felt satisfied. 'Well, you need to sort this mess out before anyone else does and you know what that means.' The woman lowered her dark glasses to the edge of her nose and gave him a knowing look.

For an instant, their eyes met. Alex knew exactly what it meant – death. He couldn't believe that his own kids had been ripping off dealers and making their own stuff. He knew his kids and it sounded absurd. He couldn't quite take it in, but he also knew the drug-dealing game and that there were some very powerful men out there, who made a lot of money and vowed vengeance on anyone who trod on their toes. 'How much do my kids owe? Do you want the money back? I'm sure it can't be that much. I haven't been in here that long.'

'Ah, Alex, you see that's the thing. How do we, or they,' she corrected herself, 'know that you're not behind all of this? You have the perfect alibi in here, behind these walls. Is it you, Alex? Do you intend to be your own mafia boss? Do you intend to take back everything you've lost in the past?'

Alex could feel the hairs on his neck rising along with his temper. He'd played cat and mouse long enough. 'No, I have nothing to do with this so I will ask you again, why are you here and what do you want? Why haven't my kids already been murdered in cold blood?'

'Calm down, Alex. It must be that hot Portuguese blood of yours.' She smiled. 'Fortunately, the men they killed have no relevance to me. In fact, as far as I'm concerned, they got what they deserved. They were thieves and not very good ones. Personally, I just wanted to see your face. Only then would I know if you were behind this – the eyes are the windows to the soul, and I believe you had no idea about what's been going on, which is why I am glad I've come to give you the heads up. On my orders, a friend who works for me has cleared your kids' mess up and there is no trail back to them, apart from this gun, the DNA and one of their friends on a life support machine. But that's nothing to do with me, I assure you. I don't like upheaval, but now everyone is at odds with each other and that makes me uneasy. People start grassing their associates up and causing problems where there are none. So, what I need you to do is finish this war or when word gets out its your kids, rest assured someone will end it – and them – for you, Alex,' she warned, while pointing her finger at him.

Alex's eyes darted around the room helplessly as he tried to think. 'What the fuck can I do in here, lady?'

Standing up, the woman calmly put her chair under the table. 'You put yourself in here Alex. Now, get yourself out. As for what I want, that's simple – peace and quiet. I want to go about my business without wondering who is pointing a gun at my friends. All that calmed down until your Silva brood stuck their noses in. I believe in second chances, and I have given the Silva family a second chance. Now you owe me and not only will you clean up your own mess but you will also clean up mine as well. Either that, or this little plastic bag containing a gun will find its way to our friendly police department. Got it?'

Slowly, Alex shook his head. 'I can't go back to that old life again. Blackmail me all you want but leave my kids out of it. Kill me, it doesn't matter. Just leave them alone. They're stupid and have made mistakes. I will swap my life for theirs, if that's what you want. And I'll make sure you get whatever money they have stolen from you,' he pleaded.

'Alex love, we're not talking pennies, we're talking hundreds of thousands. And I don't want to kill you. A man like you is worth more to me alive. Think on what I've said. The clock is ticking and I'm sure I'm not the only person who is going to work out the trail back to your kids. Bye Alex.'

Stunned, Alex felt rooted to the spot as he watched her mink coat sway behind her as she left the room. He was flabbergasted. Hundreds of thousands? He couldn't comprehend it. His two kids ripping off seasoned drug dealers for hundreds of thousands. It seemed ridiculous. So finally his past had come to bite him on the arse and he was going to end up being dragged back into a world he thought and hoped he had left behind. The very thought of it made him feel sick.

The door opened and Alex looked up, expecting to see the woman again. Instead, it was the governor. 'Ah, Silva, yes. Thank you for coming. I hope you like your new job in the kitchens because if you do, we have decided that you can stay there if you wish.'

Alex stared at the governor, suddenly understanding that the man was covering his tracks. To everyone else, he had wanted to see Alex to let him know about his job assignment. But they both knew different and the governor neither acknowledged nor mentioned the female visitor.

Not knowing how to word his next sentence, Alex felt he should just blurt it out. His hands felt hot and sticky, and he could feel the sweat running down his back. 'Governor sir, that woman who was just here, who was she?'

Flashing a glance at him, the governor shook his head. 'Oh, you mean my secretary, Miss Dyson. Well, she works here of course. Now, off you go back to your cell.'

'Governor sir, I know this is a bit random, but how would I go about getting an early release? On what conditions would it be granted, if it ever was?' Alex stammered. He knew this was clutching at straws, but he was a desperate man.

'Family problems? That's usually a basis considering the length of your sentence, which is minimal. And of course, good behaviour and a recommendation from myself. Although, the remainder of your sentence would be suspended so should you do anything out of turn, you would come back to serve it.' Standing before him, the governor looked directly into his eyes, which unnerved Alex. 'Of course, Silva, if you had something to bargain with that might be of interest to myself, the home office would look favourably on my recommendation. So keep your eyes and ears open for something that might interest me. Off you go now, Silva, if you have nothing else to say.'

Hearing the dismissal, Alex felt he had no option but to leave. He wasn't going to get any more information out of the governor and as he walked down the spiral staircase to his own landing, his first thought was to speak to Maggie. He needed her to know what was going on and for her to be on her guard. Then he would speak to his kids. Biting his bottom lip in anger, he thought about them now. He had warned Dante about hanging around with Luke. Suddenly, that conversation came back to him and he wondered if John might be able to help. He walked along, almost in a dream and entered his cell. Lying on his bunk bed, he thought about everything this mystery woman had told him. His mind raced with what he could do. He felt helpless trapped inside these prison walls.

21

HOME TO ROOST

Deana walked into the hospital and looked through the window of the room Kev was lying in. He'd survived the worst and was getting better. She had lied to the officer on the door and said she was Luke's girlfriend. Once Luke had confirmed it, she had been allowed to visit. 'How's he doing, Luke? Well, apart from all of the plaster.' She smiled weakly. 'His legs must ache being in the air like that. At least he's on the mend.'

Luke stared at her blankly. 'On the mend? It would be easier to tell you what bones weren't broken, Deana. And he's pumped so full of pain killers, he doesn't know what day of the week it is. He has spoken once or twice, but not coherently and he's having night terrors.'

Deana swallowed hard. 'Mum wants to know if you and your mum want to come to us for Christmas day?' she asked hopefully.

'That's kind of her. She's been great popping round and seeing Mum. Giving me the time to come here. She's brought so many meals from your carvery I think I've put on a stone!' Luke grinned.

'Well, when she heard that Kev had been beaten up, she had to come, Luke. Only Kev can tell his story. You know.' Deana looked at him squarely. 'What actually happened to him that night?'

Luke glanced up towards the door to where the policeman was standing outside. 'That's what he's waiting to hear. Let's be honest, Deana. None of us know what happened, do we?'

'No, but I've turned this over in my mind a thousand times, Luke. How did those blokes know where Kev lived and why wasn't any of the usual crowd there? Have you seen them before?'

'Kev has a lot of friends that I don't know about. And personally, I think that woman was covering her own arse. She was definitely in on it with them. I think we took her more by surprise, than the other way around. We haven't heard a word from her since. That three hundred quid I had to drop off was at some shitty second-hand furniture unit off the main road. I just walked in and handed over the envelope with her name on it to some bloke. Nothing was said, so I left. Must have been okay, she hasn't called to complain.'

Linking her arm through his, Deana smiled. 'I think it's over too, that's why I've been keeping the home fires burning while you've been busy. I've carried on delivering with Dante. We thought, if you needed to, you could always go to a private hospital if Kev needed it.'

Shocked, Luke couldn't believe his ears. 'You are joking me?' he snapped, in a harsh whisper. 'Haven't you learnt anything from this? These people mean business Deana.

Look at my brother. Do you want to end up like that? Really, do you?'

Blushing to her roots, Deana felt deflated. She thought this would be welcome news to Luke, but instead he was scolding her for being stupid. 'You said yourself, it's all done and dusted with now. Why shouldn't we carry on?'

'Because making so much money by treading on people's toes upsets them and they want you out of the way. Are you so blinded by money you can't see the facts? You have your own addiction, Deana – money and adrenalin. But how much is enough? You've bought the pub; you have your university fees and Dante's for Christ's sake. You even have that pink monstrosity you call a car!'

'Okay! I hear you and so will he if you keep on shouting. For Christ's sake, I thought I was helping. People were messaging asking for stuff and if we don't provide it then someone else will. Anyway, I've done it now.' She smiled hopefully.

'You can't get around me that easy, Deana Silva.' He grinned and shook his head.

'Yes, I can, and you know it.' She laughed. Suddenly, their banter was disturbed as Kev began murmuring and his eyes fluttered open. 'Luke,' he whispered. 'Is that you?'

Luke squeezed his hand. 'It is Kev, and I'm not going anywhere. You just rest and get well.'

Deana beamed. 'Oh, that's great, Luke. He's talking. Kev's coming back to the land of the living. Just wait until I tell Mum and Dante's waiting outside, too.'

Happily, Luke ran his hand through his hair and grinned. 'Too right. Christ, I think he's turned the corner. Thank God!'

As Deana ran out to get Dante, the nurse walked in. 'Well, it seems our man is waking. I'll get the doctor. Maybe he can lower the dose of his medication slowly. That alone would make a horse sleep.' She laughed cheerfully.

A policeman entered the room at the same time as Dante. 'How you doing, Luke?' By now the policeman knew Luke and had often had a conversation with him to break the monotony of the day. Luke grinned. 'He spoke. He knows I'm here. My mum will be well chuffed.'

'That's a good sign.' The policeman smiled. 'What did he say?'

'Just asked if it was me.' Luke shrugged. 'But he knows I'm here and that's enough for me.'

Dante hugged Luke. 'Oh, thank God, Luke. Are you okay? You look like shit. Why don't you go home and I'll stay here with Kev. Go and see your mum and tell her the news.'

Luke thought about it. 'I would like to but, if he wakes again, I want to be here.'

'Your friend is right, Luke.' The officer nodded. 'I'm here and Florence Nightingale keeps popping in – nice bum on her, but I never said that.' The policeman coughed and smiled. 'You only need to be gone an hour tops, get show-ered, something to eat and come back.'

Unsure of the situation, Luke thought about it again. 'Okay, but, if anything changes...'

'We'll let you know!' Dante and the policeman both shouted to him.

Deana went home with Luke to find her mum there. She had been a regular visitor since Kev had been in hospital and had taken the weight off Luke's shoulders by caring for his mum.

Exhilarated, Luke told Maggie and his mum the news. His mum started crying and seeing tears rolling down her eyes saddened Deana. She thought how awful it was that

Kev's mum couldn't see her son, although, she argued with herself, considering the state he was in, maybe it was for the best.

'And I've got news for you. I've heard from your dad,' Maggie announced. 'I get a visit next week just before Christmas. That indeed is a present of its own for me. He sounded a bit serious though.'

'Anyone would sound serious in that place, Mum. But that's nice. Can me and Dante come?'

Maggie shook her head as she cast her eyes down to the floor. 'No, the visiting order is for one. Just me.'

Maggie had a strange feeling in the pit of her stomach. She had known Alex for years and she knew the ups and downs of his voice. When they had spoken, his voice had sounded serious and urgent. He hadn't said much at all, but to her, it spoke volumes. Something was definitely wrong, she thought to herself. Whatever it was she would find out soon enough.

* * *

Since his visit from the mystery woman, Alex hadn't slept. There was no one to confide in and he had to wait for visiting times, which seemed to be forever. He felt agitated and tried time after time to think of ways of getting released from prison. During his shift at the kitchen, he stood bleary eyed peeling a huge mountain of potatoes, when he heard the familiar hoot of a horn. 'That will be the delivery, Alex,' Alfred called over.

Alex's eyes shot open, and he remembered what the governor had said. If Alex had something to interest him...

The delivery scam! Surely that would interest him. Suddenly he felt he had hope. It was better than nothing.

As always, Alex and the others formed a chain outside in the yard and passed the boxes to each other from the van. With each one, Alex counted them. Thirty-six in total.

The same warder as always attended the delivery, while another one checked the menu for the day, while scrounging a cup of tea. He didn't seem to be taking a lot of interest in any of it which seemed to please the other warder. Alex watched meticulously as the boxes were piled up and the warder ticked them off.

'Well, that seems right, Alfred. Thirty boxes. Make sure all of that stuff is put away and accounted for. Then I'll do a stock take.'

Thirty? Alex thought to himself. He knew he had counted right. So, what did the other boxes contain? More pills, more drugs? What else could it be?

Busying himself, Alex was itching to look in the pantry at the side of the kitchen where he had seen the spare boxes before. He knew he was right, but then began doubting himself. While Alfred and the others were out front serving, Alex quickly ran without being seen and glanced into the pantry. Almost relieved at the sight of them, he grinned. Six boxes put aside and all with a small black dot in the corner. Success! He felt like punching the air but contained his enthusiasm and carried on with his work.

'You've perked up a bit, Alex. You were as miserable as sin this morning,' Alfred shouted through the serving hatch when he heard Alex singing. Giving him the thumbs up, Alex smiled.

As he washed up Alex was trying to concoct all kinds of ways to ask to see the governor without causing suspicion.

'So, what is it, Alex? One minute you're up and the next down. Problems?'

'Oh, just family stuff. I can't help anyone stuck in here, can I? You just feel helpless at times.'

As though a gift from God, Alfred encouraged him in front of the whole kitchen staff to speak to the governor about his family problems so that maybe he could get a day release on compassionate grounds. 'It's worth a try,' Alfred encouraged, while the rest of the staff butted in with their own stories and advice. 'They would rather help you sort the matter out, Alex, than find you hanging in your cell. You would have to report to the police station, but I did it when my wife lost her baby.'

Alex put his request in as soon as he got back to his cell and played on the family problems scenario. His request seemed to go through much faster than expected, and he was to see the governor in the morning. Inwardly, Alex cursed, because he knew the boxes would have been moved by then, and he needed the governor to see the boxes or his story wouldn't be believed.

After helping cook and serve the evening meal, Alex looked into the pantry to see the boxes were still there. Without hesitation, Alex walked in and picked one up. He stashed the box behind the huge bags of potatoes and put one bag on top, obscuring it from sight. This was his evidence. Hopefully, that would help his case. The more he thought about it, the more he convinced himself that the governor knew exactly what he wanted Alex to find. It had been weird how Alex had landed such a cushy job in the kitchens out of the blue, and he was starting to suspect that it had been planned.

Standing outside the governor's door with the warder

beside him, Alex felt nervous, but excited. His kids were running wild and seemingly on the top of a most-wanted list, and he needed to be there to help them.

Asking to speak to the governor in private, the warder left at the governor's dismissal. Taking a huge breath, Alex blurted out his story. Saying it out loud, it didn't sound like much, but the governor listened intently. Alex then told him he had one of the boxes as evidence if needed.

'Would this information get me an early release, or compassionate leave at least, sir?' Nervously, Alex pressed his fingernails into his palms and waited.

'Well, for the record, I had an idea something was going on with our friend Mr Jones. I can't promise you anything mind... So, these family problems...'

Puzzled, Alex looked at the governor, confused at the change in conversation. Cautiously, the governor pointed to the door and then his ear, indicating someone could be listening. Relieved, Alex raised his voice a little louder and spun him a story about his family problems, which seemed to satisfy them both. Once he'd finished, the governor dismissed him and standing up, Alex let out a huge sigh. He didn't know what he'd expected. Hopefully for the governor to give him his coat and say goodbye, but instead, he was led away, back to his job in the kitchens.

That evening, a prison warder came into his cell.

'Get your things together, Silva. You're being moved out.'

'Transferred? At this time of night?' Alex looked across at Fiddler who was reading his paper.

'Whenever we think fit, Silva. Usually the morning, but tonight will do.'

'But my wife's due to visit. She won't know where I am.

Can I get word to her?' Panic rose inside him. This wasn't what he'd expected.

'She'll know in due course. But the governor wants to see you first, come on.'

Alex was marched to the governor's office, and once inside, glared at him defiantly. 'You're transferring me sir, at this time of night? What the hell is going on? Is this because of what I told you today?'

The governor dismissed the warder beside Alex. 'Actually Silva, you've got a week's pass out of here. If I get more evidence of what you've told me, maybe more. That's the best I can offer you for now.'

Shocked, Alex looked at the governor curiously. 'It's best, Silva, if the men in here think you're having a hard time and are being transferred. And when, and if, you do go back to prison, it will be a different one. We all have to cover our backs, and I don't think you'd be particularly welcome back here... do you?'

Alex's mind raced. A whole bloody week back with his family to sort some of this mess out. Smuggled out the back way with his box of possessions, Alex was almost thrown out into the dark night with only his train fare. Whatever happened, Alex thought smugly to himself, Jonesy was going to get his comeuppance. He was a parasite playing on people's loneliness. It wasn't the vengeance he'd planned but it was good enough. Years would be added to Jonesy's sentence and that smug warder friend of his would certainly face the music after abusing his position. Shaking his head, Alex couldn't believe his actions. Once again he'd grassed up other people for their shortcomings. Was that to be his lot in life?

The elation he felt at seeing his home again after the long

journey made his heart almost burst. The dark crisp night promised snow and there was a Christmassy feeling all around. Christmas trees lit up by their fairy lights could be seen in every window. It warmed Alex, to be walking down his street amongst all of this. But it also made him realise how selfish he'd been, volunteering to go to prison without a thought for Maggie and the kids. He knew they wouldn't have got into this kind of trouble if he'd been home. He felt overwhelmed with guilt. Walking into the pub, everyone stood in silence, surprised at their Christmas visitor. 'Evening all.' Alex grinned. The regulars in the pub shouted his name in shock.

'Alex! Bloody hell, it's the ghost of Christmas past,' Mark shouted. 'What did you get for Christmas, a ladder over the wall? Maggie never said you were coming home today. For fuck's sake, I would have picked you up. Come here, let me buy you your first pint in the land of freedom. You're out... I can't believe it.' Mark hugged him so tight the circulation in his body nearly stopped. But just the familiarity of being home in his own surroundings brought tears to Alex's eyes. Home... what a nice word that was, he thought to himself.

Maggie ran from behind the bar and hugged him tightly, tears in her eyes. He kissed her and was about to drag her upstairs to speak to her when a voice rang out in the noisy bar.

'I'll get that whatever Mr Silva is drinking, ladies. In fact, I'll get everyone a drink.' A woman opened her wallet and threw a bundle of money on the bar. 'The hero is home.' Turning, Alex stood rooted to the spot. It was the woman from the governor's office. Obviously, she was well informed.

Pauline passed him one of her best pulled pints of beer

and handed it over, then busily began serving everyone else with a free drink as they pushed their glasses under her nose.

Freeing himself from Maggie's grasp, Alex walked over to the woman, leaning towards her ear. 'Who are you, lady?'

Holding out her hand to shake his, she smiled. 'How do you do, Mr Silva. My name is Patsy, Patsy Diamond Carreaux.' She grinned. Alex paled; he knew of this woman and her contacts. Uncomfortably, he turned from her and took a large gulp of his drink, waving it in the air. 'Cheers everyone!'

'Hang on, Alex, the phone's ringing. I'll be back in a minute.' Answering the telephone, Maggie heard a man's muffled voice, but what chilled her to the bone was the screams of a woman in the background. 'Mum! Mum help me!' Instantly Maggie recognised it as Deana's voice, screaming and shouting for help. Maggie's blood ran cold. Then a man's voice shouted, 'Shut the fuck up! We have your daughter, Mrs Silva. Don't call the police or you will be burying her. We want our money back.' Suddenly the line went dead. What should have been a celebration for Alex was suddenly interrupted by Maggie's chilling scream. The whole pub stopped and went quiet.

'Alex! Alex!' Turning, Alex saw Maggie running towards him. Tears rolled down her face, as she trembled. 'It's Deana!' she shouted. Hastily, Alex pulled her through to the back of the bar. 'In here, Maggie, away from the customers. What is it? What about Deana?' he demanded. Standing in the hallway, he shook her by the shoulders. 'For fuck's sake, spit it out. I've only been home five minutes. Who was that on the telephone?'

Maggie sniffed, trying to compose herself. 'I think Deana's been kidnapped! Some man on the other end of the phone said they have her and they want their money back. Oh my God, Alex. We have to call the police, but they said if we did, they would kill her.' Maggie was hysterical, crying and shouting.

'We can't call the police.' Alex shook her shoulders again. 'That's why I wanted to see you alone. Our kids are drug dealers. Where's Dante?'

Maggie stood trembling and staring at Alex, shaking her head. 'Our daughter has been kidnapped. Can you hear what I'm saying? We need to call witness protection. This is that mafia lot wanting revenge. I know it, I just know it.'

Alex put his hand over her mouth to silence her. He knew people in the bar could hear her rantings and pulled her into another room, further away.

'No Maggie,' Alex whispered. 'This has nothing to do with the mob. This is different. Our kids, under your very nose, have lied to you and have been dealing drugs and have been very successful by all accounts. Maggie, they have caused mayhem. Now shut up and sit down. Tell me what the man said, and where is Dante? Did they mention him?'

Maggie stared at him in disbelief and wiped the snot from her nose. Maggie's voice was shaking as she tried to speak. She felt a pain in her chest and couldn't breathe.

'Come on, Maggie. Breathe with me love.' Slowly Alex breathed in and out, encouraging Maggie to do the same. He could see she had paled and looked like she was about to faint. Holding her hands, he carried on until eventually her breathing returned to normal. 'Sit down. I have a long story to tell you and you're not going to like it. If they weren't my kids, I would kill them myself. What the fuck have they been doing running wild under your nose?' Alex lashed out. He wanted someone to blame, anyone but himself.

'Don't blame me, Alex! You left us alone to fend for ourselves! Is it any wonder if they've gone off the rails! Dante's visiting his friend in hospital. Poor lad has been beaten to a pulp by muggers or something.' Alex took another deep breath as Maggie's words sank in. He knew she was right and all this was his fault. And he also knew he had to fix this.

'Let's not fight with each other. Not now.' Alex pulled Maggie close and hugged her. 'I'm home and we'll sort it. I've been warned about this. In fact...' Leaving Maggie standing there, Alex ran back into the bar to where Patsy Diamond was still seated. Instantly, she raised her drink in the air when she saw him.

'It's started then? Well, I've done my bit. The rest is up to you, Alex.' She smiled and winked. Alex stared at Patsy Diamond open mouthed as she raised the collar of her mink coat and walked to the doors. Turning before she left, she winked at him. 'Speak soon, Alex.' With that, she blew a kiss and left.

Alex knew trouble was about to head their way. And time was not on his side. He had a week to sort out a mess that had been going on for months. Walking back into the back room of the bar, he tried his best to give his wife a reassuring smile, but knew he didn't look convincing. The darker part of his mind wondered if Deana was still alive, but he brushed that negative thought away. He couldn't think like that.

Running his hands through his hair, he sat down. His legs felt weak and his mind was in turmoil. It had been a hell of a day and this just about rounded things up. Letting out a huge sigh, he looked up at Maggie. 'Pour us a large whisky, then sit down and tell me what you know – if anything.'

'Nothing, Alex! Deana has a job at a supermarket; she's spent a lot of time there...' Maggie tailed off.

'They are drug dealers Maggie and they have been doing it right under your nose and you haven't noticed anything – nothing at all?'

'Don't blame me Alex. I appreciate you need a whipping boy but not me. I've been deceived and lied to. How do you think I feel? Do you think that caller will call back? What about Deana? What do you think is happening to her right now?'

Suddenly a thought occurred to Alex. He knew it was a long shot as no one in the underworld would be so stupid. 'Did you do a recall on the number they called from? Have you tried it?'

Maggie frowned. 'Of course I did. As for the number, it was a private number. Nothing to call back.' Moving forward, she sat on the floor beside his chair and put her head in his lap. 'What about the police Alex? Surely it's an option? Our daughter has been kidnapped and most likely been beaten up or worse. She's a beautiful young woman to a hot-blooded male...'

Running his hand through her blonde hair and stroking it, he didn't want to think about what was happening to Deana. 'It's not an option Maggie. Two kids with the surname of Silva are drug dealers. They've caused turf wars. They have been running around selling here there and everywhere while living in a bubble thinking no one would notice. Whoever called you will call back. If they were just going to kill her, they wouldn't have called us first.' Alex almost cursed himself when he felt Maggie freeze and look up at him.

'Kill her? Our Deana? They can't do that.'

'Oh, wake up Maggie. You're an ex-mafia wife. You know how the system works. You don't tread on toes. Not in that world anyway. But they will call back, I promise, otherwise, why would they have called in the first place? They want something, possibly their money back, but who knows? We just have to sit tight until they do.'

For a moment they both stared at each other in silence.

Breaking the silence, Maggie had a thought. 'What about John? Maybe he could shed some light on it. Have you thought about that? And who was that woman?'

Alex nodded and agreed. 'John's an option and I will follow that avenue. If there are turf wars, then he will know about it. I'm sure of that. And that woman is the most powerful woman in Europe and possibly further. She's our only ally at the moment. She wants peace and discretion on the streets. She doesn't want the police sniffing around and she definitely doesn't want her name popping up in conversation. She only cares about her own business. Fortunately, she sees two opportunistic kids in Deana and Dante and wants this whole affair stubbing out before war begins and arrests are made. She will have a price but, at the moment I don't want to think about it. She tipped me off and gave me the option of getting out of prison – I realise that now.' He squeezed Maggie's hand. 'We need Dante. He is part of this duo and he can fill us in on the full story. Call him, tell him it's an emergency. He needs to get back here before someone decides to kidnap him as well. For Christ's sake, we have to move and move fast.'

Alex's eyes narrowed and he looked up as he heard someone approaching. He put his finger to his lips. Suddenly the door burst open and Mark stood there grinning from ear to ear. Seeing Alex and Maggie together on the floor, he presumed the worst. 'Oh God, sorry I didn't realise. Well, I suppose it's obvious with you being away for so long,' Mark stammered as his face reddened with embarrassment. Covering his eyes with his hands, he turned. 'I didn't see anything you two. Oh and I will tell the others you're not to be disturbed,' he shouted as he walked away.

'You lot!' Mark shouted to the bar full of people, 'I wouldn't go in there; Maggie's giving Alex a blow job!'

Hearing his announcement, Maggie and Alex burst out laughing. Seeing a familiar twinkle in Alex's eye, Maggie smiled. 'Why don't I make that call to Dante and while we're waiting for him to get back, maybe we could think of something to pass the time...'

'Aren't you going to fetch him?' Alex asked as he unzipped his trousers, smiling as Maggie's hand stroked him gently. He hardened under her touch.

Maggie shook her head and gave Alex a wry cheeky grin. 'If I did that I would have to explain the emergency on the way home. I will tell him to get a taxi and then he can be as shocked as we have been when he sees you standing here.' Picking up her mobile with her other hand, Maggie rang Dante. 'I need you home Dante. Something has come up.' Seeing Alex's response to her stroking, she winked. 'Straight away, I mean. No messing or dawdling. Get a taxi and come home now.' Hearing his worried reply, she ended the call and gave a thumbs-up to Alex.

'He's worried and on his way.' She grinned. 'You're right, Alex. I am an ex-mafia wife; it's not the first time we've been threatened and between us we will sort out this mess if I have to shoot those bastards who have our daughter myself! We've been in worse situations and survived, and I intend to man up, or woman up, and be the woman I once was. But, in the meantime...' She grinned and looked him squarely in the face.

Seeing Maggie's flushed face and her adrenalin racing, Alex felt a stirring within. This was the old Maggie. The one with fighting spirit and gumption, who faced danger with a gun in her hand. She had lived too long in the shadows and now she was going to shine. Suddenly their hunger for each other after months of separation overwhelmed them and they sought each other's lips in a passionate embrace as they tore each other's clothes off. For a moment, Alex paused and thought about what they were facing. *Fuck it, why not? This may be the last chance I ever get.* He pushed Maggie onto the floor as they writhed around and joined their bodies as one.

ACKNOWLEDGEMENTS

Thank you to all of you who read my books for your continued support on my journey as an author. May all your reviews be good ones!

Thanks to Boldwood Books, as well as my editor Emily, who never fails me, even in my darkest hour.

ABOUT THE AUTHOR

Gillian Godden is a brilliantly reviewed writer of gangland fiction as well as a full-time NHS Key Worker in Hull. She lived in London for over thirty years, where she sets her thrillers, and during this time worked in various stripper pubs and venues which have inspired her stories.

Sign up to Gillian Godden's mailing list here for news, competitions and updates on future books.

Follow Gillian on social media:

 x.com/GGodden

 instagram.com/goddengillian

 facebook.com/gilliangoddenauthor

ALSO BY GILLIAN GODDEN

Gold Digger

Fools' Gold

The Lambrianus

Dangerous Games

Nasty Business

Francesca

Dirty Dealings

Bad Boy

The Diamond Series

Diamond Geezer

Rough Diamonds

Queen of Diamonds

Forever Diamond

The Silvas

The Street

Troublemakers

PEAKY READERS

GANG LOYALTIES. DARK SECRETS.
BLOODY REVENGE.

A READER COMMUNITY FOR
GANGLAND CRIME THRILLER FANS!

DISCOVER PAGE-TURNING NOVELS
FROM YOUR FAVOURITE AUTHORS
AND MEET NEW FRIENDS.

JOIN OUR BOOK CLUB
FACEBOOK GROUP

BIT.LY/PEAKYREADERSFB

SIGN UP TO OUR
NEWSLETTER

BIT.LY/PEAKYREADERSNEWS

Boldwood

Boldwood Books is an award-winning fiction publishing company seeking out the best stories from around the world.

Find out more at www.boldwoodbooks.com

Join our reader community for brilliant books, competitions and offers!

Follow us
@BoldwoodBooks
@TheBoldBookClub

Sign up to our weekly deals newsletter

https://bit.ly/BoldwoodBNewsletter

Printed in Great Britain
by Amazon

53080587R00165